SURRENDER THE PAST

ELIZABETH JOHNS

For my mom, my number one fan, who encouraged me to dream and pushed me to be my best. She was an English teacher, walking dictionary, and editor extraordinaire. I hope I didn't embarrass you. She loved romance novels, and I hope she is enjoying this one with a big smile from heaven. I miss you beyond words.

For my dad, who has a soft spot for Jane Austen, and enjoys the long version of Pride and Prejudice as much as I do. You are my role-model and hero, a constant source of calm and strength.

CHAPTER 1

VIRGINIA, AUGUST 1814

*O*ysters. His lips felt like wet, slimy oysters. Ironically, oysters also made her feel like she was going to retch. Elinor held her mouth tight against the assault on her lips, trying to breathe through her nose despite the noxious odours emanating from his person. She stared at the wall, wondering how this could have happened. She should be safe from unwanted advances in a school of all places! How could she get out of this as quickly as possible and not hurt his feelings?

Elinor felt a cold shiver and began to sweat. She had to stop this immediately before she lost all control. She placed her hands on his chest and gently pushed.

"Mr. Wilson, please! This is hardly appropriate behaviour for friends." She hoped that got the point across, because she felt the telltale signs of clamminess and rapid heart rate beginning.

"But Miss Abbott, you must know how I feel about you! I want you to be my wife!" He slid his hand over his few remaining strands of hair atop his shiny pate, a gesture he made when nervous.

"No, sir." She paused and shook her head. She spoke more calmly than she felt. "I truly did not know. I am quite flattered by your feelings, but I am afraid I have no desire to remain more than friends. I sincerely apologize if you misunderstood my affection for you to be more than platonic."

Oh no, here they come: the stages of rejection.

Denial. The wide eyes, the mortified look, the shaking head.

"Surely you jest, Miss Abbott. I cannot be so mistaken, surely. You spend so much time here."

"I assure you, I would not jest of such a thing." She was here for the children, not him!

Anger. The red face, the veins pulsing at his temples and throat.

"But you must marry me! How could I have been so mistaken in your feelings?"

"Again, I assure you that nothing was intentionally done."

Bargaining. He began to pace the room, and threw his hands in the air.

"What can I do to change your mind? There must be something! Think of the children!"

"Sir, please." Grovelling was so unbecoming. What else was there to say?

Acceptance. His hands dropped and his shoulders drooped, his eyes on the floor.

Well, hopefully acceptance would come later, because she was not going to wait around for that. She ran toward the door, trying not to faint. "Sir, I do apologize, but I cannot stay. Take care, Mr. Wilson." She made her escape as fast as she could, stopping only to empty her stomach in the bushes behind the stable.

Elinor threw her leg over her mare and took off as if the hounds of hell were after her. She knew she should be flattered that Mr. Wilson had offered for her, but it infuriated her instead. She shuddered as she recalled the feel of his disgusting lips and clammy hands upon her person as he declared himself to her. What happened to the old-fashioned method of using words first? She had to stop thinking about it or she would retch again. Why did she keep finding herself the centre of unwanted attention from men?

She finally turned back toward River's Bend, the plantation her father had bought only a few miles outside of Washington, across the

Potomac River in Alexandria. As she rode astride across the open fields from the village to the manor house, she began to feel the panic subside. The feeling of the wind in her face and hair whipping around were a welcome comfort. She truly felt ill from her interactions with Mr.Wilson. Would there ever come a time when she could be touched by a man and not grow anxious? Would she be able to recapture her free spirit that now seemed to be trapped inside?

Elinor lowered her body down against the horse as they made their way into the trees. An afternoon shower provided little relief from the muggy August afternoon. She ducked some low-hanging branches as their leaves dripped large droplets onto her face, without slowing her pace. As she wiped the water from her eyes, she saw a man standing dumbstruck right in the middle of the path. There was nowhere for her to go with trees on one side, the riverbank on the other. She pulled up on the reins as hard as she could, and Athena reared up on her hind legs. Elinor lost her grip and flew off the back of the horse.

"Ouch." Elinor managed to get that word out while struggling to catch her breath. Now she understood what it meant to have the breath knocked out of you. She wiggled her hands and toes, still able to feel everything, and looked up to make sure Athena was unharmed, when she heard a man's voice ask if she was all right. She stood up ungracefully and wiped at her mud-covered skirts, then began to chastise the stranger.

"Of course I am not all right! Why were you standing in the middle of the path? You must have seen me coming!" she shouted with her fists balled up at her side.

The stranger stared at her from under his hat, and she caught sight of a pair of brilliant blue eyes flash at her. "I was not the one riding like a hellion!" he shouted back at her.

The nerve of the man! "I can see you are not hurt, so kindly remove yourself from our property!"

With that, she turned on her heel and marched over to her horse, which was eating grass. Once mounted, she managed to spray the stranger with mud as she urged her horse forward, taking all her frustration out on this man, knowing she was behaving abominably, but beyond caring at this point. She was so distracted, she did not even give thought to who he was or why he was at River's Bend.

Elinor rode until she felt the wind carry away some of her frustration. Finally, she slowed the horse to a walk as she reached the stables. She brushed and fed the horse before feeling composed enough to encounter others.

Elinor stopped at the door and took a few more deep breaths before entering the house, still in disbelief. She tossed her soaked bonnet on the table in the mud room off the kitchen, kicked off her muddy boots, and thrust her feet into some slippers. She went through the kitchen, drawn in by the smell of her favourite biscuits. Those always cured what ailed her. Elinor swiped a few of the treats and kissed Cook on the cheek with a half grin.

The cook looked askance at her, eyeing Elinor's sopping wet, muddy self from head to toe, but did not scold—verbally anyway. There were few things that piqued Elinor, so the staff stayed out of her way, merely handing her a towel and acting as if everything was normal. She heard Cook mumbling something about "indulged and let run wild" and "needing a man to tame her."

That actually brought a smile to Elinor's face as she walked off because she knew that was one of the ways Cook expressed fondness. Partially dry, Elinor continued on into the study where she found her papa sitting behind the large mahogany desk, absorbed in a letter. Their old spaniel lying at Sir Charles' feet, pried an eye open to see who the intruder was, then promptly went back to his nap.

Elinor stood and observed her papa from the doorway, finishing her biscuits while allowing a sense of calm to seep in. His hair was silver along the temples and receding back from his face, showing the lines of an easy smile. She walked over to where her mother's treasured tea service was laid out and touched the pot to see if it was still warm. Satisfied, she poured herself a cup and refilled her father's cup. He finally looked up, and she placed a kiss on his cheek. "Ah, there you are dear." He smiled at the apple of his eye. He must have noticed that look on her face. "What is the matter? Was something wrong with one of the children at the school?"

"No." She frowned. "Am I so obvious?" So like her father not to notice how dirty she was, or ask why, but instead notice her agitation.

"I am afraid so." Sir Charles put his work down and watched her begin to walk back and forth across the carpet, her panic now turned to vexation. He waited patiently for her to divulge her pent-up words.

"I received another offer!" she said in frustration and threw her hands out as if to ask why.

"You are supposed to be flattered, my dear," Sir Charles commented with an amused look at his daughter, while calmly sipping his tea. "Was it the schoolmaster?"

She nodded. "Why must they always offer? I thought we were friends, Papa. Am I doing something wrong that they mistake my feelings? Assume I am besotted? When I realize they—they like me in *that* way, it makes my skin crawl!" As if on cue, she shivered at the thought. "Then, *I* feel guilty for rejecting them!"

Sir Charles went and sat on the sofa and patted the spot next to him. She sat, trying to minimize the damage to the sofa, and he put his arm around her and snuggled her to him. These were the times she desperately missed her mother. Her papa did not always know how to handle these situations, other than to hold her and pat her back. Elinor often lacked feminine polish, and though she had gone to a finishing school for young ladies, it still did not come naturally to her.

"Do not stop being yourself, Elly. Just be honest and kind about your feelings. When the right man comes along you will not feel disgusted by his offer." His eyes twinkled at her, but at least he did not laugh out loud.

"Hmph," was all Elly could reply. She knew this feeling would never stop happening around men. At least she could talk to men now and be friends with them. Or so she had thought. "So it does not bother you that I have not accepted anyone? What if I did choose to settle here? Would that bother you? You did say eventually the plantation would be mine, did you not?"

He sighed. "No dearest, I am in no hurry for you to marry. I only bought this plantation as an investment. I had not planned on staying here so long, Elly. I know you are comfortable here, but I think you should give England a chance once more before you make up your mind."

After a few moments of pondering that statement over another biscuit, she dismissed it. They had already had many discussions about her not wanting to go back to England. She changed topics as she noticed a parchment sitting open on the desk. "Who is your letter from, Papa? Is that why you wished to speak to me?"

"Yes, yes. The War Office in England. It seems negotiations are being commenced." He rose and made his way back over to his desk.

"That is wonderful news!" Elinor clapped her hands together with excitement, for she prided herself on being well informed on political goings-on.

"Yes, but it means I will be away for some time. The meetings are being held in Ghent." Her excitement faded as quickly as it had come. She frowned.

"Why are the negotiations being held in Belgium? The war is between America and Britain!" Elinor exclaimed, exasperated. "It is so far!"

"Since when did logic ever enter into political negotiations? Especially Belgium being a neutral party and all," her father countered. Elinor smiled despite herself as her father tried to make light of a subject she knew he dreaded approaching her with. "Dearest, I must go. This war must be stopped, and if I can help them see how pointless it is and return the countries to their prior arrangements, then life here can be peaceable again." He paused, knowing she would dislike his next statement. "I want you to go to your grandmother while I am away."

She wrinkled her nose at him. "Next thing I know, you are going to say I need to have a come-out Season in London!"

An awkward pause ensued. He looked at her questioningly. "Actually, yes, I was going to suggest it. I presumed all girls longed to dress like a princess and dance at balls. Never mind that you push the word *dress* to its limit." He eyed her muddied, split-legged riding costume as he spoke with a twinkle in his eyes.

So he had noticed her dress. Ignoring his jibe at her attire, she said, "I am not disagreeing that you should go help make peace, merely that I must go to England while you do so. I have no desire to have a fancy come-out London Season amongst a group of idle, immoral, self-indulgent aristocrats, especially while there is a war going on here! How could I pretend to be happy while immersed in frivolity?"

"I believe you must have missed an adjective or two. Perhaps vain, greedy, arrogant...and it is *because* there is a war going on here that I insist you go." Sir Charles shook his head. He never envisioned when they came to America several years ago, for him to serve as a diplomatic minister to the King, that Elinor would transform into a fiercely independent American, almost anti-English.

Elinor smiled. "Perhaps that was a bit excessive, but you know how I feel about useless titles and people who feel work is beneath them." *Her father had earned his 'Sir,' so that was different, of course.* "I do not need to have hundreds of dresses by the finest modistes and dance at a ball every night to feel respectable. Here I have the injured soldiers, the vicarage children and the plantation to keep me usefully employed. This is my home now."

"Why, Elly, you would look beautiful in a potato sack," Sir Charles replied, shaking his head at her tenacity. "However, England is your heritage, and your mother always wanted a London Season for you." *And a nice English husband*, Elinor thought to herself. "Besides, all society is not as you describe. There are plenty who champion worthy causes and strive to do right by their tenants and the needy. If you look for the good, you will find it—just as you have here." He paused thoughtfully, wondering the best approach to take with her. He could tell she was clearly not moved thus far. "You have not been to visit our family since we left; it might be your last chance to see your grandmother."

Elinor sighed, but nodded her head, not wishing to argue. Her grandmother was the one argument that would always work. It would also be nice to see her older sister, Sarah, and brother, Andrew. Her brother was in the army, and had been fighting Bonaparte. However, she heard that Bonaparte had been exiled, so she hoped she might see Andrew.

Elinor knew she was being unreasonable about going to England, but she was beginning to feel her world crumble beneath her. Change was not her favourite thing, but she could not tell her father the real reason she did not want to ever go back to England. Her father hugged her and kissed the top of her golden blonde head.

"As long as you promise I can return here when I do not find Prince Charming at the end of the Season," she said resignedly.

"Of course. I pray these negotiations will be over quickly and I can join you to see what a toast you are." He winked at her. She rolled her eyes playfully and tried to flutter her eyelashes.

"Father, I said I would go. You did not say I had to be an actress!"

"No, dear, never an actress!" They both shared a good laugh over the thought since they both knew Elinor was no typical London debutante, and being an actress, or even knowing one, was a forbidden thought for a lady in England.

"You will do well enough, lass. You will be a refreshing delight. I am afraid your life here has been much too serious. I never intended you to put so much upon your shoulders—it was not fair of me. Just promise me you will try to enjoy yourself and know you have here to come back to if you do not take, though I know that will not be the case."

Elinor thought he might *perhaps* see his daughter's charm in a different light from the high-sticklers of London society.

There was a knock on the parlour door and Abe, their butler, came in with a message. Sir Charles scanned the note with a concerned look on his face. Elinor waited to see if everything was all right. Sir Charles stared at the paper with a look of consternation.

"Is something amiss?" she asked because of the look on his face.

"I do not know, but this message is from Commodore Gordon. They are positioned right off the coast near Alexandria."

"So what does that mean for us?" Elinor was fairly certain it would not be good news.

"I am not sure, Elly. I still hope this will end soon, but I am afraid it will get ugly first. He is sending a messenger later with details." He pinched his fingers over the bridge of his nose, a sign he was worried, but she pressed on. "I should have suspected as much with the increasing presence of soldiers around town, only I expected more warning. We must prepare ourselves."

"Why is there even a war? This war was fought once—the British lost. They need to leave America be and stop trying to control the world. If there were an evil tyrannical government here, I would understand. But these people left England to make a better life for themselves and are harming no one."

"America declared war, if you recall. You know the British feel like they are justified in retaliating for the destruction of York." He shook his head, not quite sure how to best handle his youngest when she got passionate about a cause. She was normally more even tempered.

"This is so pointless!" She threw up her hands and kissed her father's cheek. "I will see you for dinner, Papa." He nodded distractedly, so she escaped for the stables as soon as she could throw her boots back on. She desperately needed to get control over her emotions. Would today stop bringing unwelcome news? She had become an expert at hiding her real feelings from her papa. The one thing she could not bear was for her papa to know of her shame. What would he think of her then? She had hidden that awful time of her life away in her innermost depths, numbing herself to any intimacy of feeling other than with those closest to her in order to bear it.

With a heavy heart, Elly went through the motions of mounting her horse and took off riding as hard as her mare would go, while tears began to stream down her face. Once the initial dismay was out of her system, she slowed down to a trot until she reached her favourite spot overlooking the Potomac. She dismounted and inhaled the fresh scent of pine and rain, and listened to the water lapping the banks of the river below. She was thankful for the breeze off the water in the humid heat of the afternoon.

This had been her calm, her peace for six years. Would it still be here when she came back? How would she find escape in England?

The prospect of facing *him* again was the worst thing she could imagine. She threw herself to the ground and stared at the sky, searching for answers. She closed her eyes as a fresh wave of mortification closed in on her.

She remembered feeling similarly six years ago before she left her childhood home to come to America. She had left everything that was familiar while in the midst of trying to cope with the attack and the deep sense of loss from her mother's death. Now she could not imagine being happy back in England. In America, she had started over to find herself, not under the shadow of her past with constant reminders of her attack. She was free to be herself here. English society was much more rigid with unwritten rules. Would she still be English enough? Would her family understand that she could never marry—without her telling them why? Would they believe her if she did tell them why? How would she face her attacker again?

She had no idea, but that is what her father wanted, so she would try unless she could come up with a way to stop it. She had convinced herself that she could avoid ever going back. She could not even bring herself to relive that night consciously, though she did not have the luxury of controlling her nightmares. She was grown now. She could do this. She must.

Elinor sat up on her favourite rock on the riverbank, skipping rocks and thinking of how she spent most of her days and how fulfilling the work was. She helped teach the village children, and recently began helping nurse wounded soldiers at the school she used to attend in Washington, The Preparatory School for Young Ladies. She laughed out loud to think of her prim aunt's expression if she saw Elly with blood on her hands from assisting the surgeon, or with a horde of ex-slave children at her feet learning their letters. No, she thought, she would never fit in polite society.

CHAPTER 2

 ajor Adam Trowbridge, now Viscount Easton, was on his last assignment with His Majesty's Army. With his father ailing and his elder brother recently killed in a horse race, he was going to settle down after eight years of honourable service to His Majesty and perhaps work at the War Office. A desk job. He sighed. He was now his father's heir, as his brother had not seen fit to provide an heir before his death. Prinny, the infamous Prince Regent, did not like heirs fighting on the front lines. Besides, Easton did not want to be fighting in America. Fighting Bonaparte—now that had purpose. Fighting America? Well, he had seen more than enough death and destruction for a hundred lifetimes, and disputes over trade restrictions did not incite passion for more. Even the great Wellington himself did not agree with this campaign.

At least while here he would get to see his godfather, whom he had not seen in ages. He was dispatched to deliver a message tonight to his godfather, who was serving as minister to the King in Washington. He hoped to pass a rare pleasant evening with Sir Charles before heading back to the dreaded business his superiors had in mind for Washington. Apparently Sir Charles's plantation home was right on the water, and its safety from attack could not be guaranteed, so he had been sent with a warning missive.

Easton took a small boat from the ship in the harbour up the Potomac to the dock on Sir Charles's property. He let out a gasp when the plantation and property came into view. A beautiful, white manor house stood overlooking a bend in the river. The house was surrounded by enormous oaks, pines and rolling hills covered with vineyards and fields of tobacco. A more picturesque setting he could not imagine. It was as if a fine portrait came to life with sounds and fragrances in accompaniment. At least he understood why Sir Charles had stayed on in America after the war started, when most British loyalists had fled.

Standing there, Easton was struck with a longing he had never known before. He had spent eight years wandering nomadically with the army, both following and giving orders. The bonds he had felt with his fellow soldiers had been enough—an unspoken comradeship of people who never would have interacted otherwise were it not for the connection of war. He had been a mere child when he had left, invincible and arrogant, the military his destiny as a second son. He had accepted it willingly, but nothing could ever truly prepare one for the harsh realities of war.

Now he was a man, hardened by the horrors of battle and loss, littered with scars both physical and mental. Suddenly, the thought of settling down and working his own land almost overcame him. He longed to return home and never look back at this life. He had to hope that somewhere a small measure of peace existed for his estranged soul.

Easton then remembered Sir Charles's daughter: Little Elly they had called her. He wondered how old she might be now. She had been an adorable little spitfire with golden curls and charm enough for a whole army. She had followed them everywhere in her pink pinafores and dirt, and none of them had had the heart to turn her away, not that it would have deterred her. So she had gone riding, fishing and shooting with the lot of them. Of course they had teased her relentlessly by putting frogs and worms in her bed, but she had been full of pluck, reciprocating as much as she was able. He hoped she had not turned into a silly, simpering miss like most females of his acquaintance.

The noise of a galloping horse shook him from his reverie, reminding him to paste his pleasant façade back in place. He looked up to see a girl flying straight at him on her chestnut horse in a break-neck fashion, much too fast and distracted to notice him coming up from the dock on the property. She was dressed like a groom, blonde hair flowing wildly behind, riding astride in her split-legged skirt.

As he stood there gaping, he realized she did not see him and would soon run him over. He jumped back into the muddy riverbank, at the same time she saw him and pulled up on her horse to try to avoid trampling him. Instead of stopping, the horse reared, and the girl flew off, landing with an ungraceful thud at his feet.

"Ouch." Her hair in the mud and her limbs splayed in all directions, he offered his hand to help her sit up as she tried to catch her breath, but she ignored it.

"Are you all right, miss?" She looked around and spotted her horse, and then glanced at him. Clearly, the horse's well-being was of utmost importance here. Again, he offered his arm, but she shooed it off, then stood and began smoothing her mud-covered skirts. A little late to be concerned with appearances, he thought.

"Of course I am not all right! Why were you standing in the middle of the path? You must have seen me coming!" the girl shouted with her fists balled up and her arms stiff at her side.

He gaped at her from under his hat. He longed to wipe the mud off her face to see what she looked like. Of course he had been mesmer-ized watching her, but he was not going to 'fess up to that while she was trying to blame him for her reckless riding!

"I was not the one riding like a hellion!" he said to her as if she were one of his troops.

"I can see you are unharmed, so kindly remove yourself from our property!"

With that, she turned on her heel and marched over to her horse, which was lazily chomping grass. Once mounted, she managed to spray Easton with mud as she urged her horse forward. He realized she had said *our* property. He groaned. He would not call Little Elly miss-ish or simpering at least.

~

Elinor returned in time to hurriedly bathe and dress for dinner. Cook had informed her of a dinner guest, and her father had also informed Josie to dress her appropriately. She normally dressed herself, but on special occasions her maid would help. Josie had just finished filling the bath when Elinor walked in. Without missing a beat, Josie said, "I thought you went riding horses, not pigs!"

"Very clever, Josie. I will have you know I was thrown from my horse!" Elinor said, rubbing her aching backside in recollection. Then she had gone out riding again, which had not helped her pains in the least.

"Well, there is a first for everything I suppose," Josie said as she began helping Elinor rid herself of the muddied riding habit.

"There was the most exasperating man standing in the path! Where else was I supposed to go? He did not even move until I was upon him!"

Josie was only half listening, too caught up in getting her mistress ready for dinner, which was no small task. "In with ye." Josie nudged Elinor toward the bath. "How am I supposed to dress your hair proper if it is sopping wet? We do not have time to wash it, dry it and dress it."

"Can we not brush the mud out? I do not need fancy hair tonight."

Josie sighed the sigh of the exasperated and tackled the mess, while Elinor scrubbed herself with the soap. "Why must we have a guest today of all days? I am in no mood for company." She towelled herself off, then noticed that Josie had picked out an elegant pale green silk trimmed in cream, a gift her grandmother had sent her for her upcoming birthday. Elinor saw it laid out for her and shook her head vehemently when it came time to dress.

"That is indecent. It may be all the rage in London, but the neckline leaves little to the imagination! Besides, this is only a small dinner, nothing like the ones in town." She strode straight to her wardrobe and stared at all of the dresses hanging there that she had little cause to wear. Her grandmother kept sending them despite Elinor's letters protesting against them. They all looked equally inappropriate to her as she sifted through them.

"Miss Elly, it barely shows your shoulders! This is an English gent and he will expect you to act like an English lady, so we are going to dress you like one." *And hope they do not notice the rest.* "Her Grace would not send something improper anyhow, and I have my orders from Sir Charles." Josie crossed her arms as if to dare Elinor to protest. Elinor was too tired to argue and surrendered to Josie's ministrations.

Josie had been with them since they had come to America. They had found her orphaned and homeless, and had adopted her as a maid and companion. Josie and Elinor acted like sisters.

"Besides, we need to start practising if we are going to have you ready for the likes of the Season," Josie said.

"Ha! I will never be ready for the likes of the *Season*, and well you know it. Josie, I think you would fit better in than I!" They both laughed. "You care more about the latest fashions and hairstyles. I have not even looked at those magazines once, and you have them memorized." She motioned towards the stack of *La Belle Assemblées* that her grandmother had sent. Josie devoured them when she got her hands on them.

"Well, I have to be prepared when we get there, do I not?"

Elinor sighed and put her head down trying not to cringe as Josie attempted to comb out the tangles in her hair, one of the side effects of a good, hard ride.

"Josie, you know as well as I that I have no business over there looking for a husband. Even if some poor soul took pity on me and would have me, or I found someone who did not disgust me, I do not think I could go through with *it*." Josie stayed quiet for once, pretending to concentrate on brushing Elinor's hair. Josie was the one person Elinor had confided in about the attack. "I am so glad you will be with me at least. I do not think I could bear leaving here, going there and facing him without having you there."

Josie gave her a comforting squeeze on the arm. "It will not be so bad, Miss Elly. You can charm everybody, then take interest in no one in particular. You will see. And you have a London gent downstairs to practice your charm on. Now go and knock his stockings off!"

"That is a novel idea. Charm and flirt with everyone so no one notices I favour nobody. Perfect! If I only knew how to charm and flirt." She shook her head until Josie tsked at her. "But it will never work. Grandmama would see straight through me if I even remotely possessed the skills to pull it off. I cannot even pretend to keep from hurting someone's feelings." She shut her eyes as if this were some crazy dream she still had not fully awakened from. "Thank goodness you are coming with me!" Elinor stood and hugged Josie tightly, and then reluctantly dressed. After helping her into the green gown, Josie arranged Elinor's hair in an understated but elegant new style that had been featured in the most recent magazine.

Elinor gasped when she looked in the mirror, almost unable to recognize herself. Josie beamed with pride at her mistress. Even Elinor had to admit she *looked* like a lady.

Elinor walked down to dinner in a trance of denial. It was not that she was opposed to being feminine, but she was opposed to doing everything *their* way, meaning English society's. She had seen and heard enough from her sister Sarah's Season to remember. She caught herself in the hall staring at the parlour door, unable to come to terms with the fact that she had to face her biggest nightmare in England—seeing her attacker again.

Elinor gathered her wits and came into the parlour to greet her father's guest, reminding herself that she knew how to act like a lady. She watched her father filling glasses with whisky, so she did not notice the involuntary gasp that came from the visitor when he caught a glimpse of her.

"Good evening, Papa." She reached up and kissed him on the cheek.

"You have outdone yourself tonight, dear. You do look lovely." He beamed down at her.

Elinor spoke through her smile, "Do not tempt me to roll my eyes, Papa. It will ruin my act." This made Sir Charles chuckle.

"Elinor, come greet our most welcome guest. I could not be more delighted that he is here." He motioned her toward the gentleman by the fireplace with his back to them. Her interest was piqued. Her papa was delighted?

The guest then turned, and suddenly Elinor felt her heart start beating rapidly as she looked up into the most beautiful set of sapphire eyes she had ever seen since— "And this is my godson, Major Easton. Do you remember Adam? You were so young when we left, and he was away at school much of the time."

Oh dear. She caught herself staring and remembered to speak. Surely this was not the same person? She must speak…"Of course I remember the rowdy group of boys always home from school wreaking havoc with Andrew." She managed to smile charmingly, though she was in mild shock that he was the man from earlier.

Easton laughed. Was he going to humiliate her for almost running him down?

"It is a pleasure to see you again, Miss Abbott." He had mischief in his eyes as he took her hand and brushed a kiss lightly on it, which caused a lock of tawny-gold hair to fall over his forehead. She only just stopped herself from reaching up to brush it back. Gracious! What was she thinking? She had nearly run this man over in her temper, leaving him mud-covered. She had been so angry, she had not noticed how handsome he was beneath his hat.

"Please call me Elly. We are not so formal over here. Besides, once you put frogs in someone's bed, it is difficult to think of them in the formal."

"Miss Elinor, then. I do remember a scrawny little hoyden following us around all over the place." Easton smiled as if to say,

17

'What I see before me now is not scrawny.' Instead, he said, "You are utterly charming, Miss Elinor."

Was he was flirting with her? She found herself looking over this person towering over her, exuding masculinity from his gleaming Hessians to his tightly fitted breeches. She made her way up past his navy blue coat, which seemed to make his eyes even bluer, when she met his amused smirk. He had caught her staring! She began to blush and was irritated with herself for acting like a silly schoolgirl.

"I was wondering why you are not wearing your regimentals?" She could tell he did not accept that excuse but was too gentlemanly to mention it.

Sir Charles went over to greet another guest who had just arrived. There were to be two guests?

"It would not do to be conspicuous, now would it?" He leaned in a little closer and said more quietly, "Lucky for me your father keeps clothes on hand for your brother. Mine seem to have become muddied somehow on my trip here." He smiled in genuine amusement and looked her over head-to-toe as she had just done to him. She felt a blush rising from her toes. "You do clean up nicely, though the mud was charming."

"Why thank you, sir," she said as she looked up into those eyes, challenging him. Her eyes sparked deep emerald green when she was upset or cross. Had he known who she was even then and had not had the courtesy to announce himself? Was this how things were to be?

"If you ride like the hounds of hell are at your feet, you are likely to break that pretty neck of yours one day." He reached up and flicked something from her hair. "You missed a spot."

How dare he criticize her riding! He was the one who would not move out of the way! It never occurred to her that he was toying with her, or that he might be right. "Sir, I find it more dangerous to stand in the path of a galloping horse," she countered, her face flushed.

"Touché, Miss Elinor." He raised his glass to her and took a sip nonchalantly. Sir Charles handed her a glass of wine and chuckled, as Easton said, "Perhaps you are a grown-up tomboy, though you have made quite a transformation since I saw you last." His eyes surveyed her face as he said this, and Elinor felt her heart pounding in her chest. Let him mock her. Perhaps she even deserved it a little.

"I am afraid the blame for that is all mine, Adam." Sir Charles. said as he retrieved a drink for the new arrival. "I have never insisted on Elly learning the formalities and fripperies of English society. Cannot say that I cared for them much then, and I do not now," He handed the guest the drink.

"Here, here." They raised their glasses to that.

"May I present our other guest?" Sir Charles, Easton and the stranger acknowledged each other with a brief nod. Elinor held out her hand to the new arrival and offered her most charming smile, determined to be a gracious hostess. This gentleman was much closer to her father's age, but without the kind face or easy warmth.

"Captain Dyson, my daughter, Elinor Abbott." The Captain took Elinor's hand and kissed it with an elegant bow.

"The pleasure is all mine, Miss Abbott." He looked to Sir Charles. "She is the mirror image of Elizabeth!" he said with a bit of an affected air.

Elinor did not feel easy around him, even though he had apparently known her mother. She glanced sideways at her father, who nodded, and she said, "Welcome to our home, sir. Hopefully we can provide a few hours respite from your otherwise unpleasant tasks here." That sounded agreeable. It was the best she could muster up. The Captain gave her a nod with a reminiscent look after as her father led him away to discuss war matters.

Elinor did not know what to make of him as she contemplated Easton. This could not be the same smelly, dirty boy that used to put creatures in her bed! Was he now a presumptuous, overbearing black-guard? Never one to back down from a challenge, she asked, "And what have you grown into, sir?"

"I am afraid I should not answer that," he replied with a self-mocking laugh, but his demeanour turned sombre, his eyes suddenly cold. Gone was the charming flirt. Curious.

"Ashamed?" She was daring him to shock her, though by the looks

19

of him he had seen and done it all. She knew a proper lady would curb her tongue, but she found she could not help herself.

"Nothing I would dare sully your ears with, Miss Abbott," he taunted, but before she could spout clever, unladylike replies to his comments, their butler, Abe, came in to announce dinner.

Easton offered his arm to Elinor to let him escort her into dinner. How could she refuse? She longed for time to compose herself. London was going to be difficult indeed.

~

Dinner was not a formal affair, though you would never know it by the table that was laid. They sat at a large round mahogany table that the family used for private meals, preferring to see everyone there. Elinor was very conscious of being the only female present and the tension hanging in the air.

Cook had outdone herself with the meal, a matter of pride for her when she was serving London's finest. The meal was so delectable, in fact, that thus far there had been little conversation other than trivial banter about the trials of growing grapes for wine in this climate. As the soup course was removed and the fish, chicken and venison set before them, her papa tried to make small talk. Not his forté, despite being a diplomat.

"Elly is none too happy about having a London Season," Sir Charles pronounced. Elinor stifled her choke with a cough. *Papa, how could you?* All eyes looked up to her with surprise.

She played it off with the wave of her hand. "There is so much to be done here, and I am comfortable here."

"Nonsense," Captain Dyson pompously exclaimed. "What would a proper English lady want to do with the barbarians here? Your place is in England."

"Barbarians?" She did not try to mask the shock on her face.

"There are savages and slaves here!" he retorted with indignation.

"There are no savages here, sir." Well, she had not seen any savages. "I agree with you that the use of slaves is abominable; we are hoping that other plantation owners will follow suit and free their slaves and pay them wages as we do. But savages?"

Sir Charles gave Elinor a shake of his head to warn her off any further retort. She looked up at Easton and swore he was laughing into his wine. Elinor held her tongue, and Captain Dyson kept on jovially as if nothing unnatural had been said. "She'll be the Season's Incomparable, no doubt. Quite a beauty." He nodded as if to agree with himself.

She thought she heard Easton murmur, "She'll be incomparable, all right."

She might have accidentally kicked him under the table.She decided to press with issues dearer to her. She addressed Captain Dyson, "How long is this conflict to go on, sir?"

He looked up at her with wide eyes, as if he did not understand why he was having this conversation. "No need to worry your pretty head about such things, Miss Abbott."

"Indeed?" She paused. She was only getting started. "I see the effects in the village first hand. Farming is the very essence of survival outside of the cities, so when our crops are blocked and confiscated, it devastates the livelihood of the villagers. Families' sons seem to go missing at sea. I have seen and tried to help the wounded soldiers at the hospital. So, when those things that affect our daily life go away, I suppose I can stop concerning myself."

Sir Charles shifted in his chair uncomfortably. Captain Dyson looked ready to explode.

No one answered, so she prodded, "The British already lost the War of Independence, yet you still impose trade restrictions and impress American boys into your navy."

"Those are British citizens, miss, whether they claim to have emigrated or not. Deuced convenient excuse if you ask me. Besides, they are merely reaping what they sowed," Dyson replied. "I think it best you leave the particulars of war to those who know what they are about."

Elinor counted to ten and bit back a reply, realizing it would fall on deaf ears. She rose, forcing all of the men to their feet. "Forgive me, gentlemen, I seem to have acquired a headache. Enjoy your evening. Godspeed on your journey." She dropped a quick curtsy and walked gallantly from the room, head held high.

The men stared openly as she walked off. No doubt her father was feeling her mother's absence right now. As she walked out she heard her papa offer one of his prized vintages from his own vineyards to try and change the tenor of the meal, but not before hearing Dyson proclaim, "Yes, Charles, best get her away from this uncivilized society as soon as possible."

Elinor rushed out onto the terrace, hoping some fresh air would ease her pique. She was extremely frustrated with herself for losing her temper. Those stuffy prigs were exactly why she had no desire to go to England. Even Major Easton was laughing at her, the rogue! Elinor had sensed him staring at her several times during dinner. There had been nothing blatant, but she had been conscious of his eyes on her. That man was too handsome for his own good, clearly a scoundrel. Despite herself, she found his raffish manner intriguing— dangerously so.

~

When Elinor had walked into the room, time had frozen. What a cliché. But truly, Easton had felt as if there were nothing on earth except the goddess-like creature before him. Hair of golden curls, eyes of emerald green and a smile to soften the hardest hearts. Even his. Especially his. Then he had opened his mouth.

Elinor was much as he remembered, yet so grown up. *Much* grown up. He certainly had not expected her to turn into this, this Venus-vixen-virago. And then he had had to untie his thoughts and his tongue enough to speak coherently to her. That was not one of his finer moments. First, he had stared at her as if she was the last woman on earth, then he had kept saying the wrong things, though he had quite enjoyed her temper. He was going to have to find a way to control himself around her if she was going to London; otherwise, he would be a stuttering, drooling fool.

Elinor was going to cause upheaval wherever she went. She had that natural ability to draw others to herself who hoped to get a piece of her allure. She would not enjoy London. The females would detest her distracting all of the male attention, and the males would…be smitten by her. She was every man's dream, if they were honest—beautiful yet unaffected and as capable on a horse or in intellectual discussion as any man. She would be too forthright and genuine to everyone not knowing the malicious rules of the game called the Season, and they would eat her alive if she let them. She was English by birth, but would still be considered an outsider by most.

Easton stared after her as she left the dining room, having held her own with Dyson. He had remained quiet through dinner, not wishing to betray himself to his superiors. He was fiercely patriotic to the British cause, but he did not agree with this campaign. He agreed with Elinor. He needed to put her from his thoughts since he had no business having them.

He sighed. She would take London by storm all right.

∽

Sir Charles knocked on Elinor's door, then peeked his head in. "Sweetheart? Are you still awake?"

Elinor glanced up, lost in another novel by Jane Austen her grandmother had sent. "Yes, Papa, come in. Is anything wrong?" she asked when she saw his face, growing concerned.

He shook his head. "I am afraid so. Adam came to warn us. The fleet is to begin lining the Potomac along the shores of Alexandria, and they cannot guarantee our safety. He thinks we should get away while we can. The Commander of all the British forces, Admiral Cochrane, plans to send forces to attack Washington and Baltimore soon. We are practically surrounded."

Elinor gasped and sat upright. "Why am I not surprised? I suppose we are in direct danger?"

"It is too risky to stay. The last place I wish you to be is here with gunships pointed at the shores." He sat on the edge of the bed beside her. "Not to mention all the soldiers who will be about."

She flung herself ungracefully back on the pillows, dislodging some feathers. "Why, Papa? Why?" She would never understand.

"They feel they must seek reparation for the attacks at Lake Erie and York. There is very little reasoning with people at war, and I am here at the behest of His Majesty. Many of the plantations along the coast have already been ransacked and burned, and I cannot ensure it will not happen to us. I also cannot be sure of your safety. It is best for me to get on toward the peace negotiations since the British are losing patience with the war, hopefully before there is too much damage done. I will start arrangements, but we need to move quickly."

"How long?" She twirled the end of her braid through her fingers with a worried look on her face.

"Soon. If they are already mounting the attack from both directions as Adam says, a matter of days," he said quietly, sadly. He reached over and patted her hand.

"I am sorry, Papa." She felt horrible about her behaviour. She would not fight about leaving any more.

"Me too, love. Me too." But they both knew it was not for her behaviour.

Sir Charles bent over and kissed her on the forehead and tucked her covers around her as he had when she was a child. Elinor nodded in acknowledgement, but felt a sinking feeling in the pit of her stomach. She blew out her candles and tried to sleep instead of crying, but strangely, all she could see were those ridiculously blue eyes taunting her.

She had difficulty trying not to think of what would happen in England. She would have to face her demons she had so carefully repressed into the dark recesses of her mind. She had overcome so much on her own, having been only thirteen when her mother died and she had been attacked. True, she did not think herself capable of ever having a relationship with a man, but she had managed to find some purpose in life. Now faced with the imminent return to

England, she could not keep the old memories from sneaking back. She tossed and turned and finally fell into a fitful sleep.

"Please stop! You are drunk!" she said turning around to face him while trying to push him off her. He continued to hold her tightly and try to kiss her despite her protests. She began to fight furiously. Her gown was torn down to the petticoats as they struggled.

"Why are you doing this? What is wrong with you?"

He grabbed both of her wrists and looked at her, laughing maniacally. Then noticing her torn gown, the look changed to pure lust, his eyes demonic.

"Stop! You are hurting me!" she cried. "Nooooooo!"

"Miss Elly! Wake up!" Elinor started, flailing her arms. She was drenched with sweat. Josie lit a candle and placed a cool cloth on Elinor's forehead. "Shh. It is over now. Only the bad dream. He will not hurt you any more. I will not let him." Josie held Elinor until she woke up enough to realize she was in her own room and had indeed had a nightmare. She hoped Josie was right.

CHAPTER 3

Sir Charles was already done breakfasting and off to town when Elinor came downstairs the next morning, once again wearing her serviceably comfortable riding attire, her hair in a single braid down her back. She called Josie into the breakfast parlour with her so she could begin preparations for the trip to England. Josie was much more excited about seeing Elinor into society than Elinor was. Josie clasped her hands together at the thought of seeing her lady dressed for balls and rides in the parks. She dreamt for weeks after each one of Elinor's sister's letters about London—Hyde Park, galas, balls, museums—and memorized the pages of each ladies' magazine they sent. "Do not look so glum, Miss Elly! Are you not a little excited? It will not be so bad."

"No, Josie. I am not excited. I am only going because Father thinks it best. I am quite content with life here, doing good work. Not wasting money on gowns that could feed hundreds of hungry mouths." *Or seeing the man who haunts my sleep.*

"Oh, I see." But she did not. All Josie cared about was how her beautiful Miss Elly would look on the arm of a handsome lord, and surely the right man would be able to help her through the anxieties of a relationship. Josie always thought she could keep encouraging Elinor... "But can you not marry well and keep doing good work?"

Elinor smiled. "I do not have to marry to do that!" That would be most people's logical assumption. Too bad they would be disappointed.

"No, but you would have more fun doing good with a fancy-piece beside you! And you cannot very well have wee ones without a husband."

Elinor was already reconciled to that, but a quick vision of chubby babies with blue eyes flashed before her nonetheless. She wished she could have all of it over with a snap of the fingers or by meeting the man of her dreams, but that was not going to happen. She played along as usual, ignoring the part about children. Josie knew, but she did not understand without having gone through it. She could not understand. Elinor forced herself to laugh and rolled her eyes at Josie. "And perhaps a handsome beau for you?"

"Icing on the cake!" Saucy, as usual.

Josie was to spend the rest of the day packing Elinor's trunks, and Elinor headed to the stables, to spend the day saying goodbye to the children and to the soldiers and friends she had made at her old school-turned-hospital. Unfortunately, now she would have to avoid the school since she was not ready to face Mr. Wilson yet.

Teddy, the groom, already had her horse saddled and waiting. She walked over and greeted Athena, who nickered and nuzzled for her carrot she knew was waiting in Elinor's pocket. Elinor laughed and handed over the goods, stroking the mare as she munched on her treat. If only humans were so easy to deal with. She was beginning to mount up as she heard a voice from behind.

"Good morning, Miss Elinor, would you mind if I join you for a while? Your father assured me you would not mind showing me more of this splendid land," She heard Easton's smooth voice as he strode into the stable, his hair a little tousled from the wind.

"Major Easton." She tried not to show her shock. She stared off, one hand on the saddle, one foot on the stirrup, her back to him, debating.

What was he still doing here? Why had he not left? She was hesitant to be alone with him, her nightmare last night reminding her of the dangers of rakes. She also had much to do before departing for England, but showing off her beloved River's Bend was a weakness. She was still annoyed with him for criticising her, and she was determined to keep her cool and distance from the handsome rogue. She did her best to give him a non-verbal set-down with a glare, but since he was eye-to-eye with her despite her being in the stirrup, it had little effect. Bother.

Ignoring her obvious reluctance, he walked closer and began to pet Athena, who nuzzled right up to him, helping herself to a cube of sugar. Traitor, Elly thought to herself.

"Please? I would be much obliged." He smiled at her, and gracious, if a dimple did not peek at her. Dimples had to be a creation of the devil. She looked at him sceptically, wondering why he was trying to be charming. She had already seen his overbearing side last night.

"I am rather surprised you would request to ride with me after you so eloquently stated your opinion of my riding skills," she said with a smirk.

"Your riding skills are exceptional, and you know it, Miss Abbott. I rarely ride with ladies."

The nerve of the man! No, she was not going to let him get her in a temper today. She put on her sweetest smile and spoke calmly. "Ah. So you doubt the female ability to handle a horse? Or should I be pleased you are condescending to ride with me?"

There was no good answer to that, Easton thought. "Nonsense. I find from experience it a bad idea to combine emotion with hard riding." Could he never say the proper thing around her? He rarely rode with ladies, because he was never around them. True, he had never been a skirt chaser and he avoided debutantes like the plague, but he thought most females found him charming. He certainly had not earned his reputation as a ladies' man. Elinor was apparently unimpressed with his skills. Maybe he should just smile at her more. The dimples had always worked on his mother. He had never enjoyed playing the charmer or rake, but he enjoyed watching Elinor's temper flare when he did.

"I agree," she said with a raised eyebrow and lifted her chin, which he found quite endearing. "Are you implying that females only ride hard when emotional?"

"Beg pardon. I sensed you were riding that way yesterday for a reason. I use it as my personal escape, and I thought you might do the same."

Elinor found her eyes began to glisten and turned away before she betrayed her emotion. She remained silent.

"May I *pleeeease* ride with you? I will only follow you anyway," Easton said with another grin.

"Very well." She grunted and nodded in assent. Not exactly ladylike.

"How gracious of you, Miss Abbott."

She was going to scream. "Saddle up Centurion for him, Teddy." If he wanted to ride, a ride he would have, she smiled to herself. Centurion was a barely-broken stallion.

"Already done, Miss Elly." Teddy grinned at her as he handed the reins to Easton.

First the horse, now the groom. Was no one still on her side? At least Centurion would keep Easton in line. She suppressed a laugh and gave him a mischievous grin over her shoulder as she expertly mounted her mare without the assistance of a mounting block.

She heard Easton chuckle arrogantly as he looked at the restless horse. He did not look the least bit concerned by the young stallion at all.

"Why are you here and not plotting the overthrow of Washington?" she blurted out. She meant that to be as sarcastic as it sounded, but she had also meant to be a touch more eloquent.

He looked at her with surprise in his eyes. "Miss Abbott, I am more sympathetic to your feelings than I can admit." He started to say more then stopped. "I remain to accompany your father at the behest of General Ross. We will meet up with them later."

"Then why are you here? If you do not agree with what is happening, I mean?" She looked at him in disbelief, searching his face, hoping for the answer she wanted to hear.

She saw a brief flash of something in his eyes, then he was back to his cavalier demeanour.

"Because it is my duty, though I am finding the principle of this assignment difficult now that I am here. I hope it will end soon. I am selling out when we return." He looked as if he wanted to elaborate on the subject, but hesitated. "And, your father asked me to spend the morning with you, to see if I could ease any of your fears about London." Dimples. Again. She was going to kill her father. Elinor nodded as if she could accept his answer, but the thought of him fighting for something he did not agree with bothered her. She did not envy him that. She turned her mare and clicked her tongue. She took off with an easy leap over the first hedge on her favourite ride past the tobacco fields toward the river. She pondered how many soldiers felt as Easton did? Knowing they were pawns of kings and presidents who might or might not have their best interests at heart, but a desire to protect what they believed in.

She let her disturbing thoughts go and laughed as they raced through the fields. Easton easily matched Centurion to her, stride for stride, which she must admit impressed her. *He must be cavalry to ride like that. No wonder he had looked arrogantly at Centurion.* The two got lost in the ride, finding camaraderie in their horsemanship, taken with the rush from the wind in their face and the pounding of the horseflesh beneath them. Elinor cherished the escape from reality, where it felt like her worries were carried away.

They rode until the horses began to slow from exertion. Elinor finally pulled up, bringing them to a trot, and they rode in companionable silence as she led Easton down a path toward her favourite spot. She stopped at a tree where the horses could drink and graze, and Easton followed her lead. She bent down and splashed her face to cool herself from the humid August afternoon, and then she started down a path through the vineyard. Easton eventually followed after he stopped gaping after her.

Elinor picked a bunch of grapes off one of the nearby vines, then scampered down the hill back to her special spot. She did not normally share this place with anyone, but she had little time left to enjoy it. Then they sat on the river-bank in comfortable tranquillity for a while, listening to the gentle roll of the water, until Easton broke the silence. "How long have you lived here?"

"The plantation?" He nodded. "Papa bought it shortly after we arrived six years ago. Initially as an investment, then we loved it so much we moved here. He thought I needed more room to roam than we had at the city residence."

"So you are going to London directly from here?"

Elinor nodded, still staring out at the water. She tore off half of the grapes and handed them over to share.

"Is there a particular reason you are not thrilled with the prospect?" he asked, staring at her eating the grapes. She refused to look at him, for fear he would see right through her.

"Would you want to leave this?" She gestured with her hands at the surrounding river, hundred-foot-tall trees and hills in the background.

"It is undoubtedly incredible, but I agree with your father that it could be unsafe for you here for a while. It will not be so terrible. You do have many well-placed connections in society there." He refrained from mentioning the fact that she was English, though she was certain he wanted to.

She sat in silence for a while, mindlessly pulling grapes from the bunch and eating them. Then she confided quietly, "I will never be accepted there. I remember enough of Sarah's Season to know that I cannot conform to society." She sighed. "Not after living like this."

"Who says you must conform?" He looked into her eyes, and she felt her heart soften a bit. She looked away quickly, determined not to be taken in by him. Never again.

She looked back at him suspiciously. "I will disgrace my family with my hoydenish ways, as you so graciously pointed out last night."

"That was not what I meant," he said softly.

"You mean my shrewish tongue and untamed ways will be welcome in the *ton*'s drawing rooms in London?" She stared, daring him to contradict her. "You know as well as I that any hint of individuality is shunned in a female." She looked away, starting to feel overwhelmed as everything began to close in on her. She stood and straightened her skirts out.

"I must return." She turned to head back up the hill when Easton, all six feet of him, took her arm and spun her into him. She flinched at the contact. He looked down into her eyes with tenderness, but then he pulled back when he saw he had frightened her. She could not tell him why else she did not want to go back to England, or why she was afraid of getting too close to him.

She fled to Athena and took off. *He already thinks I am hellion*, she thought, so she kept going, not looking back.

Easton had no idea what had gone so wrong, but something was haunting Little Elly.

Elinor made her rounds that afternoon to say goodbye, trying to forget her encounter with Easton. She had not handled that well. It seemed that she was unable to maintain her composure around him. He likely still saw her as the little tomboy she had been as a little girl back at the Abbey, or as bad, when she had been an awkward thirteen-year-old with her body matured beyond her years and her face covered with spots. She had felt so grown up that last night in England, her first proper gown and her first dinner with the adults. Elinor had thought Easton so handsome that night, but she had not given that or him any more thought after her attack. She had worked hard on being able to maintain calm or indifference when needed, and it was as if all of those years of hard work had been wasted when she had seen him again as an adult.

Why did he affect her so? It was not as if she wanted his attentions *that way*. Heaven knew he must have much more refined tastes when it came to females. With his looks and roguish charm, she had no doubt about his abilities with the fairer sex. Perhaps she was still vain enough to want his attention, therefore proving she was not as repulsive as she felt? She had not come across many men of his ilk before, and these thoughts were treading with danger she could not afford.

She needed to shake that feeling quickly. How was it even possible to feel attraction after what a man had done to her? *Because deep down you know all men do not hurt women.*

These questions pervading her thoughts, she made her way across the bridge on Athena toward the minister's residence in Washington, hoping Easton would be gone soon and she could get back to being composed and serene. Well, maybe not serene, but calm. At least he would not be in London.

Elinor arrived at the bustling corner at Connecticut Avenue, and left Athena in the stable with her groom whom she'd brought along at Papa's insistence when she rode to town. She loved the courtyard garden full of reminders of her mother. Gardening was her mother's passion, and together Elinor and her father had filled this smallish garden in the middle of the city with her mother's favourite trees, flowers and herbs when they had first arrived from England. She sat for a moment on the stone seat in the centre and drank in the peace of her mother's presence she felt there.

She rose after a few moments, having made it there in time for tea and looking forward to her special time of day with her papa. Ever since they had come to America, tea had been their time together whenever possible, whether in town or at the plantation. She was feeling better and hummed as she made her way through the garden, bees buzzing all about. She pruned a few dead blooms as she strolled through, taking in the heady scent of the roses in all of their glory on a warm summer afternoon.

Elinor strolled through the open doors into the library and found Easton in all of his handsome splendour having tea with her father, engrossed in discussion. She took a deep breath. She would not let this man bother her. She stepped further into the room and walked to the tea service and began to pour herself a cup before they noticed her. "I hope I am not intruding?" The two men stood at her arrival.

"Of course not, dearest. We could use a break anyway." So she was intruding. So be it. She would be separated from her father soon, and she would steal every minute she could.

"Any plans for departure?" She glanced at Easton over her cup, wondering if he understood her meaning. He shot a glance back at her. She gestured for the men to sit back down.

"Nothing in stone, dear. Just be ready." Her father tried to hide the worry from his face, but she could sense it. He looked like he had aged a decade since he had tucked her in last night.

"I believe my things are packed at least." She would never be ready. "Have you more meetings tonight?"

"In a manner of speaking." Sir Charles did not look at her when he said that. Interesting. "Will you excuse me for a few minutes?" He left the room, and her keen eyes followed him with a concerned look on her face.

Easton finally broke his silence. "He is trying to spare you worry, Miss Abbott. I would play along."

She spun around and glared at him. "Beg pardon?" He was unmoved and sat there with an arrogant air of indifference. He finally turned to look at her, and she was frightened by what she thought she saw. Disgust? Annoyance? Then his look changed to contemplation, and he finally decided to speak. So he was not going to mention her behaviour earlier. That was a relief at least. Apparently he was not going to be civil either.

"Cochrane wants to move on Washington tonight, so we will be leaving shortly to meet them."

If he intended to shock her, well, he succeeded, but she did not want him to know that. "Why are you telling me this? Clearly it is against your better judgement to do so."

He inclined his head in acknowledgement. "Because your father is sick with worry—much of that worry is for your safety. I would greatly appreciate it if you would not harass him further on the matter. I gathered you would not be satisfied until you forced him into telling you."

"You, sir, are too kind." She forced the most insincere smile she could, and without further ado, she turned on her heel and left the library, taking great pains to be dignified, with her chin held high. All she wanted to do was shout, "Go away you insufferable, impertinent, arrogant, odious creature!" Granted, she had not given him reason to think her deserving of better treatment, but it chafed nonetheless. She held her tongue and made it to her horse before she let out a scream of frustration. She had a five-mile ride home to compose herself. She was far beyond the bridge before she realized she had not bid her father goodbye.

~

Sir Charles came back into the room and circled around looking for his daughter.

"She made her escape. I am afraid I scared her away," Easton said, chagrined.

"She is only upset about leaving. She is not normally so, so… emotional." Sir Charles waved his hand about, searching for the right words.

"No, sir, I apologize. I never seem to say the appropriate thing when she is around."

Sir Charles laughed. "She seems to have that effect on men. And she has no idea. She has received at least four offers of marriage this year, and she gets upset every time."

Easton felt a pang of jealousy and dismissed it. He was not fit for husband material even if Elinor were interested, which she clearly was not. As a second son, he was not expected to marry, so he had never tried to be husband-worthy. His life the past eight years held no place for a lady. He cringed when he thought of the wives who followed the drum, not knowing when there would be food, often sleeping in the open in either freezing or sweltering temperatures, moving constantly, facing the brutality of not knowing if their loved ones would return home that day… He forced his thoughts back to the present and the sadness of his brother's life that was wasted. Easton was now the heir. He needed to be husband-material.

As if sensing his thoughts, Sir Charles said, "About time for you to think about a wife, eh? I am dreadfully sorry to hear about Max's death, Adam. However, it will be your responsibility to carry on your line."

Easton swallowed visibly. "I do not know how to be a husband."

"No one does, my boy. You learn as you go. The key is to find the right lady," Sir Charles said with a knowing smile.

"But I am so set in my habits, none of the other officers even want to share quarters with me," Easton argued with a laugh. That might be a stretch, but it made the point.

"Again, you simply need the right one," Sir Charles said matter-of-factly.

Could Sir Charles be right? He thought he still had wit and charm, when he could remember to take off his soldier's hat. It would be difficult after eight years of rigid structure and rules and having the responsibility of so many lives, but he used to know how to have fun before the army. He had even laughed a little at some of Wellington's balls when he'd had the opportunity.

"I will think on it, sir, though I am not sure there is a lady alive that deserves to be saddled with me." He thought of Elinor's spirited smile from that afternoon out riding. *I would not mind being saddled with her.* He knew he should not think such thoughts. Even if he did have to marry one day, it would not be to her.

"I imagine they can decide that for themselves."

"Perhaps." He grinned back at his godfather.

"Come," Sir Charles rose and gestured for Easton to follow, "let us rest and have a nice supper before this horrid business before us tonight."

Sir Charles and Easton arrived at the scene of the attack to the stench of death and black, thick smoke rising from burning buildings. Moans of the wounded and screams of frightened women and children echoed all around them. Easton hated this. He wanted to be home. *Only a few more weeks of this, God willing.*

They stood and watched Colonel Knott shouting orders to burn everything in sight. "This is utter madness! That was not the order at all! Should I say something? Where is General Ross?" Easton searched with his eyes, barely controlling his rage. The city was teeming with innocent civilians, and they were raining down fire and brimstone as if they were on a battlefield. He could not stand by and watch any longer. He turned to Sir Charles, "I will meet you at the Minister's residence later. Please stay safe."

"Godspeed, son." Sir Charles turned and walked his horse away from the soldiers wielding their torches at Washington.

Easton dismounted and made his way toward Knott with purpose. "Sir." He saluted. "With all due respect, is burning civilian homes necessary? The orders were to preserve the unarmed and only destroy the government buildings!"

Astonished at the temerity of Easton to question his orders, Knott retorted, "They have not given us the same courtesy! Think of the Erie attacks! And Admiral Cochrane said only spare the lives of the unarmed!"

"Do we stoop to their level? Burning houses with women and children inside? What of General Ross who is directing this attack?" Murmurs of agreement sounded from the soldiers around them as a crowd was beginning to grow, which only infuriated Knott.

"Soldiers, I did not order you to cease! Unless you want to find yourself charged with insubordination, I suggest you follow orders! Now!" He turned back to Easton in full rage as the soldiers scampered off reluctantly. "Take your concerns to General Ross, but I suggest you keep your opinions to yourself unless ordered otherwise! If I catch you ordering anyone to defy my orders, you will regret it." The last sentence was spoken with quiet malice, before Knott turned and stomped away.

Easton took several deep breaths to calm himself, then went to find his men. He refused to have any part of killing innocents. The inhumanity of war would haunt him for the rest of his life, but at least he did not have women and children on his conscience, and he did not intend to start now. He spotted his batman, Buffy, up ahead and rode quickly toward him. He rapidly issued orders as directed by General Ross to limit the destruction to those armed and government targets planned and avoid unnecessary civilian casualty. He saw the relief on the faces of his troops. Easton left his deputy in charge while he went to search for General Ross.

He rounded the corner of a building heading toward the Minister's residence, where he hoped to find his leadership. He heard the crack of gunfire, and he quickly lowered himself over his horse. The Americans must be responding to the attack. He spurred his horse forward and dismounted in front of the residence. He felt an eerie sensation at his back and turned to find Knott heading toward him with sword and pistol drawn. He turned to head into the residence, then heard the crack of a pistol and felt a fiery explosion of pain in his back as he tumbled face down into the ground.

He felt a booted heel come crashing down on his head and the prick of a sword searing deep into his leg. Shouts came from nearby, and Easton felt the boot and sword be lifted from his person, and Knott was gone. Trying to rise proved futile as his head swirled and his leg buckled. He lay there in agony, feeling the blood rush from him until he could not make anything else out, and then faded into unconsciousness.

CHAPTER 4

*T*hat evening, Sir Charles still had not returned home, which was not highly unusual, since he often stayed at the residence in Washington if he was at meetings or late parties. But tonight was not usual, because there was a planned attack on Washington. Elinor had no idea what that actually meant—where her father would be or what he would be doing. What did an attack actually entail? Surely her father was not going to take up swords and pistols and aid the British against America! He was here to promote peace! She paced anxiously for a while, then she tried to read for a while. She repeated pacing and then trying to read. Elinor was also anxious about news of their departure, since her father warned her to be ready. Why did not he want to tell her what was going on? And why had she not said goodbye? Because of the insufferable Major Easton, that was why. She had teetered back and forth all night between anger at his high-handedness and guilt for her behaviour toward him.

She finally gave up on wearing a hole in the carpet and was closing down the library after waiting there into the early morning hours. She heard the familiar sound of horse and carriage and ran to the front door to greet her father. But what she saw was not her father emerging from the carriage, but the limp body of an officer being carried in by a British soldier and one of the footmen.

"What happened?" she asked as she hurried over to try to help the officer who was bleeding and appeared lifeless.

"The British attacked Washington tonight, took a torch to it," her father's coachman announced.

A collective gasp sounded amongst those now gathering in the entry. "And him?"

"He's been shot, ma'am. I was given instruction by Sir Charles to bring him here." The voice came from the well-weathered and dirty British soldier carrying the injured man.

"All the way here?" It was over five miles from the city. Why not take him to their army surgeon?

"He said you would understand—that you could help him. And said not to tell anyone he was here." The soldier looked nervous, worried that she would turn him away. Actually, she was terrified and surprised that her father would send an ailing soldier to the house. Well, he was here, and she would do what she could.

Elinor nodded and told the footmen to take the officer to one of the guest rooms, issuing orders to the servants.

"Fetch me some spirits, boiled water and bandages. Send for Dr. Harrison and tell him it is urgent. I hope we can keep this man alive that long. Send Josie to come help me, and keep pressure on the wound!" The servants scrambled to their tasks and she hurried upstairs after them.

So her papa had sent him here and not to the hospital? Something about her father's message pulled at her heart. She could not let this man die, and she would not allow herself to think about why her father had done so. She looked upward and whispered, "God, please let Papa be safe."

As she climbed the stairs, she kept trying to calm herself by remembering what her papa always said. *Do not panic.* She forced herself to go into the room to try to perform her own miracle.

"How severe is it, Josie?" Elinor asked her maid. Josie had also helped at the hospital, so she had some experience.

"He's lost a good bit of blood, but he's still alive." They understood what she did not say—for now.

Elinor looked to the soldier who had brought the officer and asked as she pointed to the hole on his back near his right shoulder, "Is this the only wound?"

The pale batman nodded, "I think so, ma'am, but it was so dark I am not certain." Then he whispered a plea, "You have to save him, miss."

"I will try my best. What's your name?" She tried to keep herself talking because the batman was clearly nervous about his master. Josie came back into the room with supplies, and they started arranging them as they talked and tried to work quickly.

"They call me Buffy." He looked at her awkwardly, but she smiled back at him as if that were a normal nickname.

"Well, Buffy, I am Elinor." He nodded and stared at her, still dumb-struck that a lady was in the sickroom. "Please help me get what is left of his shirt off and roll him up on his left side to see if the bullet went through. If not, we have to remove it. If Dr. Harrison is not here soon, we will have to do what we can."

They rolled him up, and she placed a pillow up under him. *No exit hole on his chest, so the bullet did not go through.* She sighed. *No sign of Dr. Harrison; of course, he's at the hospital. Please God, let me have the stomach for this. Watching someone else is not the same as doing it yourself.*

She took a deep breath. *But he will die if you do not, Elly.* He would likely die anyway, so anything she did was better than nothing. She nodded as if she had convinced herself, rolled up her sleeves and got to work, trying to will her trembling hands to still. She took the boiled water and began to rinse the wound that was still bleeding. *At least it is not gushing.* She started trying to explore the wound with her finger, which caused the officer to wince in pain. He could feel at least. *That is a good sign, is it not?*

"I apologize, sir. You have been shot, and we are trying to extract the bullet. I do not know if you can hear me or not, but perhaps you understand me. Please live, sir. Please."

Eventually, Abe, the butler, entered the room breathless. "Miss

Elinor, Dr. Harrison has his hands full himself, but he sent some tools if you need them. He said you would know what to do with them."

Josie began to set the tools out and clean them in the boiled water. These tools were much more useful than what Josie had managed to come up with from the kitchen. One try with the forceps, and she was able to pull the bullet out. Everyone in the room breathed a sigh of relief, until the blood started pouring from the hole. She applied pressure to the wound, but it merely slowed the flow. She had not expected that. Frankly, she thought the bullet would have lodged in the bone in his shoulder. She tried everything she knew to slow the bleeding, but the bandages kept soaking though.

"I believe I might have to sew him up to stop the bleeding," she said, so as not to get their hopes up. Josie gathered her needle and thread and handed them to her. She took the spirits and rinsed the wound out, causing the man to groan. She hated to sew up a wound likely to get infected, but he would bleed to death anyway if she could not get it to stop.

"One stitch at a time," she whispered. Elinor had seen Dr. Harrison do this many times, so she began sewing the layers and the bleeding began to slow. "In and out, in and out," she mumbled. Talking to one's self was so soothing. She detested sewing, but somehow this did not bother her as much if she imagined she was darning a pair of stockings. She laughed a bit to herself at the irony. Only she could find humour in this.

Everyone else surrounded her and watched in amazement as she worked meticulously, the work slow, as Josie had to constantly mop up the blood in between stitches. Elinor finally stitched closed the outer layer, put some basilicum on top, then wrapped bandages tightly around his shoulder and back with help. She took a deep breath, as if she had held it the whole time, then collapsed down into a chair and wiped her brow.

Buffy spoke first. "You did wonderful, miss. The sawbones in the field wouldna' done so nice, if they'da bothered at all."

"Thank you, Buffy, but we have a long way to go yet. I am not even sure what I did was correct. I know Dr. Harrison does not close

42

wounds he thinks likely to fester, but I did not know how else to stop the bleeding." She stared in silence a few moments, and then shook herself back to the present. "What is his name?" She was not sure why it mattered.

"Major Easton. Finest soldier and most respected I've ever seen next to Wellington himself. His men would follow him anywhere or do anything for him." Buffy beamed with pride describing his master.

Elinor paled. How could she not have noticed? She had been too intent on the task at hand. It was better she had not known it was him. "Do you know why Sir Charles asked you to bring him here?" she asked quietly, stunned at the revelation.

"No, ma'am. I suspect he had his reasons." The batman looked down as if afraid to make eye contact.

"And my father is safe?" He nodded. Thank God.

Elinor had to accept that was all the information she was to receive. "I will go and wash, and gather the supplies we will need the next few days. Then I will stay with him for now, and you can take a turn in the morning. If we can get through the night, then we have cause to hope." She left them bathing and changing the Major and went to rinse off her shock with a bath.

Elinor returned somewhat refreshed but dreading the long hours ahead of her. She sent the others off to rest, but Josie refused to leave her. They sat on either side of the man and watched the breath in his chest go up and down for several minutes. He still looked pale, but at least his lips did not look as blue.

Josie spoke first. "He certainly is handsome. Such a shame for such a fine specimen." She clicked her tongue and shook her head.

"Josie! This is Papa's godson!" Elinor feigned outrage, but her smile betrayed her.

Josie continued shamelessly, "It does not matter who he is. I may be a maid, but I am not blind." She blushed but grinned, and Elinor could not help but laugh. She was not blind either. She did, however, make a closer examination of the patient now that they had survived the immediate crisis, and though none of his features were individually perfect, the whole certainly made a statuesque picture. Elinor had seen men without their shirts at the hospital, but none who made her insides do flips. He was so different from her—hard where she was soft, tanned and scarred along the ripples of muscles, and had a dusting of golden hair. Her cheeks felt warm, and she looked to his face. She brushed back a dark blond lock. She never could have studied him such when he was awake. Now if only she could be this calm around men when they were awake. Elinor did not know if she would ever master that.

Elinor and Josie sat watch all night with the Major. He would start shaking as if freezing. "I think he is in shock. I have heard Dr. Harrison talk of it. I think it is because of all the blood he lost, but I do not think there is anything to do but keep him warm and try to get him to take fluids." That was not very successful. Every time they tried to get him to drink, much of it dribbled down his chin. They kept trying though, and he did swallow some. She intermittently paced the floor, knowing it would not help, but it did dissipate some of her nervous energy.

"Wearing a hole in the carpet will not make him better quicker, Miss Elly." Josie chastised.

"I know, I know, but I cannot help myself." She kept up her circles.

Again, the Major would start thrashing and shaking. They would replace his blankets and try to calm him as best they could. Elly tried singing softly in his ear every hymn and tune she could think of, which seemed to settle him. He would groan in pain from time to time, and though Elinor hated to administer laudanum, she finally gave him a small dose to try to stop his convulsing.

"It almost seems like he's having nightmares," Josie said thoughtfully.

"He might be reliving the battle. I have seen other soldiers do much the same. I cannot begin to imagine how they repress so much of what they see."

"Is that like your nightmares?"

An innocent question, but Elinor froze. "Perhaps."

"You used to have them all the time when you first came. And they have started again." Josie did not have to mention that fact. They both knew the nightmares had started again, since Josie was holding Elinor when she woke last night. Sensing that Elinor did not want to talk about it, Josie turned the topic back to the wounded man. "Can you make out what he is saying?"

"No, and likely he would not want us to. It looks like he is finally calming down. Let us change him into something dry, since we seem to have spilled more on him than into him."

Josie grinned and said, "I will do that part, Miss Elly. You can look the other way."

~

Sir Charles finally made an appearance after dawn. He visited to check on his godson and was relieved to find him alive. Elinor flew into his arms. "Papa!"

"I knew you could save him, Elly." He hugged her fiercely.

"He is not saved yet, Papa." She left his arms and went over to the window and looked out over the grounds. "Why here?"

"Colonel Knott." Sir Charles paused for an interminable silence, then decided he should tell her the whole story. "Adam stood up to him for trying to set all Washington on fire, and this is what he received for thanks."

"Dear God." Elinor gasped. "How bad is the damage, Papa?" Elinor fought back tears as she thought of all of the people she knew and cared for in the city.

"The President's House, the new Capitol, and others. Ross had ordered to minimize private casualties, but Knott wanted it all destroyed. Easton stood up to him and refused to follow those orders. The men agreed with Easton. It was so pointless, Elly." He shook his head in disgust. "I do not believe anyone else saw Knott shoot him, but I pulled him away from there as soon as I could when Knott was distracted. Knott would have found a way to finish him off."

45

"Will he be in trouble if we do save him?"

"Yes, I fear Knott is already searching for him. Knott would only look a fool, but I can testify, as can Ross and some others if it comes to that."

"But was he not insubordinate to a superior's orders?"

"Thank God he was, Elly. Hurting innocents makes us no better than what they are supposedly retaliating for! Unfortunately, now there is an outcry against the British, and we will not be safe here. We need to leave here as soon as we can. When can he be moved?"

"Do we have a choice?" Sir Charles shook his head. "Then I guess we will have to take our chances."

"I will go and make arrangements then, and help you get off tonight if possible. Where is his batman?"

Elinor indicated the dressing room attached to the bedroom. "Sleeping on a cot in there. He was exhausted."

Sir Charles awoke Buffy to take a turn watching Easton. Josie and Elinor bargained with Abe and Buffy about keeping watch over their patient. Dr. Harrison arrived and reaffirmed that Elinor had indeed done a decent job, and that all they could do now was wait. He said a shoulder wound should heal easily enough with proper care and rest. She prayed she had not done anything to make him worse! Elinor hoped Easton would wake before they had to leave. She would feel a little better about her efforts and their voyage, though at Dr. Harrison's instruction she had given him some more laudanum to help ease the pain, so he had not yet awakened.

Easton found himself trying to wake up, but he could not seem to open his eyes. A familiar female voice was sending someone to retrieve fresh bandages. Was he in a hospital? He tried to open his eyes, but his sight was foggy and the room spun about him. This female then bent over him to undress him. Was he dreaming? Was he being undressed? But then he winced in pain as she moved his shoulder. Back and forth she moved him as if removing a bandage. He managed to open his eyes, but everything was still blurry and his head throbbed. He heard a humming and what is that—a bosom? An angel? He must be in heaven. Maybe he should just see…

"Sir!" She ripped the bandage off! Nope hell. Definitely hell.

"What happened? Am I in hospital?" A pair of sapphire blue eyes met directly with a pair of emerald green ones.

For a moment time stopped.

Elinor was distinctly uncomfortable with the rush of awareness she felt in his gaze, and she turned away.

"You were brought here after being shot. You are at the home of Sir Charles, your godfather. Do you remember me?"

He gave a small nod, seemed to snap back to the present, then stared quietly out the window for a few minutes, and Elinor thought he might drift off again. Then he said quietly, "How badly did he burn Washington?"

"The Capitol, the White House and some other government buildings. Apparently he was stopped before he went further."

"Thank God," he whispered. She nodded.

"Is there anything I can do to make you more comfortable?"

"Help me forget," he said quietly. She understood that sentiment completely.

"Unfortunately, we must set sail for England immediately. Papa says it is not safe to stay here."

Josie came back into the room with the bandages, and they helped him to sit up. Elinor's hands were suddenly fumbling and shaking as she tried to dress his wound. Why was she so nervous now that he was awake? Did he notice her discomfort? She finished as quickly as possible, and as soon as his head was on the pillow he was asleep again. Elinor, thoroughly embarrassed, backed to the door without making eye contact, excused herself quickly and closed the door. Perhaps he would sleep most of the voyage.

How was she going to spend weeks on a ship with this man? She knew she was overreacting, but she kept her sanity about men by avoiding them, and there would be no way to avoid him on a ship. She did not like the way he made her feel as if she had no control over her feelings or emotions. Not to mention her body's betrayal.

Josie departed to obtain as much as she could in the way of supplies. Elinor knew taking Easton on a journey this soon was risky, but so was remaining here. He continued to sleep, and she sat in silence while awaiting Sir Charles's return to take them to the ship. Elinor was trying to cherish her last hours at River's Bend.

∼

Sir Charles returned before dinner later that night. She waited for him to speak first. He did not look pleased. "You must depart tonight," he said solemnly.

"What do you mean by 'you', Papa?" She was afraid she knew.

"I cannot accompany you to England. I must make haste directly for Ghent."

"I cannot travel with him unchaperoned!" She was not a stickler for rules; she simply did not want to be alone with him. Besides, she would need help caring for him.

"This is an unusual situation, Elinor. I was fortunate to obtain any passage with all the British fleeing at present. It is with a private shipping company that sells a few cabins to those who can afford it. There will be a few servants and a cook. You will have adjoining cabins."

"Adjoining?" She was trying to remain calm, but her voice sounded harsh.

"There is no other option, and I trust Adam implicitly, Elly. I could not anticipate what happened. Besides, he is no condition...Elly, I need you to do this. No one on the ship will know you, and you may disembark in England with no one the wiser." Her father rarely chastised her. She felt like a small child being told to remove her hands from the biscuit jar. "I am afraid Knott means to finish him off," her father continued. "There are soldiers searching for him and asking uncomfortable questions. Once you are safely on board, I will let it be known what actions I have taken, but we must get you away safely first."

"Of course, Papa." Easton would be fortunate to live even if Knott did not find him. She knew that better than anyone. And her papa did have a point. No one would know the circumstances once they arrived in England, and Josie would be with her, as well as Buffy with the Major. She could not like the idea, but they had to get away from America.

"There is not any other way?"

Sir Charles shook his head. Elinor turned away to control her tears. How could one's life turn completely upside down in two days?

～

As the carriage pulled away from the house, Sir Charles spied several British soldiers ride up to the house. He hoped they had not noticed the carriage leaving, but he directed Teddy to drive a different route to avoid detection.

"Papa, look!" Elinor spied the soldiers as well.

"Hush, dear. I told Abe what to say—that I am merely escorting you to the docks. They cannot know I sent Adam to my house." He hoped. "I am sure they are just here to pass a message on."

Elinor settled back against her seat, but was now filled with trepidation for Easton and Sir Charles. If Knott knew Sir Charles had helped Easton, would he retaliate against him too? "Papa, will you be in trouble for helping him?" she asked nervously, but she had to give voice to her concerns.

"I do not plan on anyone finding out. None of the servants save Abe know it was Adam who was brought back to the house. There are retaliation mobs burning anything British at the moment, so it is quite natural for me to remove you from here if anyone wants to know my whereabouts. I plan on full disclosure to General Ross as soon as I see you safely off. He will have good advice."

"Do you think Colonel Knott will simply let the issue be forgotten?"

"I doubt it, and it is dangerous for them to be out searching with the civilian mobs out tonight. I cannot believe even Knott would be so bold."

"So why else would the soldiers be at the house?"

"As I said, they must be delivering a message." He looked as doubtful as she felt.

Suddenly the sound of horse's hooves began to grow louder and threatened to overtake them. Elinor began to pray silently that the soldiers were not chasing them. The carriage jerked to a stop, eliciting a groan from the semi-conscious Easton, but Elinor was more worried about the immediate threat. Why had they stopped? Had the rider done something to Teddy? Sir Charles jumped from the carriage to prevent the intruder from seeing their passengers.

"Thank God it is only you, Abe." Sir Charles heaved a sigh of relief.

"Aye, sir. I would not have chased you down if it were not urgent." Sir Charles nodded, and Abe continued, "The soldiers are searching the house. Colonel Knott is with them, and he is furious."

"Does he know we have him for sure?" Sir Charles asked worriedly.

"I do not think so, but he is right suspicious. I best get back." Sir Charles nodded, then Abe turned the horse and dug his heels in to urge the mare on. Sir Charles hurried back into the carriage, and Teddy sprang the horses.

"Papa, will we make it in time?"

"Heaven only knows, love."

"Should we switch to the boat?"

"I do not think we could make it in time with only Teddy and me to row."

"Josie and I can row!" Josie nodded in vehement agreement.

"No, we could not take all your luggage. We best pray we have enough of a head-start and they do not suspect we have him with us. Abe did not tell him where you were leaving from."

They rode a few miles in eerie silence, listening for the sounds of pursuit. As the carriage drew closer to the Alexandria docks, they started smelling the stench of smoke, and saw packs of angry civilians with torches looking for anything and anyone to vent their fury on. They passed the plantation of Lord Fairfax and Elinor noticed the blazing flames leaping from the rooftops and the surrounding fields. She had to hold back her cries and pleas to God that River's Bend would not receive the same fate, hoping their efforts at freeing their slaves would count for something. If they discovered a carriage with two British soldiers, the results would not be pleasant. At least their driver, Teddy, was American.

Elinor heard Teddy urge the frightened horses on through the curving, blazing streets, through the thick smoke and angry crowds. Her heart hammered in her chest, hoping they would not be noticed and Knott and the redcoats were not in pursuit. It could not be much farther.

"As soon as we stop, head to the ship immediately. I will have the luggage sent up. Do not tarry!" Sir Charles' training as a former army Colonel was showing under duress.

They pulled up as close to the dock as possible. Sir Charles helped Buffy secure Easton, then ushered Josie and Elinor out. He shouted orders to the anxious dock workers and sailors who had been awaiting their arrival, and a fury of activity broke out as their trunks were unloaded and carried away.

Elinor stopped, full of dread. "Oh, Papa, I cannot leave you here! How will you make it back to the house?"

"Much more easily without harbouring British soldiers. We will take a different route. Now go!"

Elinor spied a group of four or five redcoats charging quickly on their horses. Sir Charles turned and saw the same thing.

"Go aboard the boat now, Elinor!" He grabbed her for a quick hug and pushed her toward the planks. "Do not worry, love, I will deal with them. I love you. I will see you in England."

"I love you too, Papa." She turned to walk the gangway with a sense of doom. There was no turning back now, come what may.

"I will be with you before you know it," Elinor heard Sir Charles call out to her.

As soon as she stepped behind the railing, a sailor pulled up the planks while workers on the dock released the restraining ropes and shouted, "Unfurl the sails!" Then they were moving.

She turned to reluctantly wave her final farewells, but the pack of British soldiers had caught up with Sir Charles. An angry man, most likely Knott, dismounted and marched over to Sir Charles, shouting and hurling accusations. Her father stood there looking nonplussed and then turned to her, waved and winked at her with a smile. She waved back and smiled, trying to play along. There was nothing she could do for her papa now, except help his godson.

Elinor looked upward to the looming masts with their sails unleashed and outward toward the bow of the massive wooden-hulled ship. Squawking seagulls mocked her plight as they circled overhead. She inhaled deeply of the briny sea air that provided no comfort as the smells near the river did. She sent a silent prayer up for her papa, their journey and for Easton. She was thankful for the darkness so she did not have to watch her beloved father and land fade away in the distance.

CHAPTER 5

The First Officer directed them from the main deck up a narrow stairway the farthest aft of the ship to two small cabins separated by a sitting room near the Officer's and Captain's Quarters. Buffy was helping Easton settle as Josie was sifting through their trunks. Elinor looked around at the tiny accommodation, a far cry from the luxurious passenger ship she and her father had travelled on six years ago. The room contained two built-in bunks and a small table with two chairs, all nailed into the floor.

There was a knock on the adjoining door, and Buffy was there with a concerned look. "Miss, I think you should check on the Major. He's burning hot."

Elinor nodded and turned to ask Josie for help. "Josie, please find the supplies and bring them to me. Buffy, go see what you can find in the way of cold water." Elinor knew more soldiers died of infections than the bullets that shot them, and there was little she could do for him, especially on a ship. *This does not bode well. The ship has barely left the docks.* She went into the adjoining chamber and found a half-conscious Easton drenched in sweat. Josie came in carrying bandages and medicines. Buffy had already removed Easton's jacket and waistcoat.

"Josie, help me remove his shirt, then we need to inspect the wound."

They finally got the bandage removed, and the area was slightly red. Then she felt around the line of stitches, which was a bit warm, but was it red enough or warm enough to cause a fever? Elinor groaned. Why was this happening? She did not have enough training for this! She rinsed the wound with the spirits and applied more basilicum, then redressed the wound and sat back in a chair. She had no thoughts other than it would be a miracle if Easton lived to see England.

The trio proceeded with the arduous task of keeping cool cloths, dry clothing and clean sheets on Easton. Elinor dripped the herbal tinctures she had made and any form of sustenance she could into his mouth and hoped he would not choke. He woke intermittently, but he never seemed to be completely aware of his surroundings.

In his delirium, Easton gave hints as to the battles that haunted him. Shouts of, "We must stop him!" or "Not the children! Save the children!" Cries of agony and thrashing accompanied these horrid visions, and Elinor could only imagine the torments that soldiers suffered long beyond the actual battlefields.

Several interminable days passed in this manner, and Elinor and Buffy would rotate who stayed with him. This cabin was smaller, holding only one bunk, with a makeshift hammock strung up for the second passenger at night. Josie was too ill with the seasickness to sleep in a swinging hammock, so Elinor and Buffy usually split night duty. Elinor began to fret to herself, partially from exhaustion, for she would barely leave Easton's side. He was no better, and his fevers seemed to be higher with little reprieve. Here there was no Dr. Harrison to give her instructions, only her own, slightly educated judgement, that was growing more questionable with each passing day of exhaustion. What would happen if he died? Elinor could not bear to think on it.

She had entirely too much time for reflection as she alternated staring at the dying man and out of the small window. She frequently thought back to their interactions since his arrival two weeks prior, and felt ashamed of herself. What vile being had possessed her behaviour? She should have been kinder to him, or even kind at all. She vowed she would try to be different if he would recover. She hoped she could figure out how to keep him from affecting her.

Josie and Buffy made their way into the room to check on Easton.

"Miss Elly, you look done for! You go for some fresh air and take a nap. I promise I will find you if anything happens."

Elinor shook her head. She was not leaving as long as he remained near death's door. She owed her father and Easton her best. She looked over at him. His face was red as a lobster, and he was burning hot with fever. She rushed over to him, and the two servants watched her with growing apprehension.

"Do you think we should bleed 'im, Miss Elly?" She heard Buffy ask. She looked at him in horror.

"Do they still practice that in England?"

"Aye, miss." He looked ashamed for suggesting it.

"I am sorry, Buffy. I did not mean to criticize. Dr. Harrison believes that bleeding does no more than drain their bodies of the energy they need to fight. I am not sure what is right. I do not have the tools to bleed him anyway. I am afraid we will have to open the wound and see if there is any sign of festering beneath the skin. There has to be some cause of the fevers." She put her head in her hands. "We should have stayed there until he was better. Where Dr. Harrison could have taken proper care of him."

"And been killed by cannon blast?" Yes, that was the alternative.

Josie came and wrapped her arms around Elinor as she began to cry. Elinor felt the overwhelming presence of an emotion teetering on hysteria welling up inside. "Miss Elly, we did not have a choice. You are doing your best, and it is in the Lord's hands now." Josie was right. She didn't have the luxury of time for emotions.

"He wouldna' had a chance with a sawbones in the field, miss," Buffy said, also trying to encourage her, but seeing Elinor so worried made him scared.

Buffy and Josie helped to remove Easton's bandages. When they pulled them off, the wound on his back still did not appear infected.

"Buffy, are you sure there are no other injuries that could be infected? This wound looks so clean."

"Well, miss, he got old wounds on his leg from the Peninsula, but I didna' look close."

"We will have to look now before we open up the one on his back." This certainly was not the time for missish modesty. They pulled the sheets back enough to examine the old wound on his leg. It was on the far side of the bunk, so she assumed that is how Buffy missed it when changing him. She herself had tried not to look, for his sake.

There were bright red streaks coming from a red wound in the middle of a mass of puckered, scarred skin. She shook her head. She should have checked him all over, but she had not wanted to. She should have known better. "Another gun shot?" she looked at Buffy questioningly.

"I do na think so. Sir Charles only saw one shot. Mebbe a knife or sword cut?"

"Those can cause infections too. We should give him some laudanum. This will hurt worse than the gunshot did." Buffy saw to that task, while Elinor took some scissors from her bag of supplies and dipped them in the spirits to clean them. She started cutting the dead skin away layer by layer. Once she had completed that, she doused the wound in whisky and took some towels and began to push around the wound. Easton started groaning loudly and began to thrash. Buffy and Josie did their best to hold him. Immediately the wound opened up and began to ooze a foul-smelling yellowish liquid.

"Oh God in heaven. No wonder he is not getting better." Elinor's stomach churned. Josie ran from the room.

"Lawks, Miss Elly, that's awful." Buffy stated the obvious, grabbing a handkerchief to cover his nose. Josie came back in looking like she had cast up her accounts.

"Sorry, Miss Elly. I was not expecting that smell. What do we do now?"

"We try to draw the poison out and clean it. He is not going to enjoy this part." She pressed and pushed until she could no longer remove any infectious fluid, cut away the dead skin, then reached for the spirits to rinse the area. Elinor felt guilty that she had even worried about being on the ship with him. Ha! At this point, she only hoped he survived. She prepared a poultice and packed it into the open wound and wrapped the bandage around it.

"Now what?"

"We wait and see."

~

Elinor could not sleep for worrying about Easton, and when she did manage to nod off for a few minutes, it was from exhaustion. Somehow she felt responsible for him—whether from a sense of pride or why she knew not, but felt it all the same. She did not know if she could bear it if he died. He had tried to befriend her, and she had been harsh because he had been a little haughty and handsome. She should not have been so quick to judge, but old habits were hard to change. After seeing his old scars, she had found a new level of respect for him. She had no idea how he had walked without a limp or ridden a horse the way he had. She could not begin to imagine what he must have been through to have those scars.

They continued to rinse the wound with whisky and pack it with a foul-smelling poultice of garlic, plantain and yarrow, and tried to force Easton to drink teas that Elinor had learned to make from Dr. Harrison. She was willing to try anything. He still had not fully regained consciousness. When she changed the dressing, Elinor was mildly encouraged that the area did not seem to be getting worse or have any more poisonous drainage.

She woke to Buffy's nudge a while later.

"Miss Elly, he's cold!" She jumped up to check for a heartbeat. It was still there. He was not cold *that* way.

"And he's soaked." *Thank God, he must have broken the fever.* They worked to change him into dry smalls and sheets. Changing linens was a difficulty at best on a ship with a person still on the bed. Easton still showed no sign of awakening, but at least there was cause to

57

hope. She fell back asleep on the hammock in his cabin, sleeping a little more peacefully than before.

～

When Adam awoke he was famished, and he hurt like the devil. The room seemed to be rocking back and forth. He finally managed to open his eyes—something he had been trying to do for what felt like days, but he had been in a hot, groggy haze he had not been able to awaken from. He blinked a few times, his eyes adjusting to the dim light. It looked like it was early morning or the late evening; he could not tell which. He was used to waking up in strange places, but he usually knew where he was.

He glanced around the unfamiliar room and saw somebody lying on a hammock next to him, but it did not look like Buffy. He cocked his head to the side trying to focus, and saw long, golden waves hanging over the side and a petite feminine form bunched up under a blanket—Elinor. Why was she in his room? He tried to turn over and, *ouch!* Pain from his shoulder and leg shot through him, and he began to remember bits and pieces of being shot, being at the plantation, and Elinor. What had she done for him? He must have been in and out of consciousness for some time. He knew she had been there. He had recollections of her voice, her scent, her touch. Nothing specific, but he knew.

His stomach growled, and his mouth felt like the Sahara Desert. He gazed around the room and spied a jug of water. Surely he could get a drink of water without disturbing Elinor. He managed to push himself up to sitting with his good arm, but found he was exhausted from that meagre effort. He flung his legs over the side of the bunk rather ungracefully. His legs were shaking, and he knew he would not be able to manage to get across the room alone, small though it was. He looked over at Elinor sleeping peacefully and did not want to disturb her, but wondered how long would she sleep? He tried not to think about that delicious, refreshing, thirst-quenching glass of water. Of course, the more he tried not to think about it, the more he had to have it. Maybe if he tickled her cheek a little. She turned over. Well, the view was nicer at least, but she did not wake up.

She did look like an angel, albeit an exhausted one. Mayhap he should try to stand another time and not disturb her. Maybe if he went very slowly. He slid his feet down to the floor and, *oof!* He grabbed on to her hammock to steady himself, but instead flipped her out, then fell right on top of her. She screamed, of course. He managed to squeak out, "Shh," though his mouth felt like it was full of dry cotton.

Elinor stopped screaming, but her heart felt like it would beat out of her chest. When she realized she was not back in the middle of her recurring nightmare, she let out the breath she had been holding. She looked up to see Easton grinning from ear to ear, and then he started laughing hysterically. "You look awful, Miss Abbott."

"Ungrateful wretch! Did you have to scare me senseless?" she exclaimed, then she smiled, too relieved to see him awake and coherent to be mad. Then she retorted, "You look awful yourself. Would you mind explaining why you are on top of me?" He would never know how much it cost her to speak rationally in this situation.

He smiled sheepishly, clearly debating what kind of reply he could get away with. He chose the safe one. "As much as I would like to claim an amorous motive, I was merely trying to fetch a glass of water, and my legs are apparently not communicating with my brain."

"It has taken me a while to get my sea legs without an injury." She scrambled out from under him and helped him to sit back up on the bunk. Then she went to the jug and poured him a glass of water. He suddenly realized he was only in his smalls and covered himself quickly while she poured.

"Thank you." He held out his shaking hand to take the water. "So we are on a ship. That explains much." She helped him take a drink, and then he held out the other hand. She stared at it as if it had leprosy. He held it out farther. "How long have I been out of commission?"

"Several days. I've lost count." She reluctantly took his hand.

"Have I been a horrible patient?" he asked as he pulled her to the spot on the bed next to him. She hesitated but sat down. Surely someone so weak would be little threat to her, physically anyway.

"The worst."

He chuckled. "But you would expect no less."

"True." My, how happy she was to see those dimples and eyes open again.

"So you helped me despite wishing me at Jericho?" His eyes twinkled, and he still held her hand.

"I would not say Jericho, because I could have easily have let you go there." She realized her hand was still in his and drew it back.

"Touché."

"Do you feel like eating? Opening your eyes and harassing me are only part of recovering."

"I am only getting started. I am famished though. Is the chef decent?" He grunted with pain and weakness as he repositioned himself gingerly.

"The chef?" She laughed. "What they have sent has been edible."

"Is Buffy around? I would love a bath." He sniffed at himself and made a face.

"One step at a time, Easton. He and Josie should be awake soon and will come check on you." There was a knock on the door, and a young steward brought in a tray for Elinor. He looked a little startled to see Easton awake.

"Shall I bring another tray for you sir? I brought the usual, ma'am." The servant appeared uneasy, not knowing what to do.

"That would be nice. Some broth and bread, perhaps? And perhaps some bath water would not go amiss either if possible." She saw Easton trying to steal the bacon from her tray. The boy nodded and slipped out. She smacked Easton's hand away.

"I want bacon. I *need* bacon." She chuckled. Men were all alike.

"Of course you do. But your stomach is not ready for that yet." His stomach growled loudly, on cue.

"My stomach says it is. Besides, everyone knows of bacon's miraculous healing powers. Well, in England anyway." He tried to cross his arms and do his best to give his dignified try-and-stop-me look, but his arm was too weak to manage the manoeuver. The look was more like that of a petulant toddler who was not getting his way, but she gave in. After a not-so-subtle glare.

"That is the most pathetic argument for bacon I have ever heard. Maybe one tiny piece. One. I do not need you upsetting your stomach too." She was rewarded with a huge grin.

"You're awake! The steward gave us the news," Buffy said as he burst through the doors. He ran to the bed where Easton sat and enveloped him in a hug. He then remembered himself and jumped back. "Sorry, Major. I am deuced happy to see ya lookin' well. I was 'fraid ya would...well, ya know." Easton nodded then obviously regretted the swift movement. Buffy was rather talkative today. "Then Miss Elinor here pulled the bullet out and sewed you up. Then you got the fever and you should've seen what she did to your leg. That gel's got bottom." They all shivered in remembrance.

"Apparently this old cat has nine lives. And a good surgeon." He gave a grin with a nod to Elinor.

Buffy and his master starting chatting together happily, and Elinor slipped into the adjoining cabin, pulling Josie in with her. Hopefully Easton assumed she was giving him some time to catch up with Buffy and to eat and bathe in privacy. Easton incapacitated was one thing. Handsome, charming, rakish Easton was a different animal alto-gether. She would have to be on her guard with him awake, for her heart and her head were waging a war about him.

After a while Buffy knocked on the adjoining door and asked if the ladies would assist him in getting the Major out to the deck for some fresh air.

"Is he strong enough?" Josie asked, surprised.

"Now that he's awake there will not be any keepin' 'im down," Buffy said proudly.

Elinor sat debating. She did not know if there were any other passengers on board, but the likelihood of them being seen together and recognized in England later was small. Besides, anyone would realize how weak he was, and it would do him good. They could always deny having shared such close circumstances.

"Are there any other passengers on board?" Best be informed.

"Aye, miss. I heard there is an older lady, but she keeps to her cabin with the seasickness. I have not seen 'er yet."

"All right, it would do us all much good to have some fresh air. I know I have cabin fever." Though she would be surprised if Easton could walk ten feet after this morning's episode, let alone up and down the steps to the deck.

Easton chuckled and smiled in appreciation of the pun. He would not be able to do more than sit in a chair on the deck, but it was a start.

Over the next few days they settled into a routine of trying to strengthen Easton with food, strolling on the deck, and taking fresh air. He was determined to get back his strength as quickly as possible, but it was not going to be easy. He had never bought into doing anything slowly.

They kept mostly to themselves, eating in the cabin and playing cards or chess in the evening. Often Elinor would read to them from one of the books she had brought, but she maintained a polite distance. Easton wondered why Elinor was different, now quiet and withdrawn. What happened to the little hoyden? Buffy had told him of her dedication—how she had never left the cabin, and how she had insisted on keeping watch at night when his fevers always had been the worst. He was dumbfounded that she had done so much. She was unlike any other female of his acquaintance. But why the change? Was she disgusted with him on some level? Perhaps she thought him a coward for defying Colonel Knott. Perhaps he was. Or had he offended her? Was she still annoyed about their last meeting in Washington? Hopefully, she was merely homesick.

According to the Captain, there were only a few days left until reaching England, if the winds remained in their favour. Easton wanted to get on better terms with Elinor before arriving, but he was not sure how. He was not sure if she was irritated with him personally, or because she was being forced to go to England and having to nurse him. Never before had a female shown so little interest in him in that way, which was perhaps what he liked best about her. Naturally. With her, he was uncertain, and he found himself uncharacteristically flirting with her or trying to get her agitated just to break down the wall she seemed to have put up.

Easton continued gaining strength. He was able to limp about on his own, and could use his arm a little. He was eating normal meals, and even had a touch of colour back in his cheeks. Once he regained some of his lost muscle, one would never know how close to death's door he had been.

The four of them were sitting on the deck as had become their custom the last few days, enjoying the brisk, fresh sea air. The day was calmer than usual, and not too chilly.

He decided he would take matters into his own hands. He was not sure what it was about Elinor that made him want to try so hard. He felt as if everything had changed since that night in Washington, as if he had a second chance. Perhaps it was the fact she was Sir Charles's daughter, but there was something about her that he wanted to help. Perhaps gratitude was what he felt.

"Miss Abbott, would you mind taking a stroll on deck with me? It is a beautiful day."

She looked up at him and hesitated. Sensing her hesitation, he said, "Come now, I do not bite. We have been through hell and back, surely we can promenade about the deck without much ado."

She capitulated and took the arm he offered. After walking in silence a few minutes, Easton could take it no more. "Miss Abbott, have I done something to offend you?"

Startled she stopped and looked at him, "Why no. Why ever would you think so?"

He laughed and looked back into her eyes, "Why, because you are offensively polite to me and you stay as far away from me as decently possible. Why the turnabout? I am unaccustomed to the docile, meek person before me."

She did not say anything, clearly pondering how much to say.

"I fear I am going to suffer a decline if she does not return soon. I am quite sure it was that Miss Abbott who induced me to fight so hard to live." He pulled out his signature cheeky smile with the dimples.

She blushed and was again speechless. He could see her mind searching for appropriate words as she worried her lower lip. Finally all she said was, "I am sorry I am unaccustomed to delivering the flattery you seem to warrant from most females."

"You think I desire that?" They stared at each other questioningly, and before he realized what he was doing, he bent down to place a simple brush on the lips, but she turned away and it landed on her cheek. She did not yell or slap him, but she did pull away while shaking her head.

No rebuke? He would feel better if she had. He searched her eyes, but was not sure what he was seeing. Why had he done that? He was not a rake, so why was he acting like one? "I am sorry, Miss Abbott. I do not know what came over me."

He sighed and let his shoulders slump a bit. "Can we please at least be friends? I promise to try not to assault your lips in the future without permission."

She reluctantly nodded and pulled away to walk back to their chairs on the deck before her resolve melted. Easton stood looking after her. He wondered what had he done wrong. And she had not actually answered him. Satisfactorily anyway. As he stood there frowning after her, he heard a voice calling his name.

"Major Trowbridge? Fancy meeting you here!"

Oh, no. He recognized that voice. What the deuce was she doing here? London's most infamous biddy. Of course, the older lady passenger. He would pray for rough seas for the remainder of the trip. He turned and bowed. "Lady Dunweather. I am glad to see you are feeling better."

"Who was that?" No greeting or how-do-you-do for Lady Dunweather. Straight to gossip, as usual.

"A relation." Of sorts. "Daughter of my godfather."

"I never tried to kiss any of my relations that way." She raised her eyebrow in suspicion. "Where is Sir Charles? I have not seen him yet." The blasted woman would have noticed that.

Easton knew how he handled his next statement would make or break Elinor's Season, so he remained quiet. Lady Dunweather was London's most malicious gossip. She narrowed her eyes as she waited for his answer.

"Her companion is with her. Sir Charles was to accompany her but was called away for official business. Unfortunately war did not allow for ideal travelling conditions and companions."

"I would have hardly chosen these conditions myself." She nodded and seemed somewhat appeased by this explanation, but it was clear she would be watching. He tried to divert her by asking after her and her favourite subject, herself. She had travelled to visit her daughter in Virginia, but left with the threat of war along the coast. This diversion did not appease her for long.

"So, Sir Charles Abbott's youngest chit? I had forgotten about that one." She eyed Elinor appraisingly across the deck, considering where to file this information for later. "I shall expect an introduction."

"Of course."

"Pray tell, why you are travelling on a passenger ship instead of His Majesty's?" she asked, hoping there might be a juicy bit of scandal involved.

He hesitated. He did not want to mention the unfortunate incident with Colonel Knott, but mentioning the injury would at least keep her from suspecting his relationship could have been improper, although he knew it would be all over town the minute they arrived. Maybe he should have worn a sling.

"I was injured in one of the American efforts, and the Abbotts were kind enough to allow me time to recuperate at their home. Even if I had wished to ravish Miss Abbott, it would have been quite impossible." He grinned the grin that showed off his dimples in order to turn Lady Dunweather up sweet. It seemed to work. He was not normally crass, but she was not a normal person.

"Major! How could you say such a thing, you blackguard!" She batted at him with her fan but seemed satisfied for now.

"That is what you wanted to know was it not?"

"Hmph. Impertinent baggage."

"And now, your ladyship, I must excuse myself, for this exalted company exceeds my prescribed activity for the day, and I am feeling quite fagged." He bowed elegantly and limped away. Perhaps he exaggerated the limp a bit for her benefit.

"You seem fine to me, you rogue!" she said, smiling after him as he turned. He walked toward his cabin, but stopped short and instead sought out a place to think alone.

Easton stood by himself for a while. He was not sure how to handle Elinor. He sensed some turmoil in her. Why did he care? He enjoyed verbally sparring with her before, but now she was barely conversing with him. She was beautiful and could ride like the wind, which enhanced her beauty, but there was something else drawing him to her. Why had he tried to kiss her? He knew he should not have. He chuckled to himself. She was adorable when flustered; he could not help himself. He had never had intentions of getting leg-shackled, though Sir Charles hinted rather strongly he would not mind a match in that quarter. He had not been the first-born son after all, and he had never intended to wed. Now, he had no business getting married despite Sir Charles' reassurances. For some reason he wanted to prove to Elinor that he was not a rogue —kill her with kindness and be a friend to her. But she deserved better than anything an old, battle-hardened soldier had to offer.

His thoughts took a more sombre turn to what had happened in Washington. He hoped Sir Charles was right that there would not be any repercussions from his actions against Knott. He was sure he had done the right thing. In fact, he would do the same thing over again. Hopefully Knott would remain silent—he had shot his own man in the back, after all, and there were gentleman's own rules for that conduct. Besides, Knott had left him for dead. Yes, doubtless Sir

Charles was correct that there would not be any more said, especially since Easton was planning on selling out when he reached England.

Easton was looking forward to spending time on the estate. He doubted he would be working at the War Office after what had happened in Washington. Surely it had nothing to do with the fact that Elinor would be spending time with her grandmother on the adjoining estate.

"Pardon me, Major." Josie tentatively approached Easton in his reverie.

"Oh, Josie. Is everything all right, or did you come to watch the sunset as well?" She stared at him as if he was mad. Maids stood enjoying sunsets with gentleman. She shook her head. "No, sir. I do not mean to be impertinent and all, but I noticed you with Miss Elinor earlier."

He turned to look at her, uncertain whether he was surprised or indignant. "Yes?"

"Well, you see. It seems to me you are sweet on her." She actually held her hand up to stop him from protesting! "And she does not react well if she thinks you are flirting. You would do better to try and befriend her. Loosen her defences that way. Good day, sir." She winked, bobbed a quick curtsy, and hurried off before he could reply. He gaped open-mouthed after her.

CHAPTER 6

*E*linor noticed Easton speaking to the garishly-outfitted older lady. Even the wealthy in Washington did not display themselves in such an ostentatious fashion. To Elinor, there was a difference in the type of quality that required display and had to be announced, versus the kind that simply...was. That, the way she gestured intimately and Easton's lack of reciprocity predisposed Elinor to dislike the woman. Easton seemed disturbed when the conversation ended, and he did not return to their place on the deck. Instead, he walked off.

Elinor groaned to herself. She hoped the woman had not seen her or did not have any place in society. She was being daft. She thought more about what Easton said. Could they only be friends? How many times had she said that herself? Elinor did not want to keep her distance on purpose, to judge him by her previous experience. It was difficult to be near a handsome man and not feel that she was somehow threatened. Was that the difference? Had she been able to befriend those men in America because she had not had any attraction to any of them? Why did she feel guilt when she found herself attracted to Easton?

Elinor still did not like the way she felt when she was near him, even though he had not acted rakishly or arrogantly since the shooting. He seemed a different Easton. Perhaps being near death had that effect. Something in her had stirred when he had tried to kiss her, something she desperately needed to shut away. Then he had asked her what had changed and she had been utterly at a loss for what to say. She could not exactly have said, 'I am afraid to be alone with you when you are awake.' Or, 'I am scared of the way I feel when you look at me like that.' She prayed that they arrived in England soon. She did not know how much of the charming Easton she could handle, but she was determined she would try to be as close to normal as possible.

Easton finally returned to the cabin to rest. Elinor was having tea at the small table in the sitting room; he sat wearily on a chair across from her. "May I join you, Miss Abbott?"

She nodded, but scooted herself to the far edge unconsciously. "Are Buffy and Josie about?"

"They are playing cards in the servants' quarters." She saw the exhausted look on his face. "You have overdone yourself, sir. Should I call for Buffy? Why do you not lie down and rest?"

"Nonsense. Just a trifle fatigued. There is something mesmerizing about watching the sun fall behind the sea. A spot of tea and a few minutes rest will have me good as new."

"Do I need to order you?" She smiled playfully and poured him a cup. She was trying hard not to act awkwardly, but how did she manage to end up with him alone all the time?

He mock-saluted her, though it pained him to lift his arm so high. "I promise I will be good from here on out." They both knew he meant more than as a patient.

"Miss Elinor, I ran into an acquaintance earlier and feel I should warn you about her, for she is a notorious gossip in London."

"Have I done something to be worried about?" She was afraid she already knew. The rules were more relaxed in America, but even she had concerns about sharing adjoining cabins. She wondered, as they sat there alone in the cabin's sitting room, if this had come to the lady's attention.

"I hope not. She was quite curious about you. I tried to ensure her about the propriety of our situation and informed her of my injury, but it would be best if no one knew our true travel accommodations."

Elinor nodded. "Well, what's done is done. Papa did not see anything wrong with it, and of course nothing improper has happened, but I suggest you not try to kiss me in public view again."

"Does that mean it is acceptable in private?" he asked, jesting, but if looks could kill, he would be dead from the daggers coming from Elinor's eyes. "I promise to behave. I suppose I should keep a proper distance from you in London so she does not get any ideas."

"Yes, that is probably wise. Unfortunately, if my Season is like Sarah's, I will be busy from dawn until dusk. I do hope I can at least get in some riding." She looked longingly at the tea leaves in the bottom of her cup.

Easton was still trying to figure Elinor out. If he had even hinted at any other ladies being compromised they would be trying to force him into a betrothal. But not her. It did not appear as if the thought had occurred to her. How different she was from all of the simpering misses he had endured on the Marriage Mart in the past! He hoped that she remained unaffected by Season's end.

They both sat quietly sipping their tea for a while. Elinor was trying not to feel awkward, and Easton was trying to think of something *friendly* to say to her. They were finally alone together, and he could not think of anything meaningful to discuss.

"Where did you learn your medical skills, if you do not mind my asking?"

She looked up from her tea curiously. Was he truly interested in that? "I am not sure I would rate them as skills. Perhaps I would call it experience. But to answer your question, I suppose by accident. My finishing school in Washington was turned into a makeshift hospital, and I began volunteering to help the wounded soldiers. I would write letters for them or feed them or sometimes only read to them. Eventually, they needed help with other things, and there were never enough people to help." She contemplated her tea. "It seemed hypocritical to sit by and watch when I had able hands to help. Many of those poor boys should have still been home with their mamas, yet they were fighting for things they could not yet comprehend." She shook her head. "Forgive me. You asked a simple question, and I went on a discourse about why."

"Nonsense. You will find me the last person to complain about how or why you garnered you medical skills. I very likely would have been in the ground in Washington or buried at sea if it were not for you." She blushed charmingly. He could watch that all day. "Besides, I find it quite fascinating. I have never been around females much, but the ones I have would be hysterical at the thought of blood."

"I cannot say that your choice of females to associate with has much to recommend it."

"That is an understatement. I would not exactly call it my *choice*. And it is one of the reasons I did not object to the army."

"For some reason I feel compelled to defend my sex!" She laughed. "Although I cannot condone hysteria or impracticality. I think there must be a compromise between army life and flighty females."

"I do hope so, since that is now my destiny. I suppose I can hide out on the estate and avoid all females, though that will not make Father happy."

"*Flighty* females," she corrected. "Well, you could place a sign at the gate that says no flighty females allowed." She chuckled. "Although I find that type rarely able to take hints."

"Exactly." He sighed. "If you find out how to avoid them or deter them, I would be forever in your debt." As if he was not already. "Now you know my deepest fear—the dreaded Marriage Mart."

She barked out a laugh. "Is that what they call it?" They shook their heads in mutual disgust. "So, where will you go after London if you are avoiding the Marriage Mart?" She asked this as if she had eaten a very sour lemon.

He regarded her question with amusement, but answered amiably. "My intention when I left home a year ago was to sell out after the America campaign. I will tie up a few loose ends in London, then head home to rusticate in the country for a while." He could not help but smile when he thought of his home. "Then I suppose I will take a seat in Parliament. I have too many opinions about how things should be improved to remove myself completely." He chuckled a little.

"That's nice to hear," she said quietly.

Easton cocked up an eyebrow and looked inquiringly at her. "What do you mean?"

"That it is nice to meet someone with a sense of purpose—of doing good, I mean."

"Do you suppose that all English aristocrats are lazy wastrels? I suppose the London *ton* could give you that impression certainly, but second sons must be productive or be impoverished," he said with a twinkle in his eye, but leaned forward as if to impart a deep secret. "We are much closer to the masses then we let on."

She regarded the question thoughtfully. "I do not suppose I thought all of them were. But I confess my memory of Sarah's Season left me with the impression the majority were." Many of her relations had also helped form that opinion, but she decided not to mention that.

"Is that why you are reluctant to have a Season? You think none of us worthy?" he asked teasingly but with an edge of truth to it. "Are we all to be judged by a few?"

She blushed to hear him speak of her thoughts in such a way and realized how intolerant she seemed. "Well, sir, when you put it like that, it does sound a bit ridiculous. But I do hope to live a life that has meaning. I *was* living a life that had meaning. Besides, I have no thoughts of forming an attachment here and have every plan to return to River's Bend when it is safe again. So it makes little difference what I think of the English gentlemen anyway."

"Then I shall have to make it my mission to show you that England and English gentlemen are worthy. We cannot have you returning to America with such an ill feeling about us."

"Very well. I wish you luck. I will try to be appreciative of your efforts." She laughed. She was grateful for being able to be more comfortable in his presence. She berated herself inwardly for not giving him a chance earlier, but she could not help but feel she was being drawn in by some force she could not control.

"That is all I can ask. I think I shall enjoy trying very much," he added softly. And the blasted dimples were back.

~

The seas were not as friendly the last few days, and they did not at all agree with Josie. With her companion feeling queasy, and knowing Lady Dunweather was lurking about, Elinor chose to lie low in the cabin for the remainder of the trip. She was happy that Easton seemed to have stopped flirting. She was actually enjoying his company, strange as it was. They would arrive in England soon and go their separate ways, and she could forget all about him, or at least the uncomfortable sensations his presence caused.

The pair and their companions eventually reached England on a brisk autumn day. Easton was feeling well enough to take command of their transportation, for which Elinor was grateful beyond words. He left Elinor and Josie in Buffy's care. The ladies were extremely happy to be on land and walked around joyfully as if it were their first steps while they waited for their trunks to be unloaded.

Easton was back shortly with a travelling carriage and a luggage cart arranged for their transport from the docks to London. This was the first time Elinor had seen Easton in his full regimentals, and the old adage was true: there most certainly was something about a man in uniform. He had regained some of the weight he had lost from those first two weeks of the journey when he had been bedridden and feverish, and filled out his uniform in a most pleasing manner. Even the limp did not hinder his allure.

Elinor shivered against the bone-chilling cold that seemed to come from the River Thames, along with a rather unpleasant odour of dead fish and rotting refuse. Josie elected to ride up on top with Buffy despite the cold, not ready for more motion sickness after her last few days at sea.

Easton handed Elinor up into the carriage, then handed her a rug to protect her from the chill. He sat on the bench across from her, but his long legs seemed to surround her, filling much of the space inside. She was shocked to find she was not afraid of him, that she did trust him not to hurt her. She pondered this as he looked out the window and realized for six weeks she had been with him almost constantly, and they knew very little about each other. She was both thankful and disappointed they had arrived, for she found herself wanting to know everything about him, despite knowing it was futile. She needed to distance herself from what could never be.

A thick fog was settling in over the city, but she stared out of the window anyway, mainly catching glimpses of street lamps and old buildings. As they rode through the various areas of London, Elinor's thoughts turned to what she would face when she arrived. She was to meet up with her family in London, then go on to Loring Abbey for the Christmas holiday. Her grandmother, the Dowager Duchess of Loring, would be her sponsor and present her at court. Elinor adored her grandmother, who, despite her age, was very warm and loving, and certainly entertaining. Some might call her eccentric, except that was normal for a duchess. Elinor could not help but smile when she thought of her grandmother. She desperately hoped she had not changed too much from age, but she did not think so based on the regular letters and gifts she received.

When they finally pulled up to the Duke's residence on Audley Street, Elinor felt that the trip had gone too quickly. Easton alighted first, helped Elinor out and walked her to the door as Josie and Buffy carried their trunks toward the servants' entrance.

"Will you come in?" She was surprised at the sudden sense of melancholy she felt about saying goodbye. My, how her opinion had changed in a few short weeks!

He shook his head. "I am anxious to greet my father. Please give my regards to your family. I will call to check on you soon." He reached for her hand and gave it a kiss. Then he looked up sheepishly and said, "I suppose I should not have done that, I promised not to kiss you any more." He looked at her in a way that made her temperature rise up within her.

"Actually, you only promised not to assault my lips without permission," she quipped. She was proud of herself for managing that clever retort.

Elinor turned toward the door preparing to greet her family whom she had not seen in six years then turned back when Easton said, "Well, I guess this is a goodbye of sorts. The rules will be different now."

She nodded. "I know."

He took her hands and looked her in the eye. "I do not know how to thank you properly, Miss Abbott. There are not sufficient words, but please know if you ever need anything at all, I am at your service." He gave her another quick bow, then turned and climbed back into the carriage.

CHAPTER 7

LONDON

*E*aston watched Elinor go in and thought staying away from her was going to be nigh on impossible. After the door closed behind Elinor, he tapped on the carriage roof, signalling the driver to proceed. He watched the familiar houses pass by as he reflected on all that had transpired since he had been here last.

Everything would be different now. His army days were virtually over, and he would have to start learning how to be a peer. Unlike many siblings, Adam had never envied his elder brother's position as the heir. He felt a wave of sadness that his brother was gone and he never had the chance to say goodbye. For despite their opposite ways, they had been close. He had seen so much death in the army that it was more painful to know his brother had been reckless with his life, either drinking too much or engaging in dangerous races.

Adam quickly felt guilty for his thoughts about his brother, Max. Was he not himself guilty of being reckless? With his actions, he had practically asked Colonel Knott to kill him. If it had not been for Elinor, he too, would be dead. He rubbed his injured leg subconsciously as he thought about all she had done for him. My, but she was hard to figure out! For weeks she had been either fuming at him or ignoring him when she had not been saving his life. They had seemed to develop a friendship of sorts over the last few days, which he was grateful for. He was not sure why they had started off tumultuously, but hopefully that was now past. He wished that he could be the one to show her about town and help her get to know the good parts of life here, but that would be too risky to her reputation. He hoped that someone in her family would be accepting of her, since she was not a paragon of the typical English debutante they would expect.

The carriage pulled in front of the family's London town house, and Easton prayed his father was in town. He had not seen his father since before Max had been killed, but he had business in town to attend to before he could set out for the country. He made his way up the steps, and the long-time butler, Hendricks, opened the door for him before he could knock.

"Hendricks." He smiled as he took off his hat and handed it over.

"My lord. Are you well? Your arrival is unexpected, but most welcome."

"Thank you, Hendricks. It is good to be home. I was injured, but as you can see I am relatively intact." He turned to shrug from his coat.

"May I say how relieved I am to have you home," Hendricks said nervously.

Easton spun about at the concerned tone in the butler's voice. "Is something wrong, Hendricks?"

The butler hesitated and then said, "The Earl is not well."

Easton's heart plummeted to his boots. "He is here, I presume?" Hendricks would not be in London if the Earl was not. The butler nodded. "How ill is he?"

"It is difficult to say, my lord." Hendricks sighed, uncomfortable being the bearer of bad news. Easton urged him on with hand gestures, anxious to hear the state of his father.

"The doctor says he has been having apoplectic spells, and they are becoming more frequent. Some of them have been very severe, leaving him weak and having difficulty speaking. He has not been the same since your brother..." Hendricks trailed off, unable to speak of the loss of the other son.

Easton nodded. "I will go and see him now. Thank you,

Hendricks." He turned and made his way to his father's chamber, dread growing with every step. He tapped lightly on the door and opened it quietly when there was no answer.

Easton stepped into the dim chamber and let his eyes adjust. He spied his father on the large bed and felt his throat tighten when he saw how frail his father was. He managed to control his emotion and walked quietly toward the bed.

"Adam?" The Earl reached out and took Easton's hand.

"Yes, Father. 'Tis I." He lovingly squeezed his father's hand. He opened his eyes wider and smiled. Though the smile was crooked, Easton was relieved to see the affliction had not affected his father's pleasant demeanour. He bent over and hugged his father as best he could.

"Have a seat, son. We have much to catch up on." The Earl's words were slurred but understandable.

Easton sat on the bed next to his father. "How are you, Father? Hendricks said you have had some spells," he said softly, trying not to make an issue of his father's illness, knowing it would tweak his father's pride.

"They are all making them out to be more than they are, though I will say, with what happened to Max and having these spells take away my strength, it makes one realize how short life is. You know in your mind you are mortal, but until you lose something you took for granted, you do not know it in your heart."

Easton nodded his understanding. He did understand. During the war, some of his best friends would be there with him for breakfast and not be there for supper. The hardest part of it all was not becoming numb to everything around him. He realized he was lost in thought when he heard his father speak.

"Tell me why you are home early, my son."

Easton began to fill him in on what had occurred, only leaving out the necessary details about Colonel Knott's retaliation. He debated how much to disclose to his father, but he seemed to still have his wits about him and would know sooner or later. The Earl was one of the most well-connected men about town, and Easton had no doubt he would be up on the latest with the war, if possible. He respected his father too much to consider lying to him.

Easton also tried to skirt around how close to dying he actually came, but he did not want to undermine how much Elinor had done for him. The Earl sat and listened to Easton's account thoughtfully without interrupting, though Easton could see him trying to hold back his emotion when he told him she had removed a bullet and treated his infection. When Easton finished his account, the Earl shocked him by only saying, "Please bring Elinor to visit me soon."

Elinor watched Easton climb into the carriage and felt abandoned and alone as she turned and found herself trapped in an unwelcome sense of recollection. She stood at the threshold of a large stone mansion. The Palladian façade remained unchanged from her last day in England six years ago. She fought off the urge to run after Easton and beg him not to leave her here. She reminded herself that she was no longer a naïve adolescent and that she had to face her demons. She took a deep breath, then brought her hand up to the knocker and tapped.

Barnes, the butler, opened the door, looked curiously at the shabbily dressed female and wondered why she had not used the servants' entrance, though he was too well trained to show it. Elinor noticed his slight hesitance and took matters into her own hands, "I gather the family is not expecting me? Barnes, if I remember correctly?" The stunned butler hesitated, so Elinor stepped into the grand marble entry hall of the Duke of Loring's house. She felt a rush of emotion engulf her. She was mentally and physically exhausted from the last several weeks, and being here brought back everything she had wanted to keep shut away forever. It had all happened so fast, somehow she felt she was dreaming and she would wake up and be back in America. It had not occurred to her how dishevelled and weary she must look, not to mention how dirty she was from travel.

Shocked by the use of his name, Barnes took another look, astonishment visible on his face. "Miss Elinor? Is that you?"

"It is, and I had hoped my arrival would not have been such a surprise, for it seemed Papa and Grandmama have been plotting my visit for some time." She smiled and handed him her bonnet and pelisse.

"Aye, Miss Elinor, that was the hope, but we did not know when you would arrive. You are all grown up." He was obviously embarrassed for not recognizing her.

"Is anyone in residence, or are they at Loring Abbey? Papa had thought I was to meet the family here." She looked around, noting the ostentatious taste of the Duchess had not changed.

"They are in the dining room," he said nodding his head toward the room.

"Well I shall not interrupt them, Barnes. It would be lovely to be shown to my room and have a bath and a tray."

"Certainly. I will call Mrs. Brown and have her show you to your room." He sent a footman off to fetch the housekeeper.

"It is nice to have you back, Miss Elinor. They've been worried about you." *They* meaning her grandmother. Elinor smiled inside to see the small crack in the normally reserved butler.

"Thank you, Barnes. It is wonderful to see you again." And she flashed him a lovely smile as Mrs. Brown came in to greet her.

"Miss Elly! Let me get a good look at you!" The old nanny, now housekeeper, knew exactly who she was. Mrs. Brown gave her a big hug, then held her hands out and checked her over from head to toe. "La, you look just like Lady Elizabeth! We had best get you bathed and out of those clothes before the rest of them see you!" Mrs. Brown turned and started to rush Elinor up the staircase, but voices came down the hall toward them.

"Barnes, who is there? What is the commotion out here?" The Duchess glanced toward the entry and saw an apparently questionable female in Elinor. She held up her hand to hush Barnes from answering and promptly placed herself where she would block the view of Elinor from her guests. She hurried the group of ladies into the parlour, whispered something to one of them then closed the door behind them to come and see who was in her house.

"What is the meaning of this, Barnes?" The Duchess gestured her hands up and down at the dirt-covered, governess-like creature in front of her.

Elinor wanted to giggle at this vision in front of her. *Badly.* Apparently her practical, navy blue muslin was not appreciated as fashionable. "Aunt Wilhelmina, how nice to see you again." Elinor said, rising from a deep curtsy.

Barnes knew that look. He rushed to catch the Duchess before she fainted, and guided her off into the nearby morning room. "I will send her vinaigrette in." Mrs. Brown called after him without the least bit of concern.

Elinor looked at Mrs. Brown and shrugged her shoulders. "I gather she is pleased to see me?" It was a rhetorical question. Mrs. Brown started to pull Elinor toward the stairs, but Elinor hesitated. "Do you not think we should check on her?"

"She'll be fine. Happens at least once a day," the plump housekeeper said without taking another look.

"That must be delightful." Elinor did not expect a reply. "Is Grandmama here?"

"She took a tray in her room."

"Oh, she is not ill, I hope?" Elinor desperately hoped not. She could not survive here without her grandmother's support.

The housekeeper chuckled. "She's still healthy as a horse. She did not care for tonight's company."

"I want to stop in and greet her before my bath." They continued up the stairs. Elinor was determined to shut away the past and not let it overcome her. She felt her heartbeat increase and felt a few beads of sweat break out on her forehead as she climbed the stairs and walked down the hallway that had last been a path to torture. But Elinor was so excited to see her grandmother that her feet barely touched the floor. She tapped on her grandmother's door and heard, "Enter!"

Elinor stepped into the room and stood there waiting for her grandmother to look up from her reading. She had aged much in six years, but was still extremely handsome. She spoke without raising her eyes from the page. "Leave it on the table, Hanson." She waved her hand to indicate without looking up. "This book is too good to put down unless it is urgent." Hanson was the dowager's maid.

"That depends on if you consider a weary traveller from America urgent..." Her voice trailed off as she saw realization hit her grandmother's face. The old lady jumped up from her chaise faster than Elinor herself could have, and embraced her like the long-lost granddaughter that she was. After she had had enough, she pushed Elinor out to arm's length to look at her. Then she went to her dressing table, grabbed a cloth and wiped Elinor's face off.

"Am I so horrible, Grandmama? Aunt Wilhelmina fainted." She laughed. "I rated seeing you first before a bath."

"That biddy did not faint because of dirt or your shabby dress." The Dowager tsked.

Elinor was perplexed. "Did I do something wrong? Other than my shabby dress, of course!"

"Look in the glass, dear. Even dressed like a governess, you will put Beatrice in the shade. She did not get an offer this Season, now your aunt Willy's nose will be out of joint for certain. Thank you dear! Life just got to be much more exciting!" She rubbed her wrinkled hands together in anticipation.

"Oh. I did not realize Beatrice had already had her come-out." That was all she needed. Here she thought she would be enjoying her cousin's company throughout all of this, and her aunt and grandmother were going to set up a competition. A maid knocked on the door to let Elinor know her bath was ready.

"Go on and rest, dear. We'll catch up in the morning." Elinor gave her grandmother another big hug and went off to escape into the luxury of a bath.

She could not remember enjoying a bath more. It had been a long month of only washing with a cloth and small basin, fresh water too precious to waste on baths. She stayed in the water until it was too cold, and then donned a soft flannel nightgown, crawled into the bed and barely made it under the counterpane before falling into a deep sleep.

~

Elinor slept harder than she ever had. When she did awaken, it took her a while to realize where she was, snuggled into a luxurious four-poster bed in a room with a warm fire and plush rose curtains hanging from ceiling to floor. She was beginning to recall that she was at her uncle Robert's home in London, as a maid peeked in from behind the large wooden door to check on her. She stepped in and curtsied, and then meekly stated her Grace would like Elinor to breakfast with her in room when she was dressed. Elinor rubbed her eyes and stretched and reluctantly pulled back the covers. She climbed down and went to the basin to splash water on her face to wake up.

"I was asked to help you dress and take you to her Grace."

Elinor nodded and allowed the maid to dress her and pull her hair up, wondering where Josie was. A pale blue muslin had been selected for her, and she debated arguing, then decided against it. After she was ready, she was led down the corridor to her grandmother's apartments.

"Good morning, Grandmama." Elinor bent over and kissed her grandmother on the cheek and took the seat beside her. A cup of chocolate and sweet roll were waiting for her.

"Already keeping London hours, I see." She chuckled as Elinor slowly sipped on her drink. "Unfortunately we have a busy day. I hate to hurry you on your first morning, but we have more work to do than I had anticipated. Did you not bring any of the gowns I sent you?" she asked, glancing over Elinor's toilette. She smiled back at her lovingly, and Elinor noticed the deep lines etched into her grandmother's face and that her hair had gone completely silver. She was still extremely handsome, but Elinor felt a pang in her heart for missing all of those years with her.

Elinor nodded and opened her mouth to protest, but her grandmother held up her hand. "Before you go getting all provincial on me, missy, your objections are duly noted but refused. I have waited six years for this Season, and I intend to enjoy it. I did not enjoy Bea's or Sarah's—they were prissy stick-in-the-muds—but I am going to enjoy yours. Humour the old lady, eh?"

Elinor sighed, but could not refuse her grandmother. "As long as it is within reason, I will try."

Satisfied, her grandmother looked at Elly and said, "Well, make haste, then! I took the liberty of scheduling appointments with the modiste and coiffeur! And we must also go to Bond Street for bonnets, gloves, slippers and the rest. I also sent off a note to the Queen to have you presented. You must be presented at court to be officially out, you know. Did you bring any of your mother's jewellery?"

"Only the pearls, Grandmama. Sarah has her diamonds." Elinor wanted to crawl back in bed, and she had not been awake an hour yet.

"No matter, I have enough to share." Elinor bit back a groan, envisioning being trussed up like the goose at Christmas.

As they gathered up their bonnets and pelisses to go to the modiste, they overheard her cousin, Lady Beatrice, and her aunt in the morning room discussing her. The Dowager held up her finger to her lips so she could listen.

"You should have seen her dress! Why, I would not have my housekeeper caught dead in that outfit. She is not fit for society. I knew letting Charles drag her off to the colonies would be a mistake!"

"Mama, you cannot expect me to take her all over town. I am not going to let her ruin my chances. Think of how they will laugh at me if I am seen with her! I will not do it!" Elinor could imagine Beatrice stomping her feet like she had as a child. They had been together much as children, but they were complete opposites then, and Elinor feared nothing had changed in that regard from the sounds of things.

"Of course not, dear. I only hope we can keep the family from being disgraced."

A sense of dread overcame Elinor. How dared they! Did they think she wanted to be here or be like them? She decided to disappoint them by being as graceful as she could remember her mama and

Sarah being. She looked up at her grandmother, and the Dowager rolled her eyes. Elinor would not give them more reason to disparage her.

"Well, dear, let us get this over with." Her grandmother gave her a slight shove.

"Good morning, Willy; Bea." The Dowager sauntered irreverently into the room. Elinor saw her aunt grimace at the Dowager's pet name for her. She had to fight back a laugh.

Elinor put her chin up in the air and glided into the room behind her grandmother with a sweet smile on her face. "Aunt, I hope you are feeling better this morning? I am sorry I startled you last night."

Her aunt had composed herself since last night's shock but was still not pleased, as Elinor could feel her aunt's examination from head to toe. Her voice was cool with indifference. "Elinor, we are pleased you could join us. Please forgive my little episode last night. They strike me at the oddest times."

"More likely convenient," the Dowager mumbled.

"And Beatrice! How beautiful you are! I am sure you must have dozens of suitors fawning over you." Elinor had turned to her cousin who was appraising her with contempt. Elinor was hoping God would not strike her down for her ridiculous flattery.

Taken aback by this charm, Beatrice looked quizzically at her mama. "Why thank you, Elinor. You have changed much since we have seen you," Beatrice said with no warmth in her too-polite reply. Beatrice looked Elinor up and down, obviously not approving her gown, but not sure if she was as ill-behaved or shabby as her mama thought. Elinor certainly was pretty and that did not make Beatrice happy.

Elinor was quite done being scrutinized.

The Dowager had had enough of the artificial hypocrisy from that biddy daughter-in-law and granddaughter of hers. "Well, girls, you can catch up later. I am taking her off to the shops to freshen her wardrobe up."

"Yes, a modiste in the States is not the same. They are all about function and modesty."

Completely missing her sarcasm, Elinor and the Dowager left Beatrice and the Duchess thinking the visit went well.

~

Elinor had very little memory of London itself, having spent most of her childhood at the country estate in Sussex. Her senses were overwhelmed as she surveyed her surroundings. The constant noise, the noxious smells, the sooty fog, the crowds, were all competing to overwhelm her sanity. She had never experienced anything like it. The extremes of wealth and poverty from one area to the next were contributing to her culture shock. She wanted to run as far away as she could and be alone for hours. But alas, the carriage came to a stop as they arrived at their first appointment.

Elinor tried to imagine places she could run off to while enduring her time with the exclusive modiste. Madame Bissette had no qualms clearing her calendar for the illustrious Dowager and her granddaughter, who she was hoping would provide her with prestige and delicious fodder for gossip.

Elinor stood like a mannequin as Madame brought fabric after fabric to drape across her, uttering "magnifique," at every piece selected, clearly pleased with her genius. The assistant measured, pinned and made patterns. After voicing a few opinions without any response, Elinor realized she was clearly not the primary actress in this scene, merely a prop. She found herself hard-pressed to think of anything else she disliked more than being fussed over. She finally put her foot down when it came to numerous flounces, laces and ribbon. She did not feel that those were required to display her assets—not to mention their ideas on modesty were vastly different from her own. The Dowager and Madame kept their heads together over the pattern books. Eventually Elinor was released, but not before having to exchange her practical dress for a ready-made one in a more-modern style up to London standards.

After ordering morning gowns, walking costumes, travelling suits, riding habits, and ball gowns, she was coerced into going on to the milliner for several new bonnets to go with the numerous gowns just ordered. Elinor could stand no more and insisted on going home before falling into a megrim.

"Enough, Grandmama! Surely Josie can go with Hanson to get the rest," she said without any tinge of anger as they climbed back into the carriage. The Dowager eyed her sceptically.

"I suppose you do look spent, Elinor. I guess I have pushed you far enough for your first day."

"I confess I am feeling homesick. I cannot see the reason for all of this fuss."

"We will head to the Abbey in a few weeks for Christmas, and you will feel more the thing there. Try to hold on a little while longer. Are you so unnatural at being a girl that you dread balls and parties?"

"Papa asked the same thing. I suppose I am, Grandmama. I do not dream of balls and dresses. I prefer smaller, more intimate social settings, and I was truly content at River's Bend."

"How is that? Did you leave a beau behind?" she asked curiously.

"None that I was interested in *in that* way." *Let us dispel those thoughts quickly.*

"So you left broken hearts." The Dowager nodded as if it were just as she suspected.

"I hope not. I did not intend to hurt anyone, but I was not interested in any of them." Elinor fumbled with the buttons on her pelisse, wishing to have almost any conversation but this one.

"Oh, dear. I hope you are not too particular?" The Dowager considered this with a concerned look.

"I am simply not interested in marriage." *Should I tell her I feel sick when men make up to me like that?*

"Nonsense. You are happy right now, but your father is very concerned about you finding the proper husband. He is not getting any younger and has voiced his growing concern to me in his last few letters."

"He has? I did not know that. I thought he was happy with me there. I thought he needed me. Who will take care of him?" Elinor felt despondent at her ignorance of her father's feelings—and at the thought that she might actually have to marry. Surely they would not force her.

The Dowager waved her hand in dismissal. "Silly child! It has nothing to do with that. We old folk start feeling our mortality and want to see things are in order for those we leave behind. That is all he meant by it; you know he loves having you there. He feels he has been selfish keeping you to himself this long. I, however, would not mind having another grandchild to bounce on my knee."

"I will try a little harder if it will please him," Elinor said resignedly, worried thoughts swirling in her head. "He never mentioned he wanted me to find someone, only that I will know the right man when I meet him." Well, she would at least try to appear as if she was trying, as Josie had suggested.

"You know that we only want your happiness and would never force you to marry. You will be well taken care of, regardless. Now tell me more about River's Bend and your trip over, and why your papa has not come to greet me."

Elinor realized she had not told her grandmother about her travelling companion. Not that there had been much time for that. She decided it would be better to tell her now than wait for Lady Dunweather to surprise her with it. "It was *interesting*. Papa's godson was injured and was forced into making the trip over with me. Papa had to go directly to Ghent."

"Lord Easton?"

"No, Major Easton."

"I see. They are one and the same. His elder brother Max was killed about a year ago, and so Major Easton became Viscount Easton, though it will not be long until he becomes the Earl. His father's health is quite poor."

"He is a lord? He never mentioned that." Elinor was not so happy about the news either, for some reason. Not that he had tried to hide anything; he undoubtedly assumed she knew all of that about him. But he had talked of second sons.

"He likely assumed you remembered he is an earl's son. I suppose we should add *Debrett's Peerage* to your growing list of things to review. Did he come in with you? Please tell me Wilhelmina does not know he travelled with you unchaperoned!" Elinor shook her head. "I assume he was anxious to get home, or to protect your reputation." The Dowager nodded in approval.

"It was very late after a long journey. He said he was anxious to greet his father. He did send his regards, though he did mention keeping his distance in town."

"I am sure we will see him soon, however. Society is rather thin here right now. Too bad Andrew is still with Wellington on the Continent."

"But Easton detests the Marriage Mart," she said doubting she would see him.

"Don't they all? But the Earl will be pressuring him for a grand-child. We best not mention your recent acquaintance with Easton, especially to your aunt or Bea." The Dowager thought Elinor had no idea that she would be considered compromised if word got out. Though the Dowager could not think of a better match for Elinor, she did not want it to happen by scandal unless necessary. She would stoop to that, however, if it kept her granddaughter in England.

"I wonder when he found out about his brother. I do not think he will be too happy to hear his father wants grandchildren from him. I would not have the heart for matchmaking if I only found out Andrew or Sarah had died. And how is Sarah?"

"Increasing. Again. Hopefully you will see her at Christmas."

"Oh my goodness, I can hardly wait!" The Dowager ignored her and already had her wheels turning as to throwing Easton and Elinor together, but she knew if she pushed too hard Elinor would run the other way. So she would scheme to herself, though she already had a feeling she knew how everything would play out.

"Time will tell what Easton will do. Let us have tea and get you prepared for your first evening on the town. The coiffeur should be here soon." Her grandmother rubbed her hands together in giddy anticipation. Elinor readied herself for battle.

The coiffeur, Monsieur DuPont, was waiting on them when they returned to the house. Elinor would have welcomed the reprieve of a nap or even tea, but instead she found herself pleading to keep her hair. Eventually Monsieur sided with Elinor. He actually listened to her when she did not wish to have her hair lopped off. And why was everyone here French? Or pretending to be? The Dowager wanted daring, but Elinor wanted to keep her long, curled locks. Her mother had always told her that her hair was part of her beauty, and that much had stuck with her. She did, however, refuse the face-framing, rigidly curled hairstyles that were so artificial in her opinion, for an *au naturel* look that she was comfortable with. Little did she realize that she would stand out more for that reason. Monsieur pulled her hair back with diamond combs, allowing a few tendrils to wisp about her face and the waves to fall down naturally about her from on high. "An original, *n'est-ce pas?*" he declared, admiring his work.

CHAPTER 8

*E*aston poured himself a drink and sank into the comfortable chair by the fire. The damp, cold weather was affecting his wounds more than he cared to admit. The day had been exhausting, and it was only mid-afternoon. Nothing was going as planned. He had stopped by the War Office to resign his commission, but was told they would take it into consideration as soon as the war was over. He was considered on leave to be recuperating from his injuries. As he was pondering soaking his aches in a hot bath, Hendricks entered to announce a visitor.

"Major Abbott to see you, my lord."

"Andrew?" Easton rose and strode over to greet his best friend.

"Adam!" They exchanged handshakes and a brotherly pat on the back. Easton winced as Andrew found his still-tender injury.

"What are you doing here? Has Old Hookey actually allowed you more than a mile away from himself, or is he here too?" Easton made a show of looking about for their commander, General Wellington. Andrew was a great favourite of the famous general.

"Very amusing. Father arrived yesterday in Ghent and sent me straight away to see to Elinor."

"He made excellent time then, for we only arrived yesterday

ourselves." He gestured for Andrew to sit and went over to fetch him a drink. He cringed as he visibly limped, knowing it would not escape his friend's eye. Andrew noticed, but did not say anything. "So have you seen your sister, then?"

"I am headed there, but I came to retrieve you first," Andrew said in his usual, unaffected manner.

Easton's head shot up at that proclamation. So many thoughts swirled through his head at that moment, the foremost being was Andrew demanding that Adam offer for her?

Andrew saw his friend's consternation and laughed. "Relax, peagoose. I simply do not want to suffer my silly female relations alone. Vernon and Fairmont are headed back and should be there as well. Thought you might want to join in the reunion."

Easton visibly relaxed. He would love to be reunited with all of their friends, but that did not make it wise. Surely Andrew had been informed about his situation with Elinor, though. He struggled with the idea. He was tempted to go, but he knew the more he interacted with Elinor, the more likely their situation would become known.

As if reading Easton's mind, Andrew explained, "Yes, Father told me about your situation. Deuced nuisance, Knott. But what's done is done."

Easton let out a laugh despite his predicament. Andrew was ever pragmatic. "And what of your sister?"

"I am not worried. I know you would not do anything improper. Besides you were injured." Andrew tossed back the contents of his drink and stood to leave. Easton should not be surprised his friend was so trusting, and he wondered how Andrew would feel if he knew Easton's true thoughts about Little Elly. "I will be by to pick you up at eight." Before Easton could protest, Andrew was out of the door.

～

Dinner that night was to be a small, family affair. Elinor allowed herself to be dressed again in the high-waisted, pale green silk with cream ribbons that criss-crossed under the bodice. She had worn the same dress the first time she had met Easton, not that she would be seeing him any time soon. Everyone knew men did not notice those things anyway. How silly of her to even think he would recall that evening as she did. She was blissfully unaware that one did not re-wear gowns in the *ton*.

She made her way down the stairs nervously, hoping she would not run into *him*. She had not heard any mention of her attacker since her arrival. However, she started to run when she heard Andrew's, voice, all nervousness replaced by excitement. She entered the parlour, her eyes searching the surprisingly large gathering, and then all conversation stopped and turned toward her. Her eyes finally found her brother Andrew amongst the sea of regimentals, and she went immediately to him for the long-awaited embrace of her dearest brother. After an embrace, she became conscious of the party assembled after someone pointedly cleared her throat, and she decided to let go of Andrew.

"I cannot believe you are actually here!" She ignored the murmurings of her aunt and cousin about atrocious colonial manners.

"Elly! I doubt I would have recognized you on the street!" He took in this picture of his little sister now grown up and astonishingly beautiful. "I met Father in Ghent, and he sent me directly to check on you, with Wellington's blessing, of course. He did not warn me I would have to be your bodyguard!" He shook his head in disbelief and then recalled their audience. Elinor almost choked at the irony of that statement. "Let me introduce you to some of our acquaintances you might not recognize." He took her elbow and led her over to a group of gentleman. Immediately she locked eyes with Easton, and her heart skipped a beat. Why was he here?

"Elinor, this is Major Lord Easton, Papa's godson. I am sure you remember Adam." He gave her a knowing glance. She made a graceful curtsy.

"Yes, I happen to recall. I am sorry to hear of your loss, *Lord* Easton. It must have come as quite a shock." She could not help herself. Why should she care he neglected to tell her his brother had died and he was now a peer?

He looked at her with sadness that he quickly disguised, took her hand and kissed it lightly. "Thank you, Miss Abbott. You look..."

"Like a reformed tomboy?" She flashed a precocious smile and then turned to greet others before he could reply.

"And our cousin, Rhys, Lord Vernon. Elinor." Elinor extended her hand to an elegant man, not as tall as Easton or Andrew, but dressed impeccably, with a fine head of wavy brown hair and chocolate brown eyes. Yes, she remembered their cousin, distant relation that he was.

"Andrew, you sly devil. You did not mention our Little Elly has turned into a diamond!" He nudged his cousin, playfully taunting him.

Andrew grumbled that he did not need to be told the implications. "It seems we have made the discovery together. My Elly always has a riding habit on, with wild hair and a tan." The gang of best friends laughed as they recalled the young hoyden they used to terrorize when they were small. "I imagine she is still a spitfire as I see her glaring at me!"

She playfully punched him in the arm, blushing adorably with embarrassment, and then noticed her cousin Beatrice fuming from across the room. "Enough with the flummery! I am delighted to see you all again, but let us be done with this nonsense, or I will never be able to take any of you seriously."

"As you wish, Miss Abbott. May I escort you into dinner before someone else steals you away?" Lord Vernon offered his arm, but Aunt Wilhelmina had no intention of letting Elinor snap up one of Beatrice's suitors.

The Duchess intervened in front all of the attention. "Now, now, Vernon. You cannot interfere with the proper order of things, or you will confuse our *colonial* guest. You are to escort Lady Beatrice." Beatrice leeched onto his arm possessively, with a warning look over her shoulder at Elinor to indicate he was unavailable.

Vernon took this as a gentleman, and he shot Elinor a look of mock apology and went off to flirt and pay homage to Beatrice. Beatrice bestowed her coquettish smile on Vernon and looked to Elinor, hoping to set her down a peg, "I am glad to see you are getting good use of my old gown, Cousin Elinor."

Unfazed and unaware of the malicious intent, Elinor replied, "It was kind of you to lend it to my cause, Bea."

The Dowager pretended to whisper, saying loud enough for all to hear, that Beatrice had done them all a favour by giving it to Elinor. She then feigned annoyance at Andrew. "Are you going to ignore your gran all evening?" Andrew smiled devilishly at her, then proceeded to adore her as if she were thirty years younger. "You know I always save the best for last, Gran." They chuckled together as he led her off to the dining room.

Elinor turned to find Easton watching her, which pleased her more than she wanted to admit. She raised a questioning shoulder slightly then took the arm he gallantly offered. "I am sorry I did not know about your brother."

"It would not have made any difference. I only found out recently myself. I am still trying to accept the changes." He waved his hand as if to dismiss the subject.

"Are you doing well? I did not expect to see you here. I thought you were going to keep your distance."

He shrugged his good shoulder. "Andrew dragged me from the house. He said it was only a small family gathering." He shrugged once more. "I also needed to speak with you."

"Oh?" She looked up at him suspiciously, waiting.

"There is someone who would like to see you before your calendar is too full. It looks as if I will have to make appointments for your time, Miss Abbott, if this evening is anything to judge by."

"Do not be absurd. There will always be time for Papa's godson," she prodded.

"I see where I stand," he said playfully. "If you and Andrew would not find it too much trouble to call on us in Grosvenor Square tomorrow?" He looked at her inquiringly.

"Who would you like me to see, Lord Easton?" She was most curious.

"Please, stop the lording. I cannot think of myself as such. I still find it hard to be called Easton." He paused and looked down.

"I am truly sorry for your loss," Elinor whispered.

He gathered himself from his momentary lapse of control and continued, "My father insists on a visit, but he is too ill to be out in this cold. If you are too busy perhaps…"

"Not at all. I would be honoured to make room for *him*." She gave him a saucy smile then took her place at the table in between Andrew and the Duke but across from Easton, trying hard not to look at him too often. Had she flirted with him a second time? She had to make herself stop! She looked up and found Beatrice glaring daggers at her, and prophesied it was going to be a long night.

Elinor had not seen her uncle in the crowd in the parlour. He sat at the table and did not seem to recognize her. He looked at her with wide eyes as if he were looking at a ghost. "Elizabeth?"

"No, Uncle, it is Elinor." She smiled up at him.

"Well, when did you sneak in here? Why did no one tell me? Get up and greet your uncle properly!" He stood to hug Elinor, and then looked down the table at the Duchess around the large centrepiece, as if about to accost her for her oversight. Elinor placed a hand on his arm to prevent any more scenes being laid at her door.

"I only arrived last night, Uncle. Then Grandmama kept me out shopping all day."

"Guilty as charged!" The Dowager chimed in saucily, quite pleased with herself. She had already imbibed in a glass or two of claret at this point.

Slightly appeased by this explanation, the Duke settled in to enjoy a conversation with his niece and caught up on her doings in America. She had always been quite a favourite of his, the exact image of his late sister Elizabeth. Unfortunately, Beatrice had taken after Wilhelmina in looks and temperament. Hearing that Elinor was still horse-mad like her mama, the Duke said, "Well then, spare a little time for your old uncle in the next day or two, and we will go riding."

That brought a genuine smile to Elinor's face. "Is tomorrow morning too soon?"

"As soon as I find you a mount. I will go and look for one at Tattersall's."

"May I accompany you, please?" That sounded much more enjoyable than a day at the modiste.

"Not the thing for a lady to go to Tatts. Not the thing." Why did she think that was not the first or last time she would hear that?

The remainder of the evening was mostly pleasant, as long as Elinor avoided the female variety of relations. She was able to hold her own with cards, having honed her skills on the voyage across the Atlantic. After the guests had taken their leave, Andrew escorted Elinor up the stairs to her chamber and bent over to kiss her cheek good night.

As he turned to leave Elinor called after him, "Oh, Andrew, I need you to take me to call on the Earl. Lord Easton said his father requested us to come." She did not notice his look of dismay in the darkness of the corridor. He was stunned into silence. "Well, are you busy? I can ask Grandmama to accompany me."

"No, I can take you."

Things were growing stranger by the minute. Andrew fell silent, obviously distracted. He followed her back into her room and fell into one of the chairs by the fire. Clearly he needed to catch up with his sister. His club could wait.

"How was Papa?" She kicked off her slippers, climbed into the other chair and tucked her feet up under her.

"Engrossed in negotiations. Says they were making a mull of it, and he got there in the nick of time." He took a sip of the drink he still held in his hand.

"I hope he can be of benefit. It was good of you to come. Tell me he is all right. I have been worried."

"Missing my little sister might have had something to do with it." He smiled. "So, Father mentioned that you saved Easton."

"I suppose I may have done. I assume he told you we travelled to England together."

"Best not to mention that, Elly. Not the thing at all. Easton will not." He shook his head vehemently to emphasize his point.

"I realize that, Andrew. Papa did not appear to consider it of any moment, though." She shrugged, as if trying to convince herself that it was not of consideration. "There was little choice. We had to get away from there. Lord Easton did say we were seen by Lady Dunweather," she added with assumed nonchalance.

Andrew groaned. "Not her! That is rotten luck. She can ruin you with one word, Elly. Though Easton and Vernon are considered the most eligible bachelors in town, which amuses me greatly, I will be happy to share the burden. Easton has always had his pick of the lot, and the ladies adored him despite being a second son. Not that he's ever been interested in the ladies much—who knows how he got that reputation. Now that he's the heir, the ladies will be on the hunt, and the old man will be urging him to set up his nursery before he sticks his spoon in the wall." He chuckled at the idea of Easton leg-shackled.

"If I am *ruined* I will have a good excuse to go back home." Yes, she mocked the English definition of the word ruined. If they only knew. Yet, Elinor's mind whirled at these tidbits about Easton, none of which fitted with the man she had spent several weeks with. He was not a rake? She could not quite reconcile what he was.

Andrew shook his head. "You best tell Gran about Lady Dunweather. You are going to need her help to get through this. I highly doubt you've heard the last from Lady Dunweather."

"I meant to tell her and became distracted." She would have to remember that in the morning. "Andrew?" He looked up at her. "Is there anywhere we can go riding? I will burst if I cannot have time to clear my head."

"You do not have a mount here."

She was not to be deterred. "Uncle said he would get me one. I am sure there is something I can borrow until then."

"If we go early, we can do a little riding in Hyde Park. They frown on serious riding there, but you can sneak a little in early if you are careful."

"Will you show me then?" She clapped her hands with excitement. How could he refuse?

He paused before answering. Chaperoning his sister was going to be a full time job. "I will once. I am not getting up before the crack of dawn every day, though."

She wrapped her arms around him. "Thank you! Thank you! Finally, something to look forward to."

Then he felt guilty and foresaw curbing his late-night habit to dance attendance on a female, and his sister no less. What was wrong with this picture?

～

Elinor rose early and dragged Andrew from his bed to make good on his promise to go riding with her. "You said it had to be early, so get up!" she said in her most chipper voice as she poked at him and tried to throw back his covers. He barely grabbed them in time.

Andrew groaned. "Did I say I missed you?"

She smiled the loving smile of a sister. "I will meet you downstairs in fifteen minutes."

Despite his grumblings, Andrew was downstairs and ready to go on time. A docile-looking mare had been saddled for Elinor. She and Andrew looked at the horse and burst into laughter. "I say, man. Who told you to saddle the Dowager's horse? Have you got anything that can walk more than ten yards?"

"Not 'un that's proper for a lady, sir. Neither Lady Beatrice or her Grace ride."

"Well, then saddle his Grace's gelding."

The groom's eyes went wide. "I couldna do that, sir. 'Tisn't fit fer no lady."

"Saddle the gelding. I know his Grace will not mind. Miss Elinor can ride better than any man I know, save Easton." Andrew used his authoritative soldier's voice. "I will take the blame if necessary."

The groom reluctantly took the mare back to go and saddle the gelding, shaking his head and muttering under his breath.

"I ride better than Easton! How could you say such a thing, Andrew?" Elinor soundly elbowed him.

The groom returned with a magnificent dappled grey gelding, but it had an odd-looking saddle atop its back. "What kind of saddle is that?" Elinor contorted her face trying to place the strange object.

"It is a side-saddle, miss," the groom retorted as if she were daft. She ignored his impertinence and looked at Andrew.

"Surely you do not expect me to ride as such?" She looked truly offended.

He hit his face with his hand in frustration. "That is how ladies ride here, Elly. If you are seen riding astride, you will be considered fast."

"I do not know how to ride that way. I have heard they are not safe. Besides, is that not why we are up early, so we will not be seen?"

"This is the thanks I get for helping." He looked heavenward in mock exasperation, then his face spread into a wide grin, and he winked at her. "All right, but only in the morning, and you have to promise to learn side-saddle and ride that way in public."

"Fine." She grimaced. "If that is what it takes." Soon the saddles were exchanged, and they were off and into the park, both horses ready to stretch their legs.

"Where can we let them go, Andrew?" Elinor scanned the park for somewhere suitable.

"There is a small space on the other side of the park. You are not allowed to gallop on Rotten Row."

"All these rules! Let us go, then." She followed, and they let the horses go to their paces as long as they dared before letting up and getting down to let them cool at the Serpentine.

"Feel better, El? I know you do not fancy it here, but it makes Father and Gran happy. Try for a few weeks, then we can be off to the country."

She nodded. "I will try. I just do not know what I am supposed to be doing or saying most of the time. Making polite chit-chat is foreign to me. Everything seems the opposite of what I am used to. Grand-mama despairs of me ever being fit for society."

"Smile and dance and look pretty." He did his best impression.

"In other words, do not speak!" She laughed and he laughed, and she almost felt normal for a minute. Then it occurred to her she did not know the dances in England. "Hm, Andrew? Do you think you could teach me to dance?"

"You do not know how to dance? Even a little?" He did not pretend his look of shock.

"Maybe a little. We learned some dances at the girls' school I attended, but I heard Beatrice talking about a new dance called a waltz being the latest craze."

"That one is simple. I can manage that. Here." He grabbed her hand and her waist and began humming and counting out the steps for her.

"This is easy, but seems rather scandalous for the old uptight tabbies."

"Yes indeed, but you are my sister."

"So I can only waltz with you?" She laughed. "Oh, Andrew, we cannot gallop in Hyde Park, but we can waltz?" This brought on another round of laughter.

"And you cannot waltz until given permission." He broke away, seeming to realize his impromptu dancing lesson should be saved for the ballroom at home.

"Permission? More rules? How many more weeks of this?" She put her hands to her temples in frustration.

He shook his head. "I would not want to be a female here, either. It will not be bad once you learn how to get on. Let us return, and I will take you to meet the Earl after lunch. I imagine Gran will have my hide for giving you dance lessons in Hyde Park." He chuckled at his witticism.

"Add that to my list of sins."

Elinor enjoyed herself immensely with Andrew that morning, and spent the remainder of time until lunch with her grandmother, being fitted for her court dress and her ball gown. Her grandmother had managed to obtain a near-private presentation of Elinor to Queen Charlotte two days hence. Her grandmother had been intimate friends with the Queen since her arrival in England.

The presentation to the Queen and the thought of a ball in her honour was enough to make her consider swooning, a habit she detested in overly dramatic females. Hopefully, the company in London was thin enough at this time for the ball to not be a total crush. Her grandmother interrupted her pondering as Elinor put her day dress back on.

"So, my dear, Andrew says you are going to meet old Wyndham today? He must be wanting to thank you for saving Adam. I cannot imagine what it would have done to him to lose both sons. Max was difficult at times, but we do love our children regardless."

Elinor was glad she had not known about Easton's brother's death. It would have been unbelievable pressure thinking she was saving the last son. "Is there anything I should know about the Earl, Grand-mama? I confess I do not remember him. Is he severe?"

"Heavens no! He's a gentle soul, much like your papa. You could do much worse for a father-in-law."

"Pardon? He's not going to be my father-in-law." She turned quickly and barely caught herself from tumbling.

"No, of course not." The Dowager smiled to herself. "I only said you could do worse." Changing the subject, she continued, "Your aunt Willy says that your uncle Robert finally summoned Nathaniel home."

At the mention of his name, Elinor felt the blood rush from her face before she fainted.

CHAPTER 9

*E*linor opened her eyes to the horrendous smell of vinaigrette and her grandmother's pearls hitting her in the face as she bent over her.

"What's the matter, child? You are not one to swoon like your ridiculous cousin!"

"I am sorry, Grandmama." Elinor sat up, but her head swirled a bit. What was she going to do? She could not bear to see Nathaniel again. Six years. She had finally learned to deal with what he had done, and she could not bear to face him again. That was one reason she had been grateful for America—to escape him.

"Elinor? Elinor?" She looked up to see her grandmother's worried face. Sensing something was wrong, her grandmother put her arms around Elinor and held her like her mama had years ago.

Elinor burst into tears and cried. Cried for her mama, cried for her beloved home and cried for her innocence that had all been stripped away. By him. She had never let herself lose this much control.

After her tears had turned into hiccoughs, the Dowager quietly asked, "Do you want to talk about it?" Elinor shook her head and hesitated, though she desperately wanted to relieve herself of this heavy burden.

"It might help."

"I have never told anyone the whole story. Josie knows a little." Elinor blew her nose and sighed.

Her grandmother held her closely and whispered, "Take your time, my love. But I hope you know you can tell me anything."

Elinor nodded. "I know."

"Is it Nathaniel?" Elinor nodded. "Did he...he, *hurt* you?" Elinor nodded. The Dowager paled. Neither of them could speak for a while. "Dear God. Before you left?"

"Yes." Her grandmother took a moment to digest this knowledge before finally speaking.

"Why did you not tell anyone?"

Elinor thought a moment, never having voiced why she had kept silent, and then shrugged her shoulders. "I was afraid no one would believe me. I was ashamed, afraid it was my fault. I do not even know exactly how it happened. I only remember him attacking me and tearing my dress and kissing me roughly. I remember he was drunk, and fighting with him, and he was rough and... touched me. I, In... Intimately." She sobbed. She could not say it out loud. "He seemed possessed. I woke up the next day with bruises, feeling awful." She could not look her grandmother in the face.

"The bruises. I remember you said you fell down the stairs," the Dowager whispered recalling that dreadful day.

Elinor nodded, tears beginning to stream down her face.

"I did not know what was happening. I still do not fully know what happened, but that is why I cannot marry, Grandmama. I cannot do it. Besides knowing I am not pure, I do not think I could ever let another man touch me that way. I could not bear it. Even if someone would accept soiled goods."

"Oh, Elly. You are not soiled goods!" Elinor could not look at her grandmother's face for fear of the disappointment she would see there.

"Please, Grandmama. Admit it. Society would never forgive this. Gentlemen expect an untouched virgin. You know everything is the female's fault. I must have said or done something to lead him on, the cunning thirteen-year-old that I was, dressed in mourning with a collar up to my chin." She held her hands up to exaggerate her point. "These things are never the male's fault." She attempted to keep the bitterness out of her voice. Her grandmother tilted Elinor's face up toward hers so she could look her in the eye.

"I will help you through this dreadfulness. I failed you, and I will help you through it."

"You did not fail me. You could not have known."

"If I had insisted they control Nathaniel, if I had not let Charles run away...we were all so overcome with grief."

"That would not have changed anything. America was good for me. I did not have to face him or anyone else and feel like a failure. I was numb for a while and uncertain, but I learned to have strength. I only have to learn how to deal with men. And, and..." She looked away and sighed. "With seeing him again."

The Dowager pondered, then sighed. "You are going to have to conquer this and face him."

"I do not know if I can." She shook her head.

"Of course you can. You have been brave for six years, and you have to have the courage to do it longer. If you run away, he wins." She stopped to let Elinor digest what she said. "But if he so much as gets near you, I will personally castrate him."

Elinor stared at her grandmother in disbelief. She made it sound so easy, as if all that had happened was as simple as being caught with spinach in one's teeth. Elinor could not risk being hurt like that again. It was not only the physical violence, it was the emotional destruction by someone she had trusted and loved.

"When is he coming back?"

"He's been on the Continent for years with the army. The Duke bought him a commission, hoping that would help him grow up, even though it is frowned upon to send the heir. He was out of control— gambling, drinking, and fighting duels. I had no idea that list included ra—" Elinor held up her hands in protest.

"Do not say it. I cannot bear that word." She shook her head, "I need some time to compose myself. Will you keep this between us?"

The Dowager nodded absently, still in shock, and Elinor left quickly.

~

Elinor tried to rest awhile before having to go and face Easton and the Earl. She could not settle her mind enough to actually sleep, so she called for a bath. She scrubbed at her skin vigorously as she had in the early days after the attack, as if that would help wash away the awfulness.

Elinor had not meant to tell her grandmother about Nathaniel, but after keeping it to herself for six years, she actually felt better knowing she was not carrying the burden alone any more. How could her grandmother think facing him, as if nothing had ever happened, was possible?

It had taken Elinor years to even look a man in the eye, even though she inherently knew most men were not like Nathaniel. She still could not be comfortable alone with a man, save her father and Andrew. But what if he stayed at the house with them? She would not be able to sleep. No, she would have to make Andrew open their town house or go to an inn, and that meant she would have to tell Andrew.

How did her grandmother think she could face her fears? Did she expect her to talk to Nathaniel like nothing had ever happened? What if he tried again?

She forced herself to take some deep breaths and relax so she could face Easton and his father with a modicum of grace. She did not feel completely comfortable with how she felt around Easton, but at least it was not the same sickening feeling she got with most men. And he had been kind and friendly since his injury.

Elinor climbed onto her bed to rest a few minutes before it was time to leave.

He pushed her, her back slamming into a tree. She felt the thorns of a rosebush tear into her flesh as she fell to the ground. She struggled to her feet and scrambled back into the house through the nearest door. She heard him stumbling behind her, breathing heavily. Despite his inebriation, he was gaining on her. Hot tears streamed down her face and her lungs ached for air as she desperately clambered up the stairs. Just when she caught sight of her door, she felt a grab at her ankle as she tried to grasp the handle. She tripped and landed face down in the hallway. Where on earth are the servants? Why is no one here to help?

Nathaniel flipped her over, and she kicked him in the groin as had been taught to her when she was younger. This only made him angry, more determined. She attempted to push him away, but her efforts were futile, his weight being nearly twice hers. He was so strong, but she refused to go down without a fight. He shoved her into her room, and she heard the key turn in the lock behind her.

She stood, paralysed with fear, staring at this delirious person, her chest heaving up and down with sharp pains from fear and exertion. She screamed, but knew it pointless, for the laughter and music downstairs was too noisy for anyone to hear her. Anyone? Please, God. Someone. As he leapt for her, she kept screaming while trying to fight him off, but felt a hard, painful fist slam against her head.

Knock, knock. "Elly? Hello? Are you all right?"

The sound of tapping woke Elly from her nightmare, thank God. She jumped off the bed and called, "Come in."

Andrew poked his head in. "Are you ready to go? I thought we might walk, since it is only two streets away. I can hear you chastising me for even thinking about taking a carriage so short a distance."

She smiled, but he could see in her face that something was wrong. "What happened, El?" He strode over to the bed and scooped her up into a brotherly hug. She hesitated, but knew he would not accept a trite answer.

"Nothing." She buried her face further into his chest.

"It does not appear to be nothing." He stroked her back in a soothing rhythm and stayed quiet.

She hesitated, but knew she had to tell him. "It was a long time ago, Andrew. Being here is stirring up old memories. I am trying to decide how best to deal with them."

"Is it grief over Mama? You were only thirteen when she passed away, then Father stole you off to the colonies." He probed gently.

"I wish that were it," she whispered, looking away. He took her hands and saw the raw, red-rubbed skin. He looked up in fear.

"Did someone hurt you, Elly? What happened? Were you violated?" He searched her face and saw the answer. He tensed with anger and jumped away.

"Tell me who, and I will kill the blackguard!" She had never seen her jovial brother in such a state. His face was red and his veins bulged from his neck. He balled up his fists at his sides, ready to inflict damage.

"Calm down, Andrew. Please. That is exactly why I cannot tell you. But you need to trust me. Promise." She rose and placed soothing hands on his arms rubbing up and down, willing him to calm.

He took a deep breath, and looked at her a long while, likely considering his actions. She saw him realizing how much more it would hurt her if he made a public display of the incident, watched the emotions parade across his face.

"I see you agree with me. I will think about telling you. I did not intend to tell Grandmama, and I need more time." She walked over to her dressing table, touched up her hair, and then smoothed her gown in front of the looking glass.

He shook his head as if trying to clear it. "You are the one who was wronged, and yet you are soothing me."

"It happened so long ago. I have had years of practice. Come, let us go get some fresh air on the way to see Lord Wyndham." She tugged on his arm, pulling him toward the door.

"Are you sure? I can send your regrets." He resisted her pulling, unconvinced.

"I am sure. Grandmama said I have to not let this rule my life and I have to face my past to move on. It will be hard, but I think she is right. I only have to determine how."

He nodded an unsure agreement, and squeezed her in another big hug. "I will do my best to help. You never have to face anything else alone. You know that, do you not?"

Elly and Andrew made their way downstairs to grab their hats and jackets. She forced herself to take slow, deep breaths in order to portray an outward calm that she did not feel.

"How can you be composed, Elly?" Andrew asked as if reading her mind, he took her arm as they made their way toward Grosvenor Square.

"I've had years of practice to rarely show emotion about myself. Others are another story." She thought back to the passionate outburst she'd had at dinner about the American War. Oh, to be back there. She looked up toward the rare, blue sky and savoured the fresh, crisp air.

"So what are your plans now that Bonaparte is captured?" she asked, turning the subject from herself as they made their way past a row of houses toward the square.

"I am trying to decide. I could work at the War Office as Easton was going to, or turn respectable and take over one of the properties."

"Any plans for a wife?" He gave her an incredulous look. How dare she say the word *wife*.

"See how it feels?" She teased and prodded him with her elbow.

"Well, I will not be pestering you about getting leg-shackled, and I would appreciate if you'd return the favour."

"I was only curious, anyway. You are quite handsome; even a little sister can see that. I imagine you have lots of marriage-minded mamas and debutantes after you."

Andrew grunted. "Let us say that anything I attend will only be for your sake."

As they made their way up the steps to the handsome Wyndham town home, Elinor put on her brave face and tried to steel herself for an afternoon of smiles and polite inanities.

The butler took their hats and jackets, then showed them into the drawing room. The decoration was elegant but understated, and Elinor unconsciously approved of the simplicity.

Easton was assisting his father to his feet to greet them. Easton smiled and made introductions. "Father, this is Miss Abbott. Miss Abbott, my father, Garreth Trowbridge, Earl of Wyndham." He and Andrew also exchanged courtesies, but they were long acquainted.

"It is a pleasure to meet you again, my lord." Elinor sank into a deep curtsy.

The frail Lord Wyndham took her hand, his shaking gently, and gave it a fatherly kiss. "I am beyond grateful you have come to visit me, Miss Abbott, but I am more grateful for you and what you have done. Will you please come sit with me so I might enjoy a chat? I knew your parents well, but I have not seen you since you were a small child. I find myself quite intrigued by all the stories Adam has told me of you." He chuckled as he shuffled gingerly back to the sofa, assisted by Easton.

Elinor raised a questioning eyebrow, but Easton simply smiled at her over the Earl and focused on assisting his father. Elinor felt instantly at ease with the Earl and his kind eyes.

"I hope I do not disappoint, my lord." She blushed lightly but looked at him directly, and he smiled reassuringly.

"There is no possibility of that. I trust your father is well?"

"Andrew said he arrived safely in Ghent and is busy trying to sort everyone out. It is early yet, but I trust we will have good news soon." She smiled, showing her pride in her father.

The Earl smiled warmly at Elinor. "Yes, Sir Charles has a way of smoothing things over. He was ever the diplomat, even when we were young."

The butler brought tea in and set it on a table before them.

"Miss Abbott, would you mind doing the honours?" He gestured lightly toward the tea service.

"Only if you will call me Elinor from now on." She smiled prettily at him.

He gave her a wink and heard Andrew and Easton laugh. She proceeded to serve everyone before seating herself again by the Earl. The men continued talking about the war and possible outcomes.

"I had thought to rejoin Father, but I will wait until after Elly's come-out ball and possibly Christmas. I will wait for him to advise me. At present, he wants me here with her," Andrew said thoughtfully.

"I am grateful for that, Andrew," she said softly to him, and they looked at each other with understanding. Easton noticed an unspoken message pass between the two.

"We did receive word that General Ross was killed by sniper fire in Baltimore, soon after you set sail. Word is we retreated after that. We have hopes that will end this, once and for all," Andrew offered, knowing Easton and Wyndham would want the latest on the war.

"Yes, the public is beginning to grumble and question the futility of the war, what with the losses on the Continent and the growing dent in the coffers," Lord Wyndham said quietly.

"I wonder what made them retreat," Easton said, staring off into the fire, contemplating. Elinor looked at Easton and saw sadness and disappointment on his face. General Ross had been one of his mentors and friends. Elinor suspected he was also wondering what affect his death might have on his case against Colonel Knott, should his actions come to light.

"Cowardice? But that is from my limited knowledge of things, of course." She managed an insincere smile. Andrew threw an astonished look at her.

"I see why my son was taken with you, Elinor. I hope you will find time to visit me again while you are here. You will always be very welcome. I owe you more than I can ever hope to repay."

"I would be honoured for your company again. And please, my lord, feel no sense of debt to me. My father loves your son as his own, and I would truly have done my best to save anyone who needed my help. The Lord guided me every step of the way, for I am sure it was not my skills that saved your son."

Easton and Andrew were silently listening to the Earl and Elinor's exchanges, though the two were unaware, fully engrossed in their conversation with one another.

"You are too modest, Elinor. I doubt you would have travelled across the Atlantic for anyone, but I admit I am biased, and I will make no qualms about telling you how much I hope you will be my daughter one day soon."

Elinor and Easton simultaneously choked on their tea. Elinor blushed. Easton protested, "Father!" But there was little reproach in his voice. The Earl smiled. He had provoked the response he had intended.

"It is not necessary for him to marry me, my lord. I understand how society would view the situation were they to know, but I assure you, your son was the perfect gentleman." She leaned a little closer, smiling sweetly and whispered not too quietly, "But thank you kindly anyway."

"That is not what I meant. But I will let you off the hook —for now."

"I think we should let you rest now, sir, though it has been a real pleasure." Elinor stood and curtsied, motioning with her hands as the Earl tried to get up. "Please, do not rise on my account." She reached out her hand, and he took it. "Until next time, my lord." She winked precociously at him.

"I will walk you out." Easton took Elinor's arm and escorted them to the entry hall. He leaned over and whispered in her ear, "Thank you. If you keep charming him like that he will never stop hinting."

She smiled up at him. "I do not think that was hinting. He is quite a charmer himself. If I can do a little to bring a smile to his face, then it is worth it. Good day, Major Easton."

"Good day, Miss Elinor. Andrew." He cast an elegant bow.

While Elinor and Andrew were visiting the Earl, the Dowager, a prudent but savvy member of the *ton,* chose to investigate Lady Dunweather's knowledge and feelings toward her granddaughter by inviting her to tea for a pre-emptive meeting. She always believed that forewarned was forearmed, and she had not planned on intervening, but she was not at all sure how Elinor would react to facing a scandal and Nathaniel's arrival. She rather feared how the *ton* would receive

Elinor and malicious gossip had ruined many a person of weaker character than Elinor, regardless of how powerful her relatives were.

Fortunately, the ball was to be at the tail end of the Little in London, and the *ton* would be retiring to their country homes for the holidays soon. The Dowager had no intention of letting her granddaughter slip off across the Atlantic again.

Lady Dunweather and Her Grace, the Dowager Duchess of Loring, had made their bows together many moons prior. There was no outward animosity between the two ladies, but neither was above using the other ruthlessly for their own aims when it suited them.

"Lady Dunweather." Barnes announced her arrival.

"Duchess, what a pleasure." She affected her most insincere smile as she swept into the room, garbed in her enormous, wide skirts and equally high turban.

"Gertie. It is lovely to see you." The Dowager wafted her fan in an attempt to disperse the overwhelming stench of gardenia mixed with Dunweather.

"To what do I owe the pleasure of being invited to tea with the Duchess?"

"Can I not invite an old friend to tea?" Barnes placed the tea service before them, and the Dowager began to pour. Lady Dunweather helped herself to several sandwiches.

She took a bite of a cucumber sandwich, and raised her eyebrow with a smirk while chewing. "Do not bother with pretences, Duchess. We are too old for that, and you would not, anyway. This would not happen to be related to my being on the ship with your granddaughter? Or the fact that she was unaccompanied with Lord Easton for weeks?"

The Dowager dismissed that with the elegant wave of her hand. "Perhaps. But, I can assure you there were no improprieties. He was injured, for goodness sake! And her companion was with her, of course."

"Of course. I have yet to meet the gel, but I am curious. She is already creating quite a buzz. As long as she behaves herself I do not see any problem."

"I do not see that there will be any problem at all." She set her teacup down with purpose. "Is not *your* granddaughter due to make her debut soon?"

"Is that a threat?" She swallowed with a gulp.

"I see we understand each other." The Duchess could have levelled a mountain with her look.

Lady Dunweather smiled—rather, grimaced—and nodded her head in acquiescence. This was all part of the game.

"You might advise her to use a bit more caution. It has become common knowledge she gallops in the park every morning astride—" She paused for effect. "—and she was seen dancing in the park." That is hardly the way to discourage speculation about one's self. The high sticklers do not like it."

The Dowager sighed and nodded. Perhaps she was too old to chaperone Elinor. She had not been paying attention, favouring reading in her room and sleeping until noon. The old ladies continued to gossip for another twenty minutes before Lady Dunweather took her leave. The Dowager was satisfied with her afternoon's work, but she was quite ignorant that Beatrice had listened to every word.

CHAPTER 10

*T*he next morning, Elinor was out for an early morning walk with Josie. Andrew had not been able to ride that morning, and she had promised not to go alone. By chance, they met Easton's batman, Buffy, and he and Josie were deep in conversation. Josie and Buffy had been finding ways to meet by accident with some frequency. Elinor chuckled.

She wandered off a bit, but made sure to keep within sight of her companion for propriety's sake. Propriety? Ha! Elinor had received quite an education with regards to London society, most of which confirmed her prior opinions to be correct. She could not care less for the opinions of the *ton* if her cousin was any representation.

There were rules about rules that were not written down, yet a social solecism if broken. Men were encouraged to whore, gamble and drink until at least the age of thirty. The only debts considered worth paying were gambling debts to other gentleman, church was merely another social event that was acceptable to be absent from, and breaking the Ten Commandments seemed to be part of the rules of successful society. In fact, Elinor thought she could rewrite them according to society:

1. Thou shall not put anyone before yourself.
2. Thy self shall be the ideal everyone seeks to worship.
3. Thou shall only blaspheme if not around ladies.
4. Remember the Sabbath day by contributing to your local parish with new organs and roofs dedicated in your name.
5. Honour thy father and mother by only marrying another member of the aristocracy.
6. Women shall not commit adultery before bearing an heir and a spare.
7. Thou shall not murder unless in a duel against another gentleman.
8. Thou may bear false witness against another until it is proven to be a falsehood.
9. Thou shall not gallop in Hyde Park.
10. Thou shall not waltz until given permission.

Elly had to laugh out loud. The sad thing was, these were all true. She needed to find something worthy to spend her time on and try to protect her soul until she was away from this Godforsaken place.

"Penny for your thoughts?"

Elinor jumped. "Easton, I did not see you there."

"Beg pardon, I did not intend to startle you. I heard you laugh, and I would give almost anything to know what brought that smile to your face."

"Truly? It is quite ridiculous."

"I delight in ridiculosity." She gave him a sideways grin for his peculiar word.

"Very well. You asked. I was thinking about society's rules. I made up a *Ton* Commandments to help me remember. It is quite blasphemous, I am sure."

"Enlighten me, please."

"Do not say I did not warn you!" She then proceeded to regale him with her list of the commandments, ticking them off on her fingers as she recited.

Fortunately, he shared her wicked sense of humour. They enjoyed a laugh and continued walking through the park together. "I suppose we should not laugh. It is quite horrendous, though true." He looked down at her with a grin.

She smiled back sheepishly. She wished he would not look at her that way. It made her insides feel like jelly. She blew out a breath and changed the subject. "How have you been otherwise? You seem to be healing well. I confess it feels odd to be so much in your company, then not at all. According to Grandmama, it is inappropriate for me to call on you, or to write to you or to be seen alone with you."

"Yes, you should add that to your list." He smiled, and they enjoyed a companionable silence for a while. "I have been staying away on purpose, so there would not be any cause for talk."

"There is only one person who would talk, and Grandmama said she would take care of that."

"You need a chance to get settled and make your own way. I am afraid if you are seen much in my company…"

"What, people will get the wrong idea? I am not trying to snare a husband, Easton," she said, a bit more sharply than she intended.

"I know that, and you know that, but the gossips here will not give you another chance. They will not allow that we could only be friends." And truthfully, he did not want to be only friends, not any longer. He would be a fool to let the one female he had ever had any interest in slip out of his grasp, now that he needed to marry. Seeing his father so ill had finally convinced him, but he needed to figure out how to convince her and learn how to be deserving of her. "The oceans are not as far apart as they used to be. Society here and there eventually catches up."

"Then I am sorry for it. Believe it or not, I have actually missed you. It seems true friendships here are hard to come by." She could not believe she said that! With that, she curtsied and turned away to collect Josie, leaving Easton standing there watching after her with an astonished smile and a sliver of hope gathering in his breast.

~

The day had finally dawned when she would be presented to the Queen. She was dressed in required court attire—an amazingly complicated gown of white crepe over satin with a long train, side hoops and a low neckline. This was followed by a headdress with a veil and three ostrich plumes attached at the back. She had almost mastered walking backward for the occasion, since you were required to back from the room in the presence of royalty. Though she was grateful for her grandmother by her side, she had never been so relieved as when she made it out of the room without falling on her face! The Queen had been lovely, at least, and had spoken kind words to her about her mother, then chatted briefly with the Dowager.

The presentation was over with quickly. All the work that went into the gown, practising the royal curtsy and walking backward, and she was not even in the room for five minutes. Most debutantes were not in there that long. If it had not been for her grandmother, Elinor would not have warranted more than a quick greeting from Her Majesty.

A tea was to be held in celebration for the few debutantes who were presented that day, as opposed to the large receptions normally held to mark the start of the Season in the spring. Her grandmother insisted that she attend these to start getting to know some of the prominent society matrons. Apparently, they would make or break her.

They entered another mansion as lavish as St. James' Palace and Loring Place, then were led to a drawing room that was already full of matrons and debutantes, all sporting the tell-tale hoops and feathers. She was more than happy to remain by her grandmother's side during her first foray into a den of dowagers, when she spotted Lady Dunweather she froze in place. Make or break indeed. Unfortunately, when she stopped suddenly, someone's wayward ostrich feather got the better of her own headpiece, and a portion of her hair spiralled down over her face. She excused herself to the retiring room to repair the damage.

Still unknown to most of the others present, she sneaked into the room before her hair fell into any further disarray. She stopped short when she heard the shrill voice that could only belong to one person. Beatrice. She quickly ducked behind a door, hoping to go unnoticed. She had not realized Beatrice would be in attendance, but Elinor did not want to add any fodder for Bea's gossip mill or have to even talk to her more than necessary. Thankful that the panelling matched her gown, she stilled herself and hid to wait it out as she heard:

"So tell me about this *cousin* of yours. I am dying to hear all about it." Not her, it.

"She is gauche. You should have seen what she was wearing before Grandmother took her in hand. She is pretty enough, I suppose, but her manners are another matter entirely! You should hear how she talks!" She laughed the signature Beatrice titter. Elinor's skin crawled when she heard her. Let Beatrice demean her. The more she was around Beatrice, she could not bring herself to care what she thought. She heard a sultry voice speak. Elinor peeked a bit to see a stunning brunette primping before the mirror next to Beatrice.

"You poor dear. I hope you are right. As long as she keeps her paws off our men. I will not let her come in here and destroy everything I have worked for. Her novelty should wear off soon enough."

"Hear, hear! I am certain I can make sure that does not happen." The laugh again. What was that supposed to mean? And would they leave soon? She did not want their men. She had experienced their paws, and they were nothing she coveted.

"Have you seen Lord Easton yet? He is back in town. I hear he is looking delicious." Suddenly Elinor felt like pawing them, except with her claws.

"Dearest, you know I only have eyes for Rhys." Beatrice examined her fingernails. "Easton was at dinner the other night. I suppose he is handsome enough for a tryst. I have never thought of him other wise, since he was a second son."

"But he is not any more. Perhaps he is due more consideration," the brunette said, with mischief in her voice.

"I thought you were looking higher. Is there something you are not telling me?" Her voice got even shriller, if such a thing were possible. "I told you Nathaniel was returning soon."

"It is always wise to have an alternate plan. Besides, it might be worth settling for Countess if he was in my bed every night," answered the gorgeous brunette with the voluptuous curves and husky laugh.

Elinor was going to be sick. She could not compete with the likes of her even if she ever thought there was a chance for her and Easton.

Elinor was finally left alone and managed to stuff the errant hair back into the headdress. Reluctantly, she made her way back toward her grandmother with a forced smile on her face.

"Ah, there you are dear. All repaired?" Her grandmother looked at her approvingly.

"I believe so." Thank the heavens she at least had her grandmother. Then the fun truly began: the parading of Elinor as though she were a mount at Tattersall's.

"Smile and play along," Her grandmother whispered in her ear as she led her from one matron to the next. "May I present Gertrude, Countess of Dunweather. My granddaughter, Miss Abbott. Elinor, this is an *old* friend." Emphasis on the word old. Never mind that they were the same age.

"Lady Dunweather." Elinor proffered her best royal curtsy.

"She ain't the Queen, gel." The Dowager tapped her gently with her fan. Elinor only smiled sweetly. All old ladies liked to be flattered.

Lady Dunweather nodded approvingly. But she could not help herself. She spoke quietly to impart her worldly wisdom. "Did you know that ladies do not ride astride in England?" The Dowager groaned.

Elinor forced herself to remain silent and managed to look astonished. "You don't say? How do you ride here?"

"Why side-saddle, of course."

"Oh dear. It was kind of you to tell me so. I will ask Uncle to teach me at once." She hoped she sounded sincere.

"I assumed you did not know, or you would not have done such a thing. I am surprised your chaperone did not see fit to tell you these things. If you need advice, I am happy to oblige." She looked smugly at the Dowager, who bit her tongue for her granddaughter's sake.

"You honour me, Lady Dunweather." Elinor hoped she had managed to appear both repentant and humble, though she was neither of those things. To think that she gave up America for this artifice. Her grandmother turned to greet another acquaintance, and Lady Dunweather leaned in to speak.

"I have my eye on you, Miss Abbott. Do not disappoint me." Without waiting for a reply, the old harridan sauntered off with her turban and skirts, leaving a sickening whiff of gardenia behind.

Easton strolled into White's gentlemen's club, nodding acknowledgement to the old doorman whose name escaped him. He had never been one to spend much time with the fashionable pastimes, but for some reason, he was not ready to go home yet. He needed time to think. He had to determine how to stay away from Elinor publicly, yet manage to convince her that he was worth staying in England for *and* make it seem like it was her idea. So much had changed in his life, yet he had not sorted much out for himself, his future. Seeing Elinor in the park this morning only made his resolve to win her greater. Never before had he been so unafraid of the thought of being bound to someone for life.

He had nothing personal against the simpering misses, other than their young age and seeming lack of intelligence. But he had been naught but disgusted by the calculating society misses and their scheming mamas. To be fair, there were a few who were intelligent and pretty, but none were Elinor. She was everything they were not. But how to convince her?

Easton mulled these things over as he sauntered past the bow window where some dandies were in heated debate over horse races. The library held the older pillars of the lords discussing Parliament's latest Bill or the best strategies to end the war with America. He'd certainly had his fill of that. He nodded greetings, but kept walking.

Another room held high-stakes card games—no thank you. He kept strolling past the notorious betting books that were surrounded by wild, young bucks with nothing better to do. Absolutely not. Then he heard the words to make his heart sink.

"Incomparable." Wagging eyebrows.

"I hear she's a bruising rider." Rounds of chuckles and nudging each other.

"American...but not." Someone remarked, followed by, "Not a shrew like our ladies."

Dear God. News of Elinor had hit the clubs. Many had not had the good fortune to view her, much less be introduced. It was more the novelty they were betting on. There were relatively harmless wagers on whom she would choose to marry, all the way to the less harmless sort about who could do other various things with her.

Easton tried to control the rage he felt, but he did not want to bring any more attention to Elinor and end up making things more difficult for her. She was beautiful, but much more so than any of these shallow fools knew. No one was deserving of her beauty or goodness, himself included, but he selfishly did not want anyone else to have her.

Instead, he marched over to a quiet corner and plopped into one of the leather chairs. He ordered a drink, hoping for a few quiet moments with himself and his whisky. Surely wisdom lay at the bottom of the glass.

"Guinea for your thoughts."

"They are not worth that," Easton replied to the familiar voice without looking up.

"May I join you?" Easton waved toward the empty chair.

"Of course." He signalled the waiter for another glass. Andrew sat down and leaned his head back toward the ceiling.

"What ails you, my friend? I have never known you to hit the drink so early."

"Nothing to bother you with. Only adjusting to all of the changes." He was not about to confess his intentions about Elinor to her brother yet, or inform him that he had been plotting how to cross her path more often. That did not mean he would not talk about her. "How fares your sister so far? She was rather clear she was not looking forward to being introduced to society."

"Well, she is being introduced to the Queen as we speak, so it is official. Our grandmother is determined to give her a full coming out whether she likes it or not."

"Well, she is quite a taking thing." That was an understatement if he had ever made one.

"Let us hope they do not discover she's an heiress," Andrew said with a large sigh as the exasperated big brother. "I am taking her to the theatre for her first real outing tonight."

"Ah. Then perhaps the speculation will die down a bit after that." *Thanks for the tip, Andrew.*

"Speculation?" Andrew's eyebrows shot up.

Easton cast a pointed glance toward the betting books.

"The devil!"

"My sentiments exactly."

Both emptied their glasses. Easton smiled inwardly. It looked like he would be attending the theatre that night. His plans to leave her alone were looking less logical by the minute. When he thought of one of those betting idiots offering for her, he told himself he would be doing her a favour by keeping the more nefarious suitors away.

Elinor was grateful to ride alone to the theatre in the carriage with Andrew. Dinner with her family had been another painful affair all about the Duchess and Beatrice. Then the Dowager decided that Andrew was escort enough for Elinor, so she could return to her book. Oh, to be old enough to do whatever she pleased again, Elinor thought dreamily. They climbed inside, each took a seat in the carriage and she slumped from weariness.

Josie had beamed with gratification as she had dressed Elinor in a cerulean blue sarsenet gown with silver netting overlay. The gown had a peasant's bodice and capped sleeves, with yet another indecent neckline that displayed more of her charms than Elinor wanted, though she looked modest in comparison to most ladies she had seen. She fidgeted nervously with her gloves, hoping she did not embarrass herself at the theatre.

"How are you faring thus far, Elly?" Andrew enquired, noticing her slump.

"I miss home. I miss Papa. It is wonderful to see you and Grandmama, but I am loath to stay in the house where I am not wanted." She proceeded to explain her interactions with the Duchess and Lady Beatrice.

"Jealous as a mama cat, I bet. She does not stand a chance next to you, especially once she opens her mouth." She chuckled at Andrew's bluntness. It was one thing she adored about her brother. "I feel sorry for the poor devil who gets caught by her." Elinor agreed. Completely. However, most men did not pay attention or notice anything beyond the physical attributes or the size of the dowry, and Beatrice was full of both.

"Andrew!" she admonished him while laughing. "She seems to view me as competition! I thought we were family, but they treat me as if I am a leper. Must I continue to stay with them? Can we not open up the town house?" She did not bother masking the desperation in her voice, and she did not want to tell him Nathaniel's return was the main reason she had to get out of that house.

"That is the way of the *ton*. Best get used to it. Once you learn the rules, it will not be so bad. I was not planning on opening the house for only a few weeks. 'Twould not be the thing for you to be at a bachelor's residence even if it is your brother's. Well, not with the normal goings on anyway." He wagged his eyebrows at her.

Elinor gave him a half-questioning, half-reprimanding look. "Do not look at me that way, Elly. I am not a saint, but I ain't as awful as that. If it gets that bad, of course we can open up the house. Grandmama will protect you. I am sure she is loving this."

"I will try, but I refuse to get used to it. Family should be held to a different standard from the *ton*." She said the last word with proper snobbish accentuation. "Any more word from Papa?"

"Unfortunately, nothing of note."

"So this charade continues indefinitely."

There was no reply as they pulled up in front of the theatre.

∽

Elinor felt like a gawking tourist. The new Drury Lane Theatre was as opulent as one would expect, but the opulence she was trying not to stare at was the people. Her very being was repulsed by the extravagance contained within the relatively small space. Men wore large jewels in their cravats, and the ladies were dripping with them. Their gowns matched the gems in splendour, and their heads were dressed with elaborate concoctions of turbans, feathers and fruits. Elinor found herself fingering her new gown with guilt, and she was fascinated despite herself.

Andrew noticed the worried frown on Elinor's face. "Now, what has got you in a pucker, sis? This is supposed to be entertaining, not disappointing. And the play has not even started yet."

"It is so, so, rich. I feel guilty, especially knowing this is the type of thing the war is supporting."

"Do not say that to anyone else, El." She was not an idiot, her look said.

"Is all of London like this?" She glanced around with an expression of dismay as they made their way toward the ducal box.

"No, only the *ton*. There is a lot of ostentatious display. Sad thing is, many of the people are below the hatches. I agree it is vulgar, but you get used to it after a while. I suppose there is not much of this in the colonies, eh? I've met some nabobs from New York, and they reek of money."

"There are rich people, I suppose. I have not been exposed to this degree of it. And it is not the colonies any more, Andrew," she gently chastised.

"There are plenty of good things you can do here, El, if it makes you feel better. Easton's family runs an orphanage in one of the slums, though he does not want everyone to know it. He's a silent deeds person."

Her estimation of Easton increased tenfold. What else might she have misjudged him for? "Interesting. Do you think he would mind if I went there? I would love to do something useful while I am here."

"It would not hurt to ask." They were interrupted by men down in the pit waving, furiously trying to gain Elinor's attention. They wanted to get a better look at the new beauty in the Duke's box. "You are supposed to ignore them, Elly, so they'll leave you alone."

"They are waving at me? Whatever for?" she asked as she waved back at the moonlings and they roared with delight. Then she turned with a questioning look to Andrew as he groaned.

"Do not wave, El. Not the thing at all. And do not mind people staring. Only want to see what the new gel in town looks like."

Not the thing again—her theme for her society debut, Elinor thought.

Andrew did his best impression of mortification. She took stock of the people around them.

"How odd! And how nosy people are!" She gasped. "My goodness, those people are staring at me through their viewing glasses!" She turned away as she felt a self-conscious blush start on her chest and rise up. She hated that part about being fair. It was hard to hide one's emotions when you blushed like a tomato.

"Oh, Elly. London society is all about the latest *on dits* and gossip. Ignore them, they will give up if you do not give them anything to blabber about." *Or wager on*, he thought to himself. He turned his attention elsewhere, clearly not interested in the play any more than the rest of them.

Ignore them. Easier said than done. Thankfully the lights were dimmed, signalling the start of the play. She had never been to a fancy play or a fancy theatre, though she had read all of them many times. She tried to settle in and enjoy the drama, for the notorious Edmund Kean was playing Shakespeare's lead character from *Richard III*. However, she was conscious of being ogled from every angle and lorgnette, and found a line of male admirers forming outside their box as soon as the first intermission began.

Beatrice, used to being the centre of attention, began talking louder and was more flirtatious than usual. It looked like she would either pull Lord Vernon's arm off from hanging on it or maim it beyond recognition, the way she kept rapping it with her fan. This did not attract any more attention her way, merely made her attentions toward Vernon look all the more vulgar.

Elinor, unused to this kind of attention, was feeling overwhelmed, and this feeling was not helped by the sneers she received from her aunt and cousin. Did they think she wanted to be here? To be like them? Either her grandmother was going to have to put an end to this nonsense, or her foray into society would be over quickly. She forced herself to submit until the second intermission, and then begged Andrew to take her home.

He leaned in to speak quietly. "Let us try taking a stroll first. You leave now, they will only talk more. Try to act naturally and enjoy the play."

She whispered back through her gritted teeth, trying to maintain a smile, "I cannot stand people looking at me. I do not want to be on parade like a freak show!"

"Touchy! Touchy!" He elbowed her in the teasing way brothers do, then dragged her to her feet to stroll about the Grand Saloon. "You have changed, El. The little sister who left here six years ago thrived on being the centre of attention." *Yes, being attacked had affected her.*

Realizing what he said, "I am sorry. I do not mean to be insensitive about what happened. I am still trying to understand it all."

"No, I am different. The reality is, our experiences change us, some for the better, some for the worse."

"Agreed. And how you deal with them shapes you into who you are." Profound. And true. She was trying at least. She squeezed his arm.

It did not take long for the group of rowdy gentlemen to take notice of Elinor. Andrew threw his best scowling look at them, and they kept their distance, but not their cat calls of approval or stares.

He procured glasses of wine, then he led her in the other direction toward the terrace, and once they were out of earshot she started giggling.

"What, pray tell, is so funny, Elly?" He looked at her glass of wine and saw it was still full. No, she was not a trifle disguised. He cocked his head and looked at her. "Well?"

She waved her hand around. "This. Me. You. All of it. It is simply too ridiculous." She laughed mockingly. "Considering how I spent my days before arriving here, I cannot quite reconcile myself to the fact that this is how I am supposed to spend my time."

"Well, it is not a dream. Unfortunately, this is your reality for a while. You might as well try to make the most of it."

"And put aside my practical, prudish, puritanical ways?" She cast a sceptical glance at him, mocking herself.

He shrugged and threw her a half-smile. "When in Rome?"

Elinor sighed. "I am doing my best. Now, can we please go?"

Andrew stared at her a moment. He threw up his hands in resignation, and grandly presented his arm to escort her. As they made their way to the carriage, he said, "You are different, El. I know you are a *woman* now, but try not to be so serious and hide that *joie de vivre* that enchants everyone."

"I am not sure I still have it." Elinor spoke softly, unsure if Andrew even heard, for Lord Vernon was calling out and coming after them.

"Leaving early? I hope all is well, Miss Abbott, Andrew?" His face held genuine concern.

"Thank you for your concern, Lord Vernon. I am still unused to crowds." As she spoke to Lord Vernon, she spotted Easton across the saloon, laughing and charming a crowd. A crowd of simpering females—including the luscious brunette from the tea earlier—was hanging on his every word. A pang of jealousy burned through her, and she tried to shake it off, reminding herself that she had no claims to Easton and never could. If he did not enjoy this though, he had an interesting way of showing it.

"Well, after all the talk this evening, I wanted to at least secure a ride in the park while I have the chance. May I call on you and take you for a ride tomorrow?"

"I already have an obligation tomorrow."

Lord Vernon held his hand up to his heart. "Already? I have been bested! Dare I ask for the day after?"

She smiled at his playfulness and consented to ride with him the day after tomorrow. "That is, if my grandmother does not already have plans for me." She said as an afterthought, remembering what she had been told to say.

"But of course. Until then." He kissed her hand and nodded his head to Andrew.

After they were back in the carriage Andrew believed he should warn his sister. He was not sure how he felt about all of his friends dangling after his sister. "Elly, I will try not to interfere too much, but I claim big brother's privilege. Some of these fellows play hard and fast with money and women. Be cautious. London's upper ten thousand play by different rules from everyone else."

"Do you refer to Lord Vernon? Or Lord Easton? The lot of you have all been thick as thieves for ever!" She was surprised by his severe warning.

"Does not mean they are good enough for my sister. It is only you are already causing a stir." He did not want to go into how much of a stir. "Besides, everyone knows Bea has been dangling after Vernon for ages. She's only waiting for him to come up to scratch." Elinor snorted. "Easton ain't in the petticoat line. Doesn't even dabble. Odd that."

That news pleased Elinor. Exceedingly.

Easton watched from across the theatre as every wastrel libertine known to man fawned over Elinor. What was Andrew thinking to allow them near her? He would have to talk to him about that later. Surely he saw the danger? Or did he not realize how beautiful his little sister was?

During the intermission, he tried to make his way through the crowds to the Duke's box, only to find Elinor and Andrew had already departed. Frustrated, he made his way out to the parlour, only to be trapped by Lady Lydia . He tried his best to smile at Lady Lydia's coquettish behaviour, but it bored and disgusted him. He fumed as he spotted Vernon flirting shamelessly with Elinor. The cad kissed her hand and did not let go! Was Andrew completely oblivious? Lady Lydia Markham persisted in her attentions despite Easton's obvious attempts to end the conversation. He ended up having to be abrupt and rude to break away, but he was not in time to catch Elinor. They were already gone.

CHAPTER 11

*T*he weather turned sour, and a cold miserable rain beat down on them for several days. Elinor was close to madness from being kept indoors, or she would have tried to refuse the invitation her grandmother put forth to a recital that night. Elinor loved music, but Andrew had sworn off recitals for various reasons, mainly because society used them to showcase their debutante daughters. Elinor was merely looking for an excuse to escape from the house. She felt like a prisoner with only her grandmother and books for enjoyable company, since she avoided her aunt and cousin as much as possible. Andrew stayed away at his club or boxing at Gentleman Jackson's, and she found herself missing Easton's company dearly.

In the carriage ride, the Dowager bemoaned another insipid recital, but explained that no one ever refused an invitation to one of Lady Ashbury's events. She rarely entertained, but when she did it was all the rage. "This is the first recital I have ever attended there. I wonder how she will make it spectacular?"

"What does she do to make her events better than others?" Elinor asked curiously, maybe this would not be as tedious as she had thought.

"She decorates the house in wild themes and such. Never seen anything so extraordinary. However, I cannot imagine what she could come up with for this. Her three daughters are apparently the attraction. They are rarely out in public."

"Are they performing?" Elinor shivered against the chill coming in the carriage despite her warm wrap.

"That is what the invitation says. I bet there will be young bucks lined up out of the door."

"They are very beautiful, then."

"And they are triplets." She snorted.

"Ah." That explained everything.

The two ladies exited the carriage, sheltered by several footmen holding large umbrellas, who guided them to the door with rain-minimizing efficiency. The bucks were not quite lined up out of the door, but there was a crush of people indoors with a definite propensity toward the male species. She had never seen triplets before, so she was quite curious.

Though she could not see much, the entry hall looked rather ordinary. If there was a theme, it did not touch this part of the house. The throng parted enough to let the Dowager through, and Elinor followed close behind, smiling as best she could. She felt the stares and whispers of many in the crowd as they passed, finding herself still the object of novelty. She was grateful to make it into the more spacious ballroom.

Elinor was handed a programme as she was directed into the room, an incredible creation in the shape of a violin, which announced a night with Beethoven by the Ladies Anjou, Beaujolais and Margaux. *Their mother must be French. Or a wine connoisseur.* Then they entered the room that had been transformed into a replica of Vienna, including Hofburg Palace, the Rathaus, St. Stephen's Cathedral and an actual water feature of the Donau River running through the 'city'. Elinor was sure her mouth was gaping open in astonishment, but she could not help herself. She tried not to ponder the extravagant cost of such an event. The chairs were placed strategically around the mini replicas.

Footmen began extinguishing candles as the guests were urged to their seats, and Elinor was entranced by the spectacle. Once the guests were seated, there was no sign of a stage or any performers. As Lady Ashbury stood to introduce the performance, Elinor saw Andrew and Easton sneak in, the rogues! Then, the building shaped like the Viennese Opera House began to rotate, and Elinor put every-thing else from her mind for the moment. On the other side of the building were the triplets, one behind a pianoforte, another sitting behind a cello and the third held a violin. Three identical, raven-haired girls looked as goddesses in their ethereal beauty. Elinor was not the only one who thought so as she gazed around at the audi-ence's faces.

Her grandmother whispered loudly, "Let us hope the music lives up to the décor." Elinor tried to cover her giggle. That notion was quickly dispelled as the girl on the cello began, then was joined by the others in Beethoven's *Triple Concerto*. She was quickly drawn in to the drama of the story being told, and was surprised when Lady Ashbury announced an intermission as the stage rotated away from the audience.

It did not take long for a crowd of men to grow near the stage, hoping for an introduction to the threesome. Elinor could not blame them. She was rather fascinated, herself. As the Dowager made her way to the retiring room, Elinor went to retrieve refreshment for them.

"May I procure something for you, Miss Abbott?" Elinor turned to see Easton standing in front of her, looking as handsome as the devil in his black tailcoat, sapphire waistcoat and black satin breeches. The clothes moulded to his muscled soldier's body, of which she knew every contour and scar of—which she should *not* be thinking about, she reminded herself. She fanned herself in order to cool her suddenly hot cheeks as she turned toward the table laden with drinks and desserts.

"I was going to gather refreshment for myself and Grandmama." She inclined her head toward the table.

"May I help you, then?" He would give a hundred pounds to know what she had been thinking just then as he caught her looking him over from head to toe.

"Of course." She smiled shyly. She had wanted to see him so much, and now she was at a loss for words!

"Do you think the wine will be French?" She laughed. "Or do you think they have a brother named Bacchus?" He threw his head back with laughter.

"Sadly, their brother's name is Charles."

"How disappointing." She feigned a disappointed look, but could not stop a smile.

"Indeed." They laughed again as they made their way toward the enormous cake shaped like a pianoforte.

"Would you prefer A minor or G major, Miss Abbott?" He waved his hand toward the cake.

"Oh, any key will do." Could the evening be any more preposterous? She felt like she had stepped into the pages of a fairy tale. They made their way toward the tables provided, past Andrew in the crowd waiting to meet the triplets.

"Now I see what brought my brother into the lion's den." She glanced over at the men making fools of themselves. "He told me he had sworn them off." She laughed and barely suppressed a bubble of champagne from escaping her.

"Yes, odd how that works. It is not my preferred cup of tea either, but I could not say no to my aunt. And, of course Andrew did not want me to have to come alone."

"No, of course not. I am sure it was a great sacrifice."

"At least the music is excellent. Usually these are bad enough to make you grind your teeth until they fall out."

"And the view is excellent, even I must admit." She smiled coyly.

He did not take that bait. "It is a shame this will all go to waste tomorrow." He looked around at the pomp and pageantry on display and shrugged.

"I am a fish out of water, I am afraid. It is a far cry from the battlefield or the tobacco fields."

"Or even the streets of London," he said quietly.

"That reminds me. I have been wanting to ask you about helping with your orphanage. If I might be allowed to sew clothes or do something while I am here?"

He looked at her, contemplating. "I suppose Andrew told you about it. We do not like to advertise who the benefactor is. It takes away from the children." She nodded and looked up at him. "Help is always welcome. There is never a lack of work to be done. I shall take you there soon, if you like."

"I would appreciate the diversion more than you know, though perhaps I should find something to do other than sewing. I am a horrid seamstress."

"I guess I should be grateful I cannot see your handiwork on my back." He dimpled at her.

They were soon joined by Lord Vernon and Andrew, who both looked disappointed. Elinor leaned toward her brother as he reached to peck her on the cheek.

"Why so glum Andrew, Lord Vernon?" She curtsied to the new arrivals. "Does this have something to do with some raven-haired triplets?"

"They will be back soon, boys." A voice with a French-tinged accent said as she chuckled behind them. They turned to find a rather amused Lady Ashbury standing before them. The men bowed, and Elinor curtsied, though she had not been yet introduced. "I am glad to see you made it after all, Adam. You have been remiss in greeting your favourite aunt since your return."

"Forgive me, Aunt Simone." He leaned over and kissed his aunt dutifully on the cheek. Elinor breathed a sigh of relief she did not realize she had been holding in. It suddenly occurred to her that meant the triplets were his cousins. Hallelujah! She heard Lady Ashbury clear her throat, and Elinor looked up to see Lady Ashbury angling her head toward Elinor. Had she been wool-gathering and missed a question?

"Pardon me, I did not realize you had not been introduced, Aunt. Marchioness of Ashbury, Miss Abbott."

"At last we finally meet," Lady Ashbury said. "I have heard much about you. I hope I will be able to make your acquaintance better when my house is not full of guests." She glanced around, indicating the crowded ballroom.

"Lady Ashbury," Andrew bowed over her hand. "May I say you have some very talented daughters. They are most lovely to…listen to." Lady Ashbury smiled with a twinkle in her eye as Andrew realized he almost embarrassed himself.

"I think so, Mr. Abbott. Thank you. I do hope you enjoy the rest of the entertainment." She flashed another smile and strode off to greet some other guests. Elinor enjoyed her cake and champagne much more now as she listened without concern to the men discussing the triplets. She found herself amused by Andrew's interest and planned to use this against him in the future if necessary. In a sisterly way, of course.

As Lady Ashbury walked away, Lord Vernon turned to engage Elinor's attentions. He bowed over her hand as Andrew engaged in conversation with Easton. "Looking most elegant this evening. I am most enchanted."

Easton and Andrew coughed their annoyance with his flummery, but Vernon ignored them.

"Are we still on for our ride in the park, Miss Abbott?" Vernon looked up from her hand and winked.

"Yes, of course. I am looking forward to it. I have been in the park in the morning, and I am sure it will be just as lovely in the afternoon," Elinor replied.

"If you think it lovely with your brother as a guide, I am sure I can do much better." He smiled rakishly down at her. Andrew had to defend himself.

"Elly can see right through you, you know, Vernon. Why would she prefer a fawning pretty face over her dashing older brother?" he parried back light-heartedly.

"Must I state the obvious advantages, Andrew?" Elinor reminded herself this was masculine banter between friends, but it was treading near dangerous waters. She glanced at Easton to see how he reacted, but he still stood there staring at her.

"I could call you out for that, Vernon." Andrew eyed Vernon to see how far his friend would take his treatment of his little sister.

"You could, but you will not. You know my actual intentions are honourable." Easton stiffened.

Beatrice approached and wound an arm through Lord Vernon's, possessively marking her territory. "Ah. Rhys, you are embarrassing my dear cousin with your teasing. You do realize he is only teasing, do you not, Elinor?" She looked from Elinor to Vernon. "You must not provoke her so, dear. She might actually think you are serious." She cackled and smirked at Elinor. Lady Lydia sauntered over in a figure-hugging dress that was low-cut to display her bosom to advantage, and she was obviously aware of the effect she made.

Nothing drew flies to honey like competition, Elinor thought.

"Why so serious? Have I missed something important?" She practically purred as she leaned too close to Easton. Elinor longed to tell her exactly what she had missed, but they had not been properly introduced, so she could not even speak to her without being improper. Lady Lydia looked Elinor over boldly with a look on her face that indicated she found her lacking. Elinor stared back just as brashly, refusing to be cowed by the scheming hussy.

Andrew made the introductions. "A pleasure, I am sure," Lady Lydia said coldly.

Thankfully, Easton saved her. Apparently her brother was too distracted by Lady Lydia's assets to recover his wits. "Miss Abbott, I see your grandmother trying to gain your attention. Might I escort you to her?"

"That would be most welcome, thank you." When they were away from the group, Easton leaned over to her. "Ignore them. They are merely jealous."

"I doubt that, but thank you for the support anyway. I confess I am not used to such open malice."

"Perhaps we should alter the sign at the entrance to the estate to include their types as well."

"I am not sure any of the adjectives I can think of to describe them would be proper for a sign."

They smiled at each other, and Elinor felt a warmth spread over her. *If only.*

~

The next afternoon arrived along with a slew of callers at Loring Place. Elinor's presence in London had inevitably become known, and many became quite curious to see the latest craze in town. Elinor did not enjoy the attention, but she was determined to be agreeable. When Lord Vernon was announced and revealed his errand in taking Elinor for a drive in the park, Beatrice gasped and glared at Elly. Lord Vernon, astutely foreseeing the impending tantrum, asked, as he bowed over Beatrice's hand, "Are you free to join us, Lady Beatrice? I promised Andrew I would show your cousin the delights of an afternoon drive in the park."

That was smooth, Elinor thought. It also meant Elinor would be forced to spend the next hour or so in a small space with Beatrice. Beatrice was pacified, for now. Elinor saw nothing but doom and destruction in her future. The Lord help her if she ever acted the shrew that Beatrice did.

Josie was delighted at another chance to dress Elinor to best advantage, and had selected a pale lilac sprigged muslin with long sleeves and a fashionable high waist. Elinor donned her robed pelisse and kid gloves to thwart the afternoon chill and placed a matching bonnet atop her head.

They made their way to the curricle, and Beatrice was clearly entering the desperation phase in Elinor's opinion. Hopefully she did not always behave like this around men. Perhaps that explained why she'd had no serious offers this past Season. When they made it outside to enter the curricle, Beatrice began shrieking. "But you cannot mean to take all of us in that!" Clearly she did always act this way.

"Of course I can. The two of you are slender enough to equal the size of one adult male. Or you can choose to stay home if you object to being in close quarters to myself or your cousin." He grinned at her, knowing she had hoist herself by her own petard. Elinor tried not to smile, but it was lovely to watch Beatrice stew. She dare not stay at home, though, so she grudgingly accepted Vernon's assistance into the contraption. It was quite small, but Elinor was enjoying Beatrice's discomfort and felt little guilt about it.

They made their way down the street and through the gates, and then they came to a stand-still. Apparently, when Lord Vernon said an afternoon drive in the park, he actually meant an afternoon sit in the carriage. There was such a crowd in the park; it was impossible to move at more than a snail's pace. For London being supposedly thin of people this time of year, Elinor shuddered to think of it when it was considered crowded. However, Lord Vernon and Beatrice seemed undisturbed with the pace, as every carriage passing stopped to greet them. Lord Vernon looked quite pleased with himself, being escort to two beauties, and was able to flaunt his good fortune in front of the other dandies in attendance.

Elinor suddenly found her hand being bowed over by numerous pinks, tulips and fops. She had never seen the likes of men wearing such ridiculous costumes! Their shirt points reached to their eyebrows and their waistcoats were bright enough to light a room. They spouted nonsense about her skin being as fair as a fresh snow and likening her eyes to lake water and oceans. Lake water? They must be thinking of different lakes than she was. Surely they jested? Was she supposed to take this seriously? She glanced at Beatrice receiving her own version of adoration, and then she turned her face so she could laugh. She actually laughed out loud.

"Thay, Mith Abbott," a man said with the exaggerated and affected lisp that was favoured amongst their set, "Ith that you I thee in the morning, galloping on the white mare?" She turned to face him, partially recovered from her laughing fit. He had decked himself out in a lime green waistcoat covered with pink flamingos and saucer-sized gold buttons. His top hat had a ribbon to match. Fascinating. She bet he would be shot if he dared to wear that back home.

Beatrice looked mortified. She murmured to Vernon, "I told you she would embarrass me."

The fop, Mr. Sinclair, continued as he looked her over with his quizzing glass; it made his eye look as big as his buttons. He nodded approvingly. "Mith Abbott, you have the finesth theat on a horthe I have ever theen."

Once she deciphered what he said, she replied, "Thank you, Mither Thinclair." She managed to speak his name with a lisp and a straight face. She knew she should not have, but she could not help herself.

This brought roars of laughter from the onlookers, and they slapped Sinclair on the back with good-natured teasing. Instead of disgusting them with her American manners, she had endeared herself to them. She heard Beatrice scream over the laughter, and Vernon only smiled and winked at her. *Poor Vernon. What did he see in her cousin?*

The next morning saw the parlour full of flowers and cards for Elinor as proof of her new celebrity. That afternoon, the flowers were joined by the parade of admirers who had sent the bouquets and trifles. She had them sent straight to the orphanage. If only they had sent the money they spent on flowers there instead. The preposterous costumes the gentlemen wore were only eclipsed by the absurd poems and odes that had been written to her eyebrows, earlobes and nose. This could not be real. She could not have made this nonsense up in her wildest dreams. The curious of London came out to see this novelty that was half American in her manners, but blue-blooded British in her pedigree.

What constituted a nightmare for Elinor was Beatrice's deepest longing—to be the most sought-after female in society. Beatrice observed Elinor's success with a growing hatred. Instead of realizing that Elinor's inner beauty and indifference were what attracted that attention, she focused on ways to put Elinor in her rightful place. Beatrice had plenty of admirers in her own right, but any attention not focused on her was attention misplaced.

~

Most days passed in a haze for Elinor. She continued to ride with

Andrew every morning the weather allowed, learning side-saddle, on the beautiful golden-white mare her uncle had bought for her. She could not wait to get her to the country to let her run loose. The afternoons were filled with more fawning gentleman callers and stuffy teas with ladies of the *ton*. She was getting more used to the silliness and tried to humour the callers, as they did seem harmless for all that. Evenings held dinners, soirees, balls or the theatre. It was exhausting and left no time to herself.

Easton had sent a note after their walk in the park, informing Elinor that he would be visiting the orphanage the next day if she would care to join him. Elinor was delighted to have a break from the constant swirl of city life. She dressed herself in one of her practical frocks from home, thankful her grandmother had not had them burned. Easton helped Elinor and Josie into the carriage beyond, then tapped on the roof signalling the driver to proceed.

Elinor had not been outside of Mayfair since the night they arrived, and it had been too foggy to see anything then. This was a clear day, and Elinor and Josie watched with wonder as they made their way beyond the hallowed streets of rich London. She only thought she had seen poverty before. The vendors and sweeps she had seen in Mayfair looked luxurious compared to the half-clothed, barefoot women and children she saw huddled in doorways and alleys, trying to keep warm. The small, soot-covered houses were falling apart, and the stench from the undisposed sewage and waste strewn about made the despair more astounding. Suddenly her problems seemed so trivial.

Elinor had not realized she was biting on her clenched fist or that her eyes were filled with unshed tears until Easton spoke and broke her trance.

"We can go back if it is too much."

Elinor shook her head. "I want to help them all. But how?"

"It is not possible to help everybody, but we are still trying." They pulled up in front of a set of buildings that were old and well used like the rest of the area, but they appeared to be in good repair. "This is it.

Shall we?" He helped the ladies from the carriage and escorted them through the front doors.

Elinor was not sure what she was expecting when she thought of an orphanage, though sad and malnourished came to mind. Instead, she was greeted with the sounds of laughter and playing children. She looked around in awe as they walked through to greet the 'house parents' as Easton referred to them. They passed a school room, a playroom, a sewing room, and then found the 'mama', Mrs. Hopkins, in the kitchen instructing a half-dozen children in the art of making bread.

Immediately Elinor's heart was filled with joy. Joy that these children were learning skills that would help them find useful employment, joy that they had enough food and clothing and, apparently, love and laughter. She had not thought this could exist in the midst of the misery outside.

When the children noticed their visitors, they immediately squealed with delight and came rushing to greet Easton. He sank down to his haunches and held his arms open to gather them in a hug. Elinor took a deep breath of astonishment. This greeting followed them as they toured the orphanage with shouts of, "Mr. Adam! Have you come to read to us? Did you bring us sweets?" and the like.

"Yes, yes. After luncheon." He chuckled at the mass of children hanging onto him.

Mr. Hopkins herded the children into the dining room. The younger children were seated near older ones who were not helping to serve the meal. Elinor stayed behind in the kitchen to see if she could offer Mrs. Hopkins any assistance. She knew that visitors made for more work. Easton reached down and gave Mrs. Hopkins a kiss on the cheek and a hug before following the others out. Elinor looked on with bewilderment. Mrs. Hopkins chuckled at Elinor's face. "I am his old nanny."

Elinor tried not to blush at her obvious lack of decorum. "The mister and I decided to take this on when the Trowbridge children were too grown to need me any more. I'd never been blessed with children of my own, and now I've got handfuls." She grinned from ear to ear. "The Earl and family were pleased to help us." Elinor did not know what to say, so Mrs. Hopkins kept going while they put food on plates and handed them to girls to carry to the dining room. "You will never find a finer family than that. My Adam visits every chance he gets, takes a personal interest in every child. His sister makes clothes for the children when she cannot be here to help."

Easton had a sister? Elinor followed Mrs. Hopkins into the dining room, her mind whirling with all the new details about Easton. She was seated in the middle of one of the tables, directly across from him. She almost dropped her jaw to the floor when she saw he held a small girl in his lap, feeding her, looking happier than she had ever seen him. She tried not to stare as the little girl traced his jaw with her potato-covered finger, and then he did the same to her and they laughed. She never would have pictured him as a wonderful father before this; he had often seemed so strait-laced. He winked at her as he caught her staring. "Miss Elinor, this is my special girl, Susie." Elinor could not help but grin back at them.

They partook of a surprisingly hearty and well-tasting meal, though simple. The children were well behaved and also helped to clean up afterward.

Mrs. Hopkins asked, as everyone finished, "Mr. Adam, a quick story before lessons?" This was greeted with loud cheers from the children. "Then, boys to the stables, and girls to sewing."

"Yes, Mrs. Hopkins!" A synchronous chorus replied. They gathered in the large drawing room around an enormous hearth with a roaring fire. Mrs. Hopkins arranged a chair for Easton, and then placed screens in front of the fire to keep curious fingers from getting too close. As Easton read to the entranced boys and girls hanging on his every word, Elinor looked around and felt truly comfortable for the first time since stepping foot back in England. This felt right. She had misjudged Easton badly and was so grateful that she was wrong. Her heart was thawing toward him in ways that made her acutely uncomfortable, and it hurt to know she would have to be content with his friendship.

She spied a little boy with big brown eyes and chubby cheeks looking at her from behind Mrs. Hopkins' skirts. He could not be much more than three years old. She smiled at the little one, and he glanced around to see if the smile was for him then immediately looked down, embarrassed at being caught staring at her. Elinor sat down on the floor to seem less threatening and motioned for him to sit by her. He only stared back at her. Oh, how she wanted to scoop him up and love away his fears!

Having finished the story, Easton sat down beside her so that she might help him hand out some treats, and talk to the children. He held out his hand to the little boy and he crawled right up in Easton's lap. Who would have thought Easton would have had the magic touch where she had failed?

"My name is Adam. What is your name?"

The little boy shrugged.

"I suppose I will have to keep this sweet for myself, then."

The boy shook his head furiously and a giant tear threatened to fall from his large, chocolate eyes. He sniffled a breath trying to be a big boy, but could not take his eyes off the confection.

"Can you talk?" Easton asked.

The boy nodded. "Don't know name," he said, and began to suck on the thumb in his mouth. He nuzzled his face into Easton's coat and refused to look up again. Easton looked at Elinor as if to say, *That was an utter failure.*

"What would you like to be called?"

The big brown eyes looked up to Easton. "Adam."

Easton chuckled. "That is an excellent choice. Adam it is. It is nice to meet you." He handed the boy the sweet and hugged him while the child devoured it.

Easton whispered into Elinor's ear. "I think I am in love."

Me too. Me too.

CHAPTER 12

The day of the ball finally arrived, no matter how much Elinor had wished it otherwise. The promising side was it would be over and she would be much closer to returning to her beloved River's Bend. She longed for home, now more than ever. She would miss her family, but she would not miss society here. This was when Elinor most longed for her mother's guidance, for she would know how to be proper and what to say to not draw attention to herself. American society had not been as difficult, not so stringent.

And today Nathaniel was to arrive, and there would be no more escaping.

Her room was filled with bouquets overflowing from the rest of the house. They had been sent with well-wishes, as was custom for a come-out ball. Many were from people she had never even met, sent by old friends of the family. There was a soft knock on the door. Josie went to answer, expecting more bouquets from a footman. Instead, Andrew entered, bearing flowers and a small box.

"You look beautiful, Elly." He paused, looking uncomfortable.

"That was difficult for you, was it not?" She laughed as he stood there trying to think of what to say. He had the decency to look sheepish.

"I am not sure I like the thought of everyone seeing you in that." He surveyed her gown of ivory satin with a green velvet bodice that fit her perfectly. She even poked her feet out to show off her matching green slippers. She had picked out the design for this dress and was quite proud of it. He cleared his throat and shook his head.

"Yes, well, Elly, these are for you." He handed her a bouquet of her favourite calla lilies. "And this is from Father." He handed her an envelope and a box that held a pair of diamond earrings, which had been her mother's.

Elinor felt tears pool in her eyes. She accepted the gifts, then reached up and pecked him on the cheek. "Thank you, Andrew."

"I am not very good at formalities or advice, but tonight just be yourself. I was wrong to tell you to smile and look pretty. Even this group of ninnies will see what a treasure you are."

"Thank you, Andrew, I think." He smiled a boyish grin and kissed her on the forehead.

Josie knew Elinor was becoming overwhelmed, and she ushered Andrew out. "Are you all right, Miss Elly?"

Elinor nodded. "I cannot do this."

"It is what your mama wanted," Josie said softly.

"I know, but this is not me. I cannot stand the thought of everyone staring at me."

"You will be perfect. Be yourself, just like he said. If you get overwhelmed, imagine yourself dancing with your papa back home." Elinor nodded.

Josie proceeded to finish Elinor's hair, placing in beautiful combs lined with deep green emeralds, allowing her golden curls to cascade down the back. "Where did you get those? No, do not tell me. Grandmama, of course." Josie coughed. "Josie?"

"He was afraid you would not accept them. He made me promise. And now it is too late to redo your hair." She grinned unrepentantly.

"Who?" Her stomach churned.

"Why, Lord Easton of course. He gave me a note in case you asked." Josie pulled the beautiful card from her pocket. Elinor snatched it from Josie and opened it.

Please save a dance for me. Yours, E

She blushed. "May I have a few moments, you devious girl? I need a little quiet before the storm."

Josie quietly escaped with a smile. Her work was done.

Elinor was alarmed by the pleasure she felt at Easton's gift and note. She could not allow herself to feel more than that. She knew he only meant the gift in friendship and encouragement, knowing how much she was dreading being on display tonight. She could not allow herself to have hope in that quarter anyway, knowing she could never marry. She did not know how she was going to get through seeing Nathaniel again. Trembling at the thought of what the evening was to bring, Elinor opened the note from her papa. She should wait to read it, but she needed the false courage it would bring.

Dearest Elinor,

It breaks my heart to miss your debut. Now the whole world will know what I have always known—that you are the most beautiful girl in Christendom. Do not hide the light that shines within you. Or break too many hearts. I will be there soon. We have made a peace offer I am hopeful will be accepted.

All my love,
Papa

Fortunately, she had been kept busy to distraction the entire day, and she somehow found herself in the receiving line between her uncle and her grandmother. How had that happened? She barely recalled dinner or noticed the hundreds of flowers that adorned the ballroom, though every niche was filled with beautiful floral arrangements, and the wall sconces and chandeliers were littered with glowing candles. Obviously her requests to limit the extravagance were not heeded. The orchestra was strumming the sounds of preparation somewhere in the background. She was led along in a daze, trying to affect the façade of *ennui* she detested in this society. But for tonight, it would help her detach her emotions, and therefore, cope.

Her uncle gave her a crushing hug, as was his non-gentlemanly custom. "I have no doubt of your success, Elly. Are you ready? You will be wonderful." He gave her a fatherly look making her feel like the most special girl in the room, despite the battles being fought in her stomach.

She nodded and flashed him a brilliant smile. "I suppose it must be done. I only wish Papa were here."

"Yes, that cannot be helped, but the rest of the family is here. Nathaniel has arrived and should be down shortly. I kept him talking so long, I did not leave him time to make it to dinner."

She felt a steadying squeeze on her arm from her grandmother, and a whisper in her ear of, "Courage, dear." But she had already steeled herself for the moment, determined to be visibly unaffected. However, she could not control what she felt on the inside. Nothing could be worse than those imaginings, which had infiltrated her dreams so often through the years.

Then she knew, just knew, he was standing there. Despite her mental preparations, she was momentarily paralysed with fear. She took a deep breath, then willed herself to turn. But her reaction was not at all what she expected. Her gaze locked with his, and she saw remorse in his grey eyes, not the possessed eyes that had haunted her for six years. She was afraid to speak, her entire body tense with anticipation and—sorrow?

"Cousin." He bowed.

"Nathaniel." This was said with false confidence and a slow curtsy, every inch of her trembling.

"I would speak to you, if you would permit." He spoke softly, but she heard.

Their grandmother intervened, speaking in a low quiet voice, "This is not the time, and you will only see her afterward in my presence. Is that clear?"

Nathaniel nodded and took his place in the receiving line. Her uncle looked back and forth between the two in confusion, but resumed his place without a word as guests were shown in. Elinor was proud she had appeared calm, though her nerves were fluttering. Having had time to prepare for his arrival had helped. She found herself running through a variety of emotions inside, while outwardly trying to paste a genuine smile on her face. However, when Lord Easton arrived, wheeling in Lord Wyndham in a bath chair, there was no effort required.

"Lord Wyndham! I am very pleased to see you here!"

Elinor did not notice the confused look on the faces of her family who were quite unaware of her recent acquaintance with the Earl. Her grandmother gave her a polite nudge to remind her.

"I am thrilled you remember me after all these years, Miss Abbott. You are looking as beautiful as I would have expected." He gave her a little wink, and she tried to mask her horrified expression as she realized her slip.

"Yes, my lord, I have an excellent memory. I am pleased you were able to join us." She fell into a graceful curtsy.

"I would not have missed it for the world, my dear," he said quietly. "Save a dance for me?"

"You may have all of them, my lord." She smiled charmingly.

He laughed loudly. "I think a few young bucks might have something to say about that."

It was Lord Easton's turn. He took her hand and brushed his lips lightly across her gloved hand. "Enchanted, Miss Abbott." Their eyes met, and his twinkled as he glanced at the combs. She blushed.

Elinor stood at the top of the stairs surveying the crush of people filling the ballroom. Her every instinct told her to turn and run when she felt her uncle take her arm and lead her to the dance floor. His presenting her put the stamp of approval on her acceptance in society. She had not been brought up looking forward to this occasion as her sister and cousin had been. Would she have revelled in this moment if her path had been different? She could not bring herself to think so.

The opening dance came and went. Her uncle's talking kept her at ease, so she was able to forget she was in a crowded ballroom full of strangers and that everyone's eyes were on her. Including Nathaniel's. That is, until her uncle led her straight to him. Nathaniel was standing with Andrew, Easton and Lord Vernon, catching up on old times, no doubt.

"This looks like the right sort for your next few dances, Elly. Who is first? I quite forget the order of things. Nate?" The Duke looked at Nathaniel, trying to give him her hand.

Elinor was horrified, but how could she refuse in front of everyone without creating a big scene? She unconsciously looked at Andrew, and instantly he knew. Nathaniel held out his hand to lead her to the floor, but Andrew grabbed her wrist gently and said quietly through clenched teeth, "You do not have to do this."

"Yes, I do, Andrew." Even though her hands were trembling and clammy and she felt a cold sweat wash over her.

Easton and Vernon stood there watching curiously, but made no comment. It took all of Easton's strength to hold himself in check. He felt fairly certain Nathaniel was the source of Elinor's anxiety, but not the nature of it.

Elinor took deep breaths. *Stay calm. Stay calm.* One dance, then she would beg Andrew to take her away. The Duke murmured something to Andrew, but she could not make out the words over the noise of her blood pounding in her ears. She was willing herself to remain calm, but her hands trembled at his touch anyway.

"Cousin." He bowed and she curtsied, as was customary to begin the dance.

"Please do not ask me to speak with you right now. Not tonight."

The dance separated them for a few steps. When they were rejoined, he said, "Very well. I cannot blame you for feeling that way." He looked disappointed.

The dance separated them again. Whatever Elinor thought would happen when she encountered Nathaniel again, this was not it. He seemed so different. Is it possible he could have changed?

"I know my presence here is distressing to you. Only say the word and I will leave again."

The dance was ending, but their conversation had only begun. They both had words they needed to say; she was not prepared to speak them right now. Nathaniel led her back to Andrew, who was scowling with his hands clenched by his sides. He turned to leave her and said quietly in a whisper, "I am sorry." He looked at her, tears filling his eyes, then walked away.

"This is not over, Nate." Andrew fumed.

Nathaniel nodded and kept walking toward the terrace.

Elinor grabbed Andrew's arm to prevent his leaving the dance floor, trying to avoid the scene Andrew was obviously trying to contain within him. "This is not your battle to fight."

"I disagree," he said more calmly than he felt.

"Six years ago I would have agreed with you. Now I need to heal. I think he is truly repentant."

"Time will tell."

"Please, Andrew. I am begging you. Let me deal with this my own way."

He stood there for an eternity, searching her face before answering. "Is he to have no consequences then?" he asked with disgust, but the look on Elinor's face convinced him. "As you wish. I would never want to see you hurt more."

She could tell it took enormous effort for him to concede. "Thank you." Then she forced herself back onto the dance floor with her next partner, to pretend a little longer.

Elinor gathered she would be considered a success, based on the crowd. At least that should make her grandmother happy. The suitors were lining up to have their turn with the American-flavoured novelty. At least being occupied kept her thoughts from Nathaniel. Three tulips had already asked Uncle for her hand. However, the arrival of Nathaniel, Viscount Fairmont, was the biggest news in years. The long-lost prodigal son and heir to the Duke of Loring had returned home, which deflected some of the attention from Elinor. Well, the female half anyway. For that she was extremely obliged to him. The attention one garnered from the *ton* females was something she could happily do without. But one female in particular was watching her cousin's every move that night, waiting for the right moment.

Elinor paused for a dance to take refreshment and watched with amusement as Andrew led one after the other of Lady Ashbury's triplets to the dance floor. He could spend all night never dancing with anyone outside family. They all seemed equally charmed by him, but which one did he fancy? He must have one of them in mind to go to so much effort with marriageable misses.

Lady Lydia was twirling about the floor with Nathaniel, wearing another clingy dress with a wide, low neckline. Elinor wondered if he was the high prey she had overheard Lydia discussing with Beatrice. Could one speak so coldly about one's brother with a potential suitor? She supposed if anyone could, it would be Beatrice. She watched as Lydia led Nathaniel out to the terrace. If Elinor did not know better, she would think the lady a skilled courtesan.

"I believe the next dance is mine, little Elly," Lord Vernon whispered seductively in her ear. He was standing entirely too close. She tried to hide her reluctance and ignore the pain that her feet were already protesting. She smiled and offered her arm. He spent the entire quadrille unabashedly flirting with her. Believing he must be deep in his cups, she tried to hide her embarrassment and hoped no one noticed his shameless behaviour.

She and Easton came together during one of the exchanges of the dance, but he looked stern, almost angry. As did Beatrice, who was partnering him. No surprise, there. Perhaps they were ashamed for their friend's behaviour. Would that this dance would be over soon, and she could be done with him! She hoped Easton might ask her for the next dance, but he did nothing more than speak about civil trivialities when they met during exchanges in the dance. He was the one person she had hoped incapable of such tedium. Lord Vernon eventually deposited her back at her grandmother's side, and Easton headed in the other direction.

The remainder of the evening kept Elinor dancing with partner after partner—except the one she truly wanted. When would he claim his dance? Elinor thought that surely he could have danced once with her without any impropriety or remark if that was his concern. He had certainly danced with every other single miss there tonight! When it was finally her turn to sit out with Lord Wyndham, she congratulated herself on choosing the supper dance, until she saw how tired he looked. Then she no longer felt so proud.

"Forgive me, my lord. You must be out much later than you are accustomed to. I had selfishly procured your company for supper with little regard to the lateness of the hour or the fatigue you must be feeling."

Easton, suddenly by his father's side, looked at her with gratitude, seemingly recovered from his ill-humour. Perhaps it was merely from dancing with Beatrice, she thought cruelly, and then chastised herself for being as bad as Beatrice in her thoughts.

"Nonsense. I quite feel like a young chap again. I have the prettiest lady for supper, which is a welcome change from all the old bores my age. What news have you got for me?" he asked eagerly, hoping to get news on the war from her father, as had become their custom during their visits together.

They chatted happily throughout the meal, unaware of their surroundings. Elinor felt a peace she had not felt in years, having faced her biggest fear and survived. She actually felt like she would make it through. She was unaware of the stares and snickers that were being circulated, timed perfectly to give them credence while seated with Lord Easton and his father.

CHAPTER 13

The Dowager Duchess of Loring had a plan. She had anticipated this happening, though she assumed Lady Dunweather to be the culprit. That woman had some nerve, and she would be dealt with later. She dispensed Andrew to speak with Easton so he could be prepared. Then she asked Elinor to accompany her to the retiring room. However, she led her, not into the rooms made available to the guests, but to where they could speak in private.

"Are you all right, Grandmama?" Elinor looked at her grandmother's face and saw that she was not. "Can I fetch you something? Sit down. I will ring for Hanson."

"No, dear. I am fine, but the news of your voyage with Easton is out. The rumours are not kind. In fact, they are more vicious than I would have expected from Gertie."

"Do not worry about me, Grandmama. They cannot hurt me. We are leaving for the country anyway. I can return to America when Papa arrives, and everyone will forget about me."

"Unfortunately, dear, it is not that simple. It will affect those of the family whom you leave behind. It will reflect poorly on your father, and your brother's chance of a good match will be lessened. The high sticklers will cut Sarah."

"That is so unfair! None of them had anything to do with this!" She clinched her fists indignantly at her sides.

"'Tis the way of things here," she said matter-of-factly.

"Is there anything to be done?" Elinor pleaded.

The Dowager thought she would never ask. "Marry Easton."

"What?" Elinor's heart stopped.

"You heard me, gel."

"I refuse to force him into a loveless marriage for this…this ridiculous reason! And, Grandmama, he does not know."

"It will not matter with the right man." The Dowager took her objections as a good sign. Elinor had not said she did not want to marry him.

"Somehow, I think it would matter with him. That he would want, no, *need*, a wife who would be willing…" She was not able to speak the word.

"I understand your meaning. But what I meant was that with the right man you can overcome your fears."

"And you think he is the right man." Elinor stated with a sigh. She could not expect her grandmother to understand.

"You seem to be handling Nathaniel's return well."

"I was not given much choice." She paused and stared thoughtfully at a spot on the wall. "He is much changed—I think."

"Your uncle has been keeping informed on him while he was away. He would not have asked Nathaniel to return, were he not reformed."

"He apologized. But that does not mean that I can forget."

The Dowager nodded and came over to Elinor and hugged her, knowing that was what she needed more than words. After a few minutes of letting Elinor compose herself, she readdressed the topic that could no longer be avoided. "I hope Nathaniel has changed, and that you can begin to heal. But I hope you will consider Easton if he asks. He seems to care for you." Elinor looked startled. Noticing her surprise, the Dowager added softly, "Do not presume to know how another will feel without hearing it from them."

"I cannot tell him, even if he does ask me to marry him out of honour." She tried to force back the tears she felt threatening.

"Consider it, my love."

～

Easton knew when the Dowager Duchess took Elinor away, and before Andrew sought him out, what had happened. He had no problems whatsoever with becoming betrothed to Elinor; in fact, he wanted it very badly. But he suspected she would not be so delighted. There were undercurrents to Elinor he could not make out, and he suspected it had to do with Nathaniel, Lord Fairmont.

He had watched her all evening, the dazzling transformation from adorable tomboy to elegant debutante complete. She was comporting herself gracefully; the pinks and tulips were fawning over her making great spectacles of themselves. That amused and disgusted him at the same time. He had also noticed the awkward interactions between Nathaniel and Elinor. They had once been as brother and sister, long ago when he had visited the family estate during school holidays, but Nathaniel had changed into a rakehell at Oxford, despite his cousins' efforts, and was capable of anything. Easton saw Andrew approaching as they were rising from supper.

"Easton, may I speak with you?" The people around them quieted, hoping for something delicious to erupt. They were to be disappointed.

"Yes, of course. May I arrange for my father to be sent home?"

"I will call for your carriage."

The men saw Lord Wyndham on his way and then headed to the Duke's study for some privacy. Easton spoke as soon as the door was shut behind Andrew. "Whisky?" Easton nodded.

"This is about Elinor, is it not? I am happy to offer for her."

Andrew was a bit stunned. He nodded. He knew Easton would do the right thing, but he did not realize the self-proclaimed, eternal bachelor would be quite this willing. "It appears Dunweather did not keep her trap shut after all. At supper, the rumours were circulating faster than wildfire."

"Where is Elinor? I will go and speak to her." Easton rose to go, but Andrew stopped him.

"I do not think it is going to be that simple, Adam." Easton stopped and turned to face Andrew.

"You mean she will not consider me because she wants to go back to the plantation?"

"There is more to it than that." Andrew hesitated. He could not give away Elly's secrets, but they were in a difficult situation.

Easton spoke before Andrew could decide what to say. "Fairmont?"

Andrew's eyes flew up in surprise. "How did you know?"

"I cannot say that I know precisely, but it is obvious to me that something occurred between them, watching her reaction around him. I spent a fair bit of time with her, if you remember, and she does not act like other females do around men."

"It is not my secret to tell, Easton, but she will undoubtedly put up quite a fight."

"She is worth the fight."

"Well, well, Easton. Has Elly finally managed to dent the armour around your impenetrable heart?"

Easton stared at the amber liquid in his glass as though fascinated. "It appears that way."

Easton pondered his strategy as they went to find Elinor. If he asked her outright she would refuse, as Andrew had confirmed his suspicions. But what did he mean about her putting up a fight? Because she did not want him and wanted Nathaniel instead? He guessed he would find out sooner or later. She was socially ruined because she had saved his life, and he would do what he could to help her now.

They found the Dowager Duchess and Elinor emerging from a private parlour, and Easton strolled over and offered Elinor his arm. "I believe this is my dance."

"I do not believe I am up to dancing right now, Easton. There are rumours…" He cut her off before she could finish.

"I know." Their eyes met, and he smiled. She wanted nothing more than to be swept away in his arms, far from the ridiculous predicament. "Trust me."

Trust was not something she gave easily, but she did trust him, she realized. He dragged her off to the ballroom before she could mount a protest and led her on to the floor as the orchestra began to thrum the opening tunes of a waltz.

"I have not been given permission!" Elinor protested, trying to draw back. He bent his head down and whispered, "It does not matter now." She looked at him questioningly.

"Go along with me, and we can talk later." He was still so calm.

He saw the Dowager and Andrew watching after them, trying not to grin.

"I never thought I'd see the day Adam was caught—and by Elly, no less!" Andrew laughed.

"I might have to thank Gertie after all." The Dowager beamed.

Easton danced beautifully, leading her through the waltz as if she were a fairy princess. She became lost in the moment despite herself and almost forgot about being homesick, about Nathaniel, about the rumours. For the first time in years, she did not panic being in the arms of a man. But, all good things must come to an end, and the waltz drew to a close too soon. Instead of leading her from the floor, Easton stood in the middle of the floor still holding her hand.

Oh, no. No! No! No! She knew what he was going to do. "Please do not do this. Please." She pleaded with him. "May we speak first?"

"Nothing you can say will change what has to be done right now. Remember, I said go along and we will talk later. Trust me." There was that word again. "Now smile and act as if you like me." The crowd had been watching them expectantly while they danced. It now parted in silence leaving them in the middle of the ballroom. Alone.

"Ladies and gentleman, it my pleasure to announce that Miss Abbott has consented to be my wife." He looked down at her lovingly and most charmingly. He mouthed, "I am sorry," but his eyes told another story. He then raised her hand and kissed it, sending heat straight to her core.

~

The remainder of the ball was spent in congratulations and toasts. Strange how people go from spouting vicious rumours to smiling congratulations in the blink of an eye, Elinor mused.

Weary after finally ushering the last of the guests out, Easton sat Elinor down on a settee in the parlour. "Would you like to talk now or wait until the morrow?" Most of the family eyed them together, but decided to let them talk, since they were betrothed, and went on to their rooms. The Duke stopped on his way up and shook hands with Easton. "I will speak with you in the morning, my son." Easton nodded, and the Duke took his leave.

"It will not change anything." Elinor looked down at her hands, afraid of looking up and betraying herself.

"What will not change?" He did not understand.

"Easton, I cannot marry. Ever." Elinor subconsciously took her slippers off and began to rub her aching feet, trying to do anything but look him in the eye. "Though I am grateful for your willingness to sacrifice yourself."

"Nonsense." He was not willing to push her yet, or tell her that he knew something had happened with Nathaniel. He wanted her to trust him and tell him when she was ready. "I have a plan." He bent down and rubbed her aching feet. It was all she could do not to flinch at the intimacy, but she took a deep breath and tried to relax. He noticed her reaction, and thought she was worried about impropriety. "We are betrothed now, I believe I may touch your feet. Why do ladies wear those painful contraptions they call slippers?"

She shook her head as if he would never understand and then looked up at him with those big green eyes. It took all his strength not to kiss her. He knew that would be the worst thing he could do at the moment.

"Why did you do it?" asked Elinor.

159

He took a deep breath and then let it out while shifting his weight off his bad leg. "It will quieten the rumours. You might have noticed how fickle the crowd was." She started to protest, but he hushed her with a finger to her lips. It almost unnerved him to touch her so. "You can cry off if you want to and go back to your home when it is time. But the betrothal will allow you more freedom while you are here, and we can spend time together again without any talk. Like old friends." He had no intention of letting her leave, but she did not have to know that now.

"What will that do to you?" She was considering, at least.

"A man can stand to be jilted, especially one who will someday be an earl. It is unfair, but it is the way of the world." Elly nodded, knowing 'the way of the world' all too well. "It is the very least I can do." And that was the crux of the matter for her—she thought Easton felt indebted to her, and she did not want him acting from a sense of debt.

"You do not owe me anything, Easton." He looked at her as if she could not understand.

"I owe you my life, Elinor. Can you not see that?" He pleaded, taking her hands in his.

"I do not want you to feel that way. I do not want you doing anything out of sense of honour to me or indebtedness. Neither of us did anything wrong!"

"Please understand that I am doing this because I want to. No one is forcing me." Her heart skipped a beat. She dared not hope.

He held her hands gently and looked so genuine that she actually believed him. But why would he do this? She looked long and hard at the wooden planks in the floor before answering. "All right. I suppose I owe that to my family. Thank you."

～

Elinor was so exhausted, she struggled to make it to her room without stumbling. Everyone else had retired, and she tried not to think about the fact that she was alone in a large house in the dark with only a single taper to light her way. Not to mention being in the house that haunted her every nightmare. She shook her thoughts off, knowing that the physical exhaustion, added on top of the emotional upheaval she felt was making her rationale muddy. She finally reached her door and jumped when she heard a noise. She opened her door, went in and shut the door as fast as she could. She lowered the latch, then pushed a chair in front of the door for good measure. She had been here for weeks, but simply knowing he was in the house made her lose all sense of stability.

Wishing she had not sent Josie to bed early, she struggled out of her ball gown, loosened her corset with a deep breath, then climbed into the bed and crawled under the counterpane as fast as possible. She buried herself up to her chin and left the curtains open so she could see the fire. She was exhausted, but could not sleep. Seeing Nathaniel again reopened all her old wounds; while not as bad, they still hurt. She finally drifted off into a restless sleep.

She heard a door open behind her, startling her peace and causing the hair on the back of her neck to stand up. She had hurried out into the garden, hoping to go unnoticed, desperate for some fresh air. She attempted to duck behind a tree and catch a glimpse of who was outside. She heard footsteps, but before she could turn around, the smell of heavy whisky overtook her and she felt arms encompass her.

"Elly, dearest. Come with me," the voice said, slurring the words. He was trying to kiss her neck.

"Dearest? Please stop! You are drunk!" She said turning around to face Nathaniel while trying to push him off her. He continued to hold her tightly and try to kiss her, despite her protests. She began to fight furiously. Her gown was torn down to her petticoats as they struggled.

"Why are you doing this? What is wrong with you?"

Her cousin grabbed both of her wrists and looked at her, laughing maniacally. Then noticing her torn gown, the look changed to pure lust, his eyes demonic.

161

"Stop, you are hurting me!" she cried out as tears streamed down her face, not understanding what he wanted or why someone she loved would hurt her.

Ignoring her, he immediately began pulling at her petticoats, trying to force himself upon her. He pushed her, her back slamming into a tree, and she felt the thorns of a rose bush tear into her flesh as she fell to the ground. She hurried up and scrambled back into the house through the nearest door. She heard him stumbling behind her, breathing heavily. Despite his inebriation, he was gaining on her. Hot tears streamed down her face, and her lungs ached for air as she desperately clambered up the stairs. Just when she caught sight of her door, she felt a grab at her ankle as she tried to grasp the handle. She tripped and landed face down in the hallway. Where on earth are the servants? Why was no one here to help?

Nathaniel flipped her over, and she kicked him in the groin as she had been taught to her when they were younger. This only made him angry, more determined. She attempted to push him away, but her efforts were futile, his weight being nearly twice hers. He was so strong, but she refused to go down without a fight. He shoved her into her room, and she heard the key turn in the lock behind her.

She stood, paralysed with fear, staring at this delirious person, her chest heaving up and down with sharp pains from fear and exertion. She screamed, but knew it was pointless since she could hear the noise from the laughter and music downstairs. Anyone? Please, God. Someone. As he leapt for her, she kept screaming while trying to fight him off, but felt a hard, painful fist knock against her head.

She had passed out for a few moments, and woke dizzily to find her attacker with his breeches down, over her, parting her legs. When she realized what he intended, she began trying to push him off with her legs and arms. He pinned her arms down and put his face next to hers. He reeked of spirits, and his eyes were possessed. This could not be happening! She shivered and screamed again, hoping this was some awful nightmare. He tried to hush her with his mouth, but she bit his tongue when he tried to intrude.

"Nathaniel, stop!" she pleaded.

"Damn you, little whore. You want to play rough?" He sat on top of her, still holding her arms down, and thrust his tongue into her mouth, forcing it wide enough that she could not bite. She gagged and trembled beneath him,

caught in some indefinite circle of hell. Would it never end? He pulled out of her mouth and when she thought she would finally be free, he thrust into her and she passed out again from the ripping pain.

"Elly! Elly! Wake up!" Elinor heard a banging on her door until she woke up enough to realize she was in her own room and was having a nightmare. She hurried out of her bed, she pushed the chair from the door and lifted the latch. She peeked her head out to see her grandmother standing in the hallway, her face ashen and her eyes wide with fear.

"I am sorry, Gran. I was having a nightmare."

"Are you all right?"

Elinor nodded. "I have them from time to time. I am sorry I disturbed you."

"It was seeing Nathaniel again."

"Perhaps. Please try to go back to sleep. I should not have another nightmare," Elinor said as she kissed her grandmother good night on the cheek. Only it was not just a nightmare, it was now her reality.

Easton left the Loring residence having had the most awkward experience of his life. He had met with Elinor's uncle, the Duke, but nothing had gone as he had planned. Sir Charles had given his permission for him to court Elinor, even though he had not asked, yet this morning her uncle implied he would prefer Elinor marry his son, Nathaniel! The Duke would make sure Elinor was not forced into an unwanted marriage! Did Sir Charles know this? Would he feel the same way? If there had been something prearranged, his godfather would not have hinted that he wanted him for a son-in-law. He shook his head. He had been trying to protect her for goodness sake! This was too strange.

Elinor had been tight-lipped about all of it, but she had been rather adamant about the fact that she did not want to marry here. Could she be harbouring some hidden affection for Nathaniel? It was not as common for cousins to marry as it used to be, but it was still done. His heart sank as he thought about his father's delight when he told him their voyage together had been found out and he had announced their betrothal. The Earl seemed as smitten with Elinor as he himself was. What a horrible fix they were in!

Easton found that he was rather pleased to be betrothed to Elinor. Of course, the thought of marriage itself was a bit daunting, but spending his life with her was not. The waltz they shared had been magical; she felt right in his arms. He could not see himself with anyone else. He would simply have to show her that she needed him as much as he needed her.

~

The next day did not bring the happiness that Elinor should have felt at finally being able to leave for the country. She had been given a few minutes to speak with Easton once he had met with the Duke that morning. He had merely informed her that he and his father were also removing to the country for the holidays and he would call on her there.

Then her uncle had insisted on a family meeting after speaking with Lord Easton. Elinor waited for the rest of the family to join her in the drawing room when Easton left. She stood by the window, pondering how they were to manage to fool their families into believing in their false betrothal. Elinor turned quickly when she heard the door click, and Nathaniel stood in front of the door. Her heart pounding, she searched the room for a means of escape. Panic threatened to overwhelm her. Her worst fears had come to life. Sweat broke out on her forehead; her breathing became laboured. Somehow through the haze of fear, she heard him speak

"Elinor? Are you all right?" He looked at her with genuine concern as he crossed the room toward her.

The sound of his voice and his rapid approach snapped her out of her trance, and she stepped back to halt his progress. "I am quite well."

He looked at her sceptically then decided to proceed while he had the opportunity. "Is it all right if I speak? The others should be joining us at any moment. I promise I offer you no threat."

She nodded hesitantly. What else could she do? She sat in a nearby chair, but could not meet his gaze. She was struggling to control her fear.

He cleared his throat and began. "May I offer my sincerest apologies?" he spoke quietly, but she heard.

"Pardon?" This scenario was not one she had ever imagined.

"I do not wish to embarrass you or make a scene, but I am afraid I will have no other opportunity to beg forgiveness."

"I am afraid I do not know what to say." In her heart, she wanted to forgive him, but she did not know if it was possible. She had released her anger a long time ago, for her own sake, but she did not know if the fear would ever go away. And he was the cause of that. Fighting tears, she shook her head.

"I have no excuses to offer you. What I did..." He took a deep breath, obviously struggling to find words to make her understand. "This was much easier when I rehearsed it in my mind every day for the last six years. Now, I find myself quite at a loss for the proper words."

"I do not know if I can, Nathaniel."

"I would like to make it right by..."

Andrew burst into the room. He looked from one to the other as if assessing the situation. Colour highlighted his cheekbones and he glared at Nathaniel. Striding past Elinor, he slammed his fist into Nathaniel's jaw. Nathaniel stumbled backward, but did not look surprised.

"Andrew, stop! It is all right." Snatching at his arm, she pulled him over to sit beside her on a settee. He continued to scowl at Nathaniel and, if the fact he was pounding his fist into his hand were any indication, was struggling with a strong desire to further pummel her cousin.

Beatrice, Aunt Wilhelmina and her grandmother entered, oblivious to the undercurrents in the room. All took seats and stared awkwardly at each other, as if wondering what they were doing there sitting in a circle. The Duke strolled in purposefully, and stood by the fireplace without speaking. He seemed to revel in the discomfort his silence was imposing. No one dared speak when he had that look on his face. He glanced around at everyone, noticing the bruise beginning to darken on Nathaniel's jaw.

After her uncle seemed satisfied he had their attention, he shut the door, then cleared his throat and began.

"It has come to my attention that Elinor has suffered grievously at the hands of both my children."

"Uncle, no. Please do not do this." Elinor's face burned red with mortification. How could he do this to her? She plucked nervously at one of the buttons on the gold velvet cushion near her lap.

"Elinor, I am sorry to speak of such things openly, but this is your family. I insist on correcting these wrongs." He turned toward Beatrice whose face was red with furore and embarrassment. "Firstly, Beatrice, have you anything to say to Elinor?" Elinor wanted to die. She could not look up.

"I have nothing to say," she said defiantly, arms crossed, chin up.

"Very well. Your pin money shall be cut off for one year, and you will remain in the country for the next Season in order to think about what you have done. You will have to prove to me you are reformed before I allow you out in society again."

"You cannot do that to me!" She leapt from her seat and began to pace furiously before throwing an accusing finger out at Elinor. "She was supposed to be ruined! Now she is going to be a countess? It should have been me! But no, she sails in from living with barbarians, has the manners of an ox, and the men throw themselves at her!" She turned to Elinor. "You will pay for this!" She stomped from the room, slamming the door.

The Duchess stood to go after her, but the Duke said, "Sit down, Wilhelmina. You will hear the rest. You bear as much responsibility for our children's actions as I." She sat down and closed her mouth. He turned to address his niece.

"Elinor, Beatrice spread the rumours about you last night. She was not very circumspect about it, however. I overheard her boasting of it to one of her friends." He crossed his arms over his chest and stared at the door his daughter had retreated through.

Elinor could not speak. She knew Beatrice had taken her in dislike, but had not imagined her capable of this. How had she found out? The Duke continued, "And I wanted you to know that you will not be forced to marry Easton unless that is your wish. I will do whatever is necessary to correct the wrongs against you." He glanced at Nathaniel and indicated with a nod of his head for him to speak. Everyone in the room remained remarkably silent.

"What is going on, here? Robert?" The Duchess whined, but the Duke held his hand up to quiet her.

Nathaniel went over to Elinor and knelt down before her in a submissive position, careful not to touch her. "Cousin, I have already begged your forgiveness, but I would also like to offer you my hand as a small peace offering for having stolen your virtue. Perhaps in time I will be able to make it up to you. "

Wilhelmina swooned. The Dowager was stunned. Andrew leapt swiftly from his seat and punched Nathaniel again.

"I should call you out!" he shouted over Nathaniel's prone form.

Elinor fled the room.

CHAPTER 14

SUSSEX

To her grandmother's credit, they were loaded in the carriage and off to the country estate in record time. Andrew chose to ride, saying he needed time to cool his temper. Why could she not have the luxury? Elinor's head was spinning. She had no idea how this horrible chain of events had come to pass as though from the pages of some horrid Gothic novel. She had never asked, even invited, any of this, had she? Why did these things not happen to the Beatrices of the world who revelled in drama? Not that she would wish rape on her worst enemy, but the rest would be no less than Beatrice deserved. If Elinor were not concerned for the repercussions on her family, she would be on the next boat back to America; English society be damned. Her grandmother must have been reading her thoughts.

"This will blow over, my dear. I know it feels like nothing in the world will ever be right, but it will. Country air and good sleep will help go a long way to help. You will stay with me at the Dower House and only see them if you wish to."

If only it were that simple. Her secret was out. Her papa would know, Easton would know, and no one would look at her in the same way again. It was like a raw wound with salt being rubbed into it.

Everything she had worked hard to repress would now be forced into the open, for others to accuse and pass judgement. With the rape out and then the accusation of being compromised by Lord Easton, she knew she would be thought terribly fast, that surely she brought it all on herself. Society considered anyone without a spotless reputation ruined, and now she had two marks against her. People would cross the street to cut her, if not her family, pointing her out as the type of female to avoid as a corrupting influence.

"After you left, your uncle Robert threatened everyone to keep silent on what happened with Nathaniel."

"He should not have mentioned it in front of everyone. He made it sound like we merely made a mistake and had relations because we wanted to! As if I agreed, and Nathaniel is doing the honourable thing! How could he? I still do not understand his motives. Aunt and Beatrice will only seek to use it for their own gain." Elinor could barely get the words out because of the hurt she felt about her uncle's tactics.

"Robert will make sure it does not go beyond the family. Once they are able to be reasoned with, they will realize how much it would hurt them to make that public. As malicious as they can be, I do not believe they would do anything to hurt themselves."

Elinor snorted. "One can hope. I cannot see how it will be kept from Papa or Lord Easton, though I would give my life were it otherwise." Elinor knew how this would devastate her papa and how personally he would feel his failure of her. She would do anything to spare him that.

"Charles is stronger than you give him credit for. I imagine he will be more hurt that you did not feel safe in telling him."

Elinor looked up, shocked at her grandmother's pronouncement, then quickly averted her eyes. How could she think such a thing? Elinor simply nodded and watched the country pass by through the window, as she tried to reconcile herself to what lay ahead.

"He did not mean to hurt you, you know. He thought it would help to reprimand them in front of you, to try to right the offences against

169

you." Elinor could not bring herself to reply. It was kind of everyone to think of what was best for her.

"Couldn't he have asked?" The answer to which was obvious and received no reply.

Thankfully, the country estate was roughly six hours from London, so they could barely make it by dark with good weather. Elinor felt a bit of the stress of being in the city lift off her shoulders. In the country, she would not be confined to a house with every person who seemed to despise her, and she could take walks and rides without the strict chaperonage required in town. She had mixed emotions about returning to her uncle's estate. She had spent most of her pleasant childhood there, before her mother became ill. She watched the grassy hills covered with grazing sheep alternate with lush woodland as they made their way further from the city.

They stopped to change horses in Crawley, then pressed onward, sampling the food and wine in the hamper Cook had packed for their journey. Elinor regaled her grandmother with stories of her life in America, and they napped intermittently to pass the time. It was dark by the time they pulled through the gates to the Dower House, and they both took to their beds shortly after their arrival.

The next morning, Elinor rose early and rushed from the house. She did not ride, seeking the privacy that walking on foot would afford. She sought out many of the places where she had found comfort as a child, but she soon realized, everywhere she went, most of those safe places and memories had included Nathaniel. She shook her head in disbelief. Surely she could find somewhere for refuge during her stay here.

She found herself wandering into an area she was not very familiar with. She had not been allowed in this direction as a child, since there were steep cliffs plunging down into the Channel water below. The scene fit her melancholic mood perfectly. She knew nothing positive would come from writhing in self-pity, but for now it was the best solution she had to accommodate her feelings.

She climbed the path from the trees through the meadow until her breathing was heavy with exertion. She found a large boulder at the edge of the cliffs overlooking the sea and settled herself where she could watch the sun rise above the horizon across the Channel. She looked around in wonder, a calm easing through her. She inhaled a deep breath of moist, salty air and watched the waves spray the cliffs until a mind-numbing bliss overtook her.

She was so engrossed that she did not hear footsteps approaching. Easton eased himself down beside her. "I see you have found my special place. May I join you?"

She jumped slightly at the intrusion. "I am sorry. I can leave."

He gently put his hand on her arm to stop her ascent. "Please stay."

She relaxed back against the rock. "It is beautiful. I was never allowed to come this way as a child."

"This was what kept me sane all of those years away. I would close my eyes and take myself here. The smell of pine and sea, the crisp morning air that fades as the warmth of sun rising overtakes the horizon, the waves spraying the rocks, the birds singing their good mornings…though one would be hard-pressed to describe seagulls as singing."

Elinor had closed her eyes, and this made her smile. She opened her eyes and surveyed the landscape as if to compare it with his description. She leaned back to watch the clouds dance across the sky.

The air was damp, and the ground was quite cold, and she shivered despite herself.

Easton began to remove his coat, but she held up her hand in protest. "I am perfectly well, thank you." She sat back up. "You are fortunate to have these spectacular views. I think I was drawn to the sea by some subconscious force. I did not realize this was part of your lands."

"Our lands are not as large as your uncle's, but I prefer the views from ours. The family bed chambers all have spectacular views. The waters lull me to sleep at night." Easton sighed and hesitated, not wanting to disturb the peaceful moment, but finally spoke because he could no longer stand the suspense. "Have you reached a verdict?" She looked at him questioningly. He responded quietly, "Are you to be my betrothed, or Nathaniel's?"

"Ah, yes. You spoke with Uncle yesterday." Easton nodded. She stayed silent a moment, afraid to know what he had been told. He would find out if he did not know already. He did not look at her any differently, so she suspected he had not been told why. "What did he say to you?" she asked quietly.

"That you would not be forced into marriage with me, and that you may have reason to want Nathaniel instead." He gazed out over the Channel, afraid to see rejection in her eyes.

"Is that all?" she asked.

He nodded. "Is there anything you would like to tell me, Elinor?" He looked back into her eyes, willing her to trust him. But she would not hold his gaze. Instead she looked away and shook her head. She said, "I am not betrothed to Nathaniel."

It was clear that was all he was going to get from her on the subject, but she had not said she wanted Nathaniel, and that she did not want him. That was a small glimmer of hope for now. "Well, no good deed goes unpunished," he said trying to lighten the mood.

"Please do not feel I am being punished because of you," she said, as the wind whipped some strands of hair into her face.

"Well, you certainly do not seem thrilled with the turn of events."

She chuckled. "Now that is an understatement." He brushed the hair from her face, and she gazed up at him, captivated by his enchanting smile. He did not take his hand from her face, and she did not flinch. She felt her pulse quicken, but she was not afraid. She realized he was the first man to break beyond her self-imposed wall. She paused, considered telling him what he would inevitably find out, but decided to delay the conversation. She was not ready to see this disappointment in his face, to give up this new-found friendship. "Please do not feel it has anything to do with you," she pleaded.

"Why do I feel I was just told I have a lovely personality?" he said good-naturedly, although he pulled his hand away. She felt a twinge of disappointment at the loss of contact.

She laughed, but was still shivering from the cold December morning. He stood and held out his hand to help her up. She looked at his hand, and then accepted his assistance, her hand warming where his grasped hers. "I do not want to go back yet."

Understanding her need for this place of reprieve, he said, "You can come here any time you like, but for now you should return to the house before you freeze." She nodded, knowing he was right, but not wanting to let go of the peace she had found. She accepted his escort most of the way to the Dower House, walking in companionable silence, with only the sounds of nature and their breathing.

As they reached the gate to the house, he stopped short. "Will you come for tea today? Father would love to see you again." He paused, then turned to face her. "And I would like you to be the one to tell him about the betrothal." He hesitated. "Or the non-betrothal, whatever you have decided. I told him about the circumstances at the ball, but not of our agreement for you to jilt me."

She tried not to wince at how the arrangement sounded and looked up at him and smiled. "Coward." She turned to walk the remainder of the path to the house, and he laughed and called after her, "Good luck telling Father no."

He turned on his heel and returned to Wyndham Court with a smile planted on his face.

Elinor made her way into the house. It was late morning by now, and her grandmother would be down soon. However, she bumped into Andrew as she went into the breakfast room.

"Where have you been? I have looked everywhere for you!" He had a look of exasperation, to go with his mussed hair and wrinkled neck-cloth as if he had been pulling on it.

"Only out for a walk. Why? Is something the matter? Is it Papa?" She made her way over to the fire to warm her hands.

"Papa is fine, last I heard. It is you I was worried about! The last time I saw you, you were hardly in a normal state." He paced the floor and threw his hands up in exasperation.

"You were the one who got to let your temper out on a ride. I was stuck inside a carriage for hours until I thought I was going to explode. Forgive me for taking a walk to clear my head." Dumb-founded, she looked at him.

He scooped her up into a hug. "Do not ever scare me like that again. I was afraid you had..."

"Of what were you afraid? That I had jumped over the cliff?" The thought had occurred to her.

"I have not had a chance to speak with you to know your mind, and yes, I was worried you might find that the better option." He gave her a relieved look. "We need to talk about this, El." He stood back and went back to pacing with his fists clenched at his sides. "It is taking every ounce of strength I have to not call him out or beat him to a pulp."

Elinor understood the sentiment completely. Andrew was still furious. She had felt that way for years, until she had not been able to take being angry any more. She rubbed her hands together closer to the fire. "I do not know if I can talk. I am still hoping I am going to wake up from this awful nightmare; instead, it just keeps getting worse." She took the poker and jostled the logs around, throwing sparks into the air.

"I think we should tell Papa. He will know what to do. I do not want you to sacrifice yourself because of what you think will happen to us. You have to talk about this. I know from personal experience it is not good for you to keep evil locked inside. I have watched soldiers try for years now, and it eats them alive."

"I have had a lot of practice. I want to relieve myself of the burden, but it is not that simple. It is unbearable what people will think of me. Then the thought of marrying, of being expected to...to..." Her voice trailed off, and he hugged her close, shushing her and rubbing her back gently. He let her go and began to pace the room furiously.

"No one who matters will think less of you. You were only a child, for God's sake! We do not expect you to be perfect, either." He sighed and tried to hold back his emotion. "You have suffered enough. If you want to go back to the plantation, I will take you."

Her head jerked up. "You would do that for me?" She dropped the poker and went over to hug him. She needed the reassurance. "Oh, Andrew, how did all of this happen? What have I done wrong that these awful things never stop?"

"I wish I knew. I still cannot fathom it all." He pushed her away and held her at arm's length. "If you understand nothing else, El, understand that you have done nothing wrong." He shook his head. "Nathaniel went through a…" He paused searching for the right word. "…A period. I will never forgive myself for what he did to you. We should have stopped him, but we were young, stupid, arrogant fools ourselves. He got heavily into drink and opium, though, and lost his mind. Uncle sent him away not long after you left, to force him to reform himself."

She drew a long breath in contemplation. "I am glad he is better, and I hope to forgive him one day. Unfortunately, I cannot forget. But, oh, how I want to!"

"Elly, you are too good. I do not know how you were able to remain sane."

"Neither do I." She shook her head. "I am not sure I am."

That afternoon, Elinor wandered over to the Wyndham estate with Josie. She was already more at ease, being allowed more freedoms than in the city. She was surprised how much closer the Dower House was to the Wyndham manor house than the Duke's as she followed a neatly-pebbled path, which led from one estate to the other. Elinor had baulked when her grandmother suggested she take the carriage. Luckily, her grandmother did not baulk when she only took a maid as escort. The luxuries of being betrothed, she had stated. *Ha!* Elinor thought—*a mock betrothal.* How was she supposed to explain that to the kind Earl she was so fond of? She had not even brought herself to tell her grandmother or Andrew yet.

She kicked some of the little pebbles from beneath her boots as if they could summon the answers to this conundrum in which she found herself entwined. She rounded a hedge, then stopped to take in her surroundings as the house came in to view. She beheld a quadrangular stone edifice, rising out of an expanse of lawn. There were Doric columns and corner towers, slightly elevated from the remainder of the structure, and tall, arching windows covered the front façade. She continued on the path toward the house, past a small lake, and then made her way to the front where she had views of the sea. It was breathtaking, serene.

She approached the large, wooden doors, which dwarfed her, yet seemed small compared to the rest of the house. The door was opened by the butler before she raised her hand to knock. "Welcome, Miss Abbott. We were expecting you." She smiled, then handed him her bonnet and pelisse.

"Thank you—" she paused, waiting for his name.

He gave her a small bow. "Hendricks, miss. This way please."

Elinor followed the butler from the entrance hall with natural light flooding through the large windows. The butler showed Elinor into a cosy parlour, and she had barely had time to take stock of her surroundings before Easton came in with a concerned look on his face. She had not seen him look so forlorn since the day he was shot.

"What is it Easton?"

"Father." He saw the look of terror on her face and reassured her. "He is alive, but has had a bad spell. The doctor is not sure how severe yet, but he says it is only a matter of time before one takes him. I suppose the journey was too much for him, but he insisted."

"I am sorry. I know how close you are." Tears begin to glisten in her eyes despite her efforts to restrain them. "I am rather attached to him myself, already."

He smiled a little at that. "And he to you."

"I will come back another time if you will send word when it is convenient. Or if I can be of any assistance."

"Actually, he has asked to see you." Easton paused awkwardly and drove his hands into his pockets. "I wanted to ask a favour first. Would you mind carrying on the charade for my father? He is so enamoured with you and the idea that you will be his daughter...well, he is rather set on it. I am sorry to ask it of you, but I cannot bear to take away the one thing that gives him hope right now."

She looked out of the window, unsure how to answer. "What if he recovers? What will we tell him, then? I could not bear to hurt him."

"I am afraid there is no chance of that," he said quietly. How could she refuse? She nodded, and he held out his arm. "Shall we?"

He led her up a grand, central staircase that curved toward the family's private apartments in one direction and guest apartments in the other. They walked silently down a long mahogany-panelled gallery lined with portraits of Wyndham's past, male and female. The end of the hall led to the Earl's suite of rooms, and Easton led her quietly into a large sitting room while he went to see about his father. He walked back in and motioned for her to follow.

She was taken aback by how small and frail the Earl looked in his huge, four-poster bed. How quickly he had changed in the few days since her ball. He noticed her and immediately started struggling to sit up and greet her. She hurried over to the bed to stop him.

"My lord, do not exert yourself on my account. You did not have to receive me when you are feeling poorly."

He cleared his throat and struggled to try to speak. When he did, it was barely audible, and one side of his face was drooping. "The sight of you is better than any medicine they can offer."

Elinor smiled and blushed prettily, not sure how to respond. "Thank you, my lord." She sat in the chair Easton placed next to the bed, but it was so far down that she could not see his face, so she stood next to the bed. Lord Wyndham reached for her hand and held it, though he was trembling slightly from the exertion. She wrapped her other hand around his. He felt her hand and frowned.

"Adam!" He weakly summoned Easton to his side.

"I am here, Father."

"Have you not proposed properly? She wears no ring."

Easton had the grace to look embarrassed. "I have not had the chance to purchase a proper ring. I will remedy that soon." He threw Elinor an apologetic smile.

"I am in no hurry, my lord. Jewellery is merely a symbol."

"Nonsense. Adam, go and fetch your mother's ring from the vault. She wanted it for your bride. Nothing would make me happier than to see it grace Elinor's finger."

Easton nodded and went to retrieve the ring.

177

"I am glad the two of you were finally able to see how well suited you are. I knew it as soon as he walked in the door from America. He had a peace about him I have not seen since before he left for the Peninsula. Then he could not stop talking about you, and I was certain. If I were younger, I would be tempted to run off with you myself," Lord Wyndham said with the most impudent smile he could muster, though it was a struggle for every word, and she knew it was important for him to say them.

Easton entered the room and said jovially, "Why, Father, are you trying to steal my betrothed?"

"I would if I could. Now, my son, let me see you do this properly."

Easton and Elinor both turned and looked at the Earl in shock. She moaned inwardly. She could not do this.

"Please humour me. I missed all of the fun at the ball."

Elinor could not look up at him. Easton reluctantly went down on one knee before her and took her left hand in his. "Miss Abbott, would you do me the great honour of becoming my wife?"

She looked in his face and was startled by the sincerity in it. Her heart started to race, and she stood there staring at him. "Go on, Elinor, you cannot back out now." The Earl nudged her hand.

"Yes, yes of course. I would be delighted." She forced herself to smile.

Easton let out a sigh of relief and slid the ring on her finger. It was a beautiful, deep green emerald, rectangular in shape with two diamonds on either side. The colour was similar to the ones on the combs he had given her for her come-out ball. She gasped at the ring, which had once graced his beloved mother's hand, and somehow felt she was betraying her by wearing it.

"Now seal it with a kiss," the Earl said softly.

The devil, you say! Elinor thought, panicking. She wanted to turn and run from the room. She looked at Easton to save her, but his eyes twinkled, and he shrugged. She sighed and leaned forward resignedly for a peck. Easton, however, took full advantage and took her face in his hands and placed a gentle, if longer than necessary kiss on her lips. She pulled back and looked at him, eyes open wide, and he winked at her and grinned boyishly. He bent over and whispered, "You did give me permission. Of sorts."

"I—I think we should let the Earl rest now. I know I have had enough excitement for one day," she said trying to regain her composure.

The Earl grinned lopsidedly. "Promise you will come back tomorrow, and we can make plans for the wedding."

Easton rushed her from the room before she could faint.

He walked her back to the Dower House, Josie and Buffy trailing a discreet distance behind. Neither Elinor nor Easton was eager to discuss the scene they had just enacted. "Would you be interested in riding in the morning? I am going to visit some tenants, and I thought you might like to come along."

This brought a genuine smile to Elinor's face. "You said the magic word. What time shall I be ready?"

"Is nine too early?"

"It is perfect. Until then, Lord Easton." She turned and walked into the house. Easton smiled, and thought his plan was unfolding rather nicely.

CHAPTER 15

*E*linor donned her new riding habit of dark green wool and could not help glancing down at the betrothal ring Easton had placed on her finger the day before.

Josie smiled. "What are you fidgeting about, Miss Elly? You are going to ride, and with a handsome lord, I might add."

Elinor had to laugh at Josie's efforts. "It is rather early for such insolence."

"It is never too early! Now, have a seat and let me dress your hair so you will not be late. Then you can tell me why you are in such low spirits when you are to spend the morning with the handsome Major who dotes on you so."

Elinor shrugged. "I do not know what to do, Josie. I am not good at pretending, and I feel guilty."

"Do you enjoy spending time with him?"

Elinor thought for a minute, then glanced at the ring, twisting it around her finger. "I do, actually. I feel more comfortable with him than I ever thought possible."

"No need to feel guilty then. Enjoy yourself and then see how you feel. You talked to Lord Fairmont, and now you have to move forward."

That was a lovely thought. *Enjoy yourself.* Could she?

"He will not hurt you. I think you know that. You might even have fun." Josie giggled. Elinor blushed. Why the thought of having fun should make her blush she did not want to examine too closely. She leaned forward and slipped her kid half-boots on.

"Josie, I think that might actually be a good idea." Elinor stood and started pulling on her gloves. Taking one last look in the mirror, she thought her grandmother had made a good choice when selecting her riding habit. Perhaps she even looked a little fetching. She had never considered being fetching before.

"Course it is."

Elinor stood up to give her a hug. "I am not sure where you got to be so wise."

"From you, of course. You only have to learn to follow your own advice."

Elinor laughed. She made her way downstairs and found Lord Easton in the breakfast room, chatting with Andrew and charming the Dowager.

"Good morning, everyone. To what do we owe the honour of everyone's presence before noon?" Elinor smiled as she proffered this greeting and curtsied to them as Lord Easton bowed to her, the men both rising from the table when she entered the room. She went over to kiss her grandmother on the cheek.

"I am not at all sure, dearest. I will not make a habit of it. Now are you not glad I picked that riding habit for you? It is quite charming, if I do say so myself."

Elinor blushed at hearing her own recent thoughts spoken out loud. "Yes, Grandmama, it is quite lovely. In fact, it seems too lovely for riding."

"Nonsense. If you cannot ride in that, then you are not riding properly." She waved her fork dismissively.

Andrew and Easton both erupted into laughter. The Dowager shot an inquisitive look at them, and they both tried to control their shaking.

"I refuse to countenance that remark." Elinor glared at them, but could not be cross and smiled despite herself. "Besides, I thought I might be permitted a bit more leeway in the country."

Andrew, still trying to control his laughter, strolled to the sideboard. "Bacon, anyone?" *Always a successful diversion, bacon.* Easton held out his plate for another rasher.

Elinor chose to change the topic. "Where shall we ride today, sir?"

"I think you will be pleased. I wanted to visit the village, after we let the horses stretch their legs, of course."

"Of course." She needed no more encouragement. She was going to enjoy herself. *Today. Here. In England. With him.*

After breakfast they donned their hats and capes and gathered their riding crops. They made their way down toward the stables as a groom was leading their horses out. Easton, in his usual fashion, was bribing the horses with pieces of apples.

"Are you trying to make them feistier, Easton?" Elinor prodded.

He replied with a mischievous grin. "Cannot handle them spirited, Miss Abbott?" He would turn that against her.

"I was trying to be considerate of a wounded veteran." Two could play this game.

He sighed dramatically. "Yes. Perhaps you will be able to keep up with me now."

That was all the taunting she needed. She mounted her mare and urged her horse on without looking back. Yes, today would be about having fun. She giggled as she bounded away. Easton caught up with her within a matter of minutes, slowing beside her long enough to flash her an indulgent smile. Then he called over his shoulder, "Race you to the river."

They both took off at breakneck speed, Easton with military precision, and Elinor with reckless abandon. They stayed evenly matched until they came to the river at the same time. They were both out of breath and began laughing as they pulled up to let the horses rest. "Very chivalrous of you to give yourself a head start, Easton. Next time we will let you try riding side-saddle, as well."

He pulled a couple of apples from his saddle-bags and fed them to the horses. "I think the lady doth protest too much." Then he winked at her. Elinor crinkled her eyes in a very ladylike fashion.

"That was nice. Thank you, Easton. I needed that." She stopped and took time to repair her unruly hair and replace her bonnet. It had long since flown off and was barely hanging on by the ribbons.

"My pleasure. Could we please dispense with formalities? I think a betrothal warrants the use of first names."

"Please go first."

He gave her an exasperated look. "Very well, *Elinor*. I have some tenants I need to see about some repairs. Would you care to join me? I am sure the tenants would appreciate a female perspective on what their needs are, instead of an old soldier's." He looked at her, awaiting her response.

"I would be happy to help, *Adam*. Are you thinking of gifts for the festive season?"

"Yes, and anything else that might need attending to. My brother... well, Father was not so ill when I left. My parents both took such pride in the village and its people, but I am afraid Father has not been up to managing the estates lately."

"Does he not have a steward?"

"Yes, of course, but Father has always felt the need for the family to be involved."

"I am not surprised." She smiled. "How far to the village?"

"Only a couple of miles, following the river. Shall we?"

They remounted their horses and took a more sedate pace in order to enjoy their surroundings. They had mainly been riding on a path through a heavily wooded area, but had now come into a meadow of sorts that led down into the village. It was a picturesque scene before them: small, frost-covered houses with smoke billowing up from the chimneys and shops in rows surrounding a central lane. They dismounted at the Crown and Bull Inn, and a groom came out to stable the horses. Easton held out his arm for Elinor and began to lead her around the town.

If Elinor had ever doubted what kind of lords of the manor the Wyndhams were, she no longer wondered. She was rather awestruck as the villagers recognized Adam and came up to greet him. They were more than a little curious about her. It was not every day the Viscount came strolling through with a female on his arm. They all assumed that she and he were betrothed, and he did nothing to dissuade them. Well, they were betrothed, were they not?

He led her into each shop to greet the tenants, addressing each person by name and asking after their children. Elinor took care to mentally document their surroundings and their possible needs, though it was obvious this was a well-cared-for village.

They turned to make their way back toward the inn, having finished one side of the village street.

"Would you care to stop for tea? I find myself a bit thirsty after the ride. We can come back this way after, or I can visit later if you have grown weary."

"Tea would be most welcome, and no, I have not tired of this."

"I do appreciate the help, but the people are most curious about you. I must admit, I had not thought of how they would perceive your accompanying me." A hint of a blush crept onto his cheekbones. "If it makes you uncomfortable..."

Was he nervous? Easton? She reached out and touched his hand before she realized what she was doing. Too late. "No. I am not uncomfortable." At least she was not until she grabbed his hand! He placed his over hers and relaxed.

"Good. I want you to feel welcome here." They made their way into the inn, and Easton requested a table, there being no private parlours in the small establishment. Again, Easton was met with open arms and genuine camaraderie, which made her see a whole new side of him. How he must have been laughing at her when she was having on about lazy aristocrats!

Elinor realized she felt at home amongst these people, acknowledging it was not that different from America. The village people worked hard here as well as there. They looked to their lord of the manor for their livelihood in a similar manner that the Americans did their landowners. The main difference was legacy. In England land ownership was a birthright. In America, anyone had the opportunity to achieve the same, regardless of birth.

Elinor sipped her tea and reflected on the similarities and differences, while Easton chatted with his tenants.

"Elinor?" She looked up and saw Easton was looking at her expectantly. "Care to share your thoughts?"

"I beg your pardon, sir. I was wool-gathering."

"I was asking if you would mind looking at a wound of the blacksmith's. Judd here says he had a nasty cut that is not healing properly. Unfortunately, we have no doctor in the village. I will send for the nearest one, but I have no idea how long it might take."

"Of course, if he does not mind me looking, I would be happy to do so."

Easton favoured her with a brilliant smile, as did the innkeeper, though Judd looked more astonished than anything else. They finished their tea then headed for the blacksmith's cottage. They made their way through a quaint wooden fence and were greeted by two youngsters playing fetch with a frisky puppy. Upon noticing the strangers, the two youngsters stopped and stared open-mouthed at the pair. Elinor knelt down to the little girl and asked if her mama was home.

"I am Elinor Abbott, and this is Lord Easton. We have come to visit your mama and papa. Could you please tell them we are here?" The little girl nodded her head, bobbed a nervous curtsy and ran inside.

Easton had joined in playing fetch with the boy and continued to play until the little girl returned to usher them into the cottage.

"Well, Major Trowbridge! I never!" The woman appeared little older than she did, Elinor thought, but she already had at least two children and looked extremely tired. She wiped her wash-worn hands on a towel and removed her apron, then swept across the room and gave Easton a peck on the cheek.

"Maddie! How wonderful to see you after all of these years. What is this I hear about Sam?"

Elinor shut her mouth as she realized it was gaping open. Maddie turned to look at Elinor, and Easton realized his omission.

"Pardon my manners. Miss Elinor Abbott, this is Maddie Smith."

Maddie curtsied. "I am pleased to meet you Miss Abbott." She grinned up at Easton.

"I had hoped this to be merely a social call, but Judd said Sam is ailing. Miss Abbott is rather useful with some injuries, having helped nurse soldiers back in America—myself included. I thought she might be able to help if you are not opposed to it. I have sent for the doctor, but in the meantime perhaps she can help."

Maddie looked Elinor up and down, first with surprise, then with approval. "Aye. 'Twould be appreciated. He has not been able to work for two weeks and is only getting worse. 'Tis a hard time of year for no work." Easton nodded. Elinor made a mental note to send a basket of goods over to help ease Maddie's worries. "I will let Sam know."

Maddie came back out and led Elinor and Easton into the small bedroom, where a large man swallowed up the small bed he lay in. He was scarlet and burned with fever. Elinor's stomach sank as she smelled then spied the festering wound on the man's left arm. Easton looked at Elinor gravely and went over to the bed to greet the man.

"Sam, it is Adam. Remember your old playmate?" The man groaned but did not wake up. "Sam? My friend is going to take a look at your arm. Is that all right?" Sam made a noise that sounded like a grunt of assent. Elinor moved closer to take a look and was immediately met with the putrid smell of an infected wound. A nasty cut indeed.

"Easton, can you send to the Dower House for Josie and my supplies? Mrs. Smith, can you set some water on to boil and gather some towels or rags and spirits, if you have some? If there is any way to find ice, it would help to bring the fever down. If not, some cool water. And Easton—send for the surgeon now." The two set off to perform their given tasks, and Elinor began to pray, with a strong sense of déjà vu striving to overcome her, though this wound was much worse than Easton's had been.

While waiting for Josie and her supplies to arrive, Elinor began the arduous task of cleansing the wound, then finally removing the dead tissue bit by bit while fighting to contain her stomach. *Keep breathing through your mouth. Through your mouth.* Fortunately Maddie had elected to wait outside with Easton, for Elinor could not contain all of the gagging and groans that escaped her.

Josie arrived at last and got to work helping Elinor. "Oh, lawks, Miss Elly!" She immediately covered her nose to prevent breathing the noxious fumes. Elinor gave her an exasperated look. "You certainly find yourself in some fine pickles!"

"Yes, well. There's nothing to be done but do our best now that we are here. Pour some spirits over that, would you? I think I have about got all of the dead tissue removed." Elinor stood up to soothe her sore back that was weary from bending over the bed to work on the man's arm. The patient let out a loud groan as Josie cleansed the wound with brandy.

"What's next?" Josie looked doubtfully at the mess of flesh on the man's arm. "Pack it with a poultice?"

Elinor nodded. "Then wait and pray that the surgeon does not cut it off when he arrives." Elinor turned and left the room, desperately needing to breathe some fresh air. Easton found her out in the small yard, trembling as she tried to hold back her tears. He put his arms around her in a comforting hug, with his chin on her head. He whispered, "I am sorry." Elinor was not sure what he was sorry for, but she had so much pent up emotion that she let the tears fall and relaxed her head on his shoulder, grateful for the comfort.

After a few minutes she had composed herself and pushed back from him wiping tears and laughing at the same time. "Now it is my turn to apologize. I am not sure what came over me."

"I never would have asked you to look in on him had I realized the extent. The surgeon should be here in an hour or two." She shook her head.

"No, please. It is not only that. I cannot even explain. It is so many emotions built up over the past few weeks. Then the gravity of his condition brought back all that you went through...then the smell. I— I did not think I could do it." She paused and took a deep breath, not wanting to say what had to be said. "Easton, I am not sure he will keep his arm or if he will even live." He was searching her eyes, as if trying to accept the reality of the situation. "I would have the surgeon's opinion before I told Maddie, though," she finished quietly.

"I will stay here and wait for the surgeon, if you do not mind going home unescorted. I have sent for a groom from the inn."

"Not at all." She shook her head, feeling guilty for leaving, but acknowledging the necessity due to her exhaustion. "Josie volunteered to sit with him tonight. I would appreciate it very much if you would let me know what the surgeon says." Easton nodded, and they returned inside for her to say her farewells.

~

Elinor made her way back to the Dower House, grateful for the time alone to clear her head and enjoying the guilty pleasure of riding alone—if one did not count the groom following behind. Her time alone had been so limited in London, especially after being virtually independent in Washington. Emotions she did not completely understand came upon her from one extreme to another. She was angry for being put in this situation in the first place. She had not wanted to come back to England, be thrust into society, and forced to face Nathaniel. She had not wanted to play doctor and accompany Easton and 'be ruined' because she was on a boat with him.

Then her thoughts swung toward melancholy; she wished for the simplicity of life she'd had with her papa at River's Bend, before feeling guilty because she was enjoying Easton's friendship—too much—and wishing there could be more, but knowing there could not. She laughed mockingly at herself, at her feelings and at the way she had chastised Easton for the *ton's* indolence. Though she had not been completely inaccurate, she should not have judged all by the actions of a few. The fact was, she was enjoying this part of England; it was refreshing to acknowledge that she was wrong. She must not let herself become more attached, or she would be sad to leave. Did she actually think that? She shook her head and urged her mare back to the house.

Early the next morning, Elinor gathered a basket of goods, with help from the cook and housekeeper, of things they all thought would be useful for Mrs. Smith. She loaded up her mare and the groom's horse with goods and set off for the village to look in on Mr. Smith. The frost crackled underneath the horses' hooves, and their breath condensed into the chill air as they rode down the path to the village.

The village was already bustling with the activity of labourers at work as she hurried up to the Smiths' cottage, leaving the groom to unload their offerings into the kitchen. She was anxious to know how Sam Smith had fared during the night. The note she had received from Easton did little to comfort her or ease her concern. It had merely stated the surgeon had not taken Mr. Smith's arm and would reassess him in the morning. The door opened to a home not full of sickness, but of warmth and cheer, the sounds of playing children, the smells of frying kippers and freshly baked bread. Upon seeing their newly-arrived guest, the children ran to greet her.

"Miss Abbott, Miss Abbott! Papa's better!" The two dirty children pulled at her arms and shook them as they bounced up and down happily. She nodded to Josie, cooking in the kitchen, as they passed, and noticed Buffy was in there as well. She smiled and made a mental note to investigate them later.

"That's wonderful news! May I see him?" They nodded and dragged her toward the room where she had left him sick and feverish yesterday. She was astonished to find Easton sitting in a chair, dishevelled in yesterday's clothes and a day's growth of beard. He must have stayed all night! And next to him, sitting up in bed and talking with him was Sam Smith. Thank heaven.

"Miss Abbott," Easton rose upon noticing her entrance. "It is my pleasure to introduce you to a fever-free Samuel Smith. Mr. Samuel Smith, your healer."

Sam Smith grinned and looked shyly up at Elinor. "Miss Abbott, I would like to thank you. The doctor said I would have died if you had not helped me."

"You are most welcome, but I am sure he would have managed."

"You are too modest, miss." That was about the extent of what he was comfortable speaking around her.

189

Easton chimed in, "Indeed. The doctor did not arrive until late, and he said he could not have done a better job himself. He said Sam would have lost his arm, if not his life, had you not acted so quickly."

Before Elinor could stumble out a reply, Maddie Smith hustled into the room and threw her arms around Elinor, tears of joy streaming down her face.

"Forgive me, Miss Abbott, but I am ever so grateful." Elinor returned the embrace fully. "First you work miracles on me Sam, then you bring enough food to feed an army, and your Josie cleaned the house and made breakfast. I feel like a queen, I do!"

"It was the least we could do. I am glad it helped a little." Elinor stood back from the embrace, but held Maddie's hands and looked her in the eye. "Assure me you will let me know if you need anything at all." Maddie nodded and tears streamed down her face. "Now let me change that bandage for you, Mr. Smith."

"Major Trowbridge, you best not let this one get away." Maddie nudged Easton on her way out of the door.

"I do not intend to," he replied softly and winked at Elinor. "I only hope I get a say," he whispered after she walked out.

CHAPTER 16

*E*aston decided to escort Elinor home now that Mr. Smith was improving. They made their way through the village content to remain silent, neither of them sure what to say. So much had happened in one day. Easton had spent a great deal of the previous night thinking over the situation between himself and Elinor. He was more convinced than ever, when he saw her walk in that morning, that he would do almost anything to keep her. Could she not see what a difference she was making in the lives of people here? Could she see what a difference she was making to him? If only she could come to care for him as he did for her.

Once they were outside the village, Elinor managed to speak. "Are you so familiar with all your tenants?"

He looked at her sideways with a small smile. "No, I had the good fortune of playing with the Smiths as children."

"Ah, I see. Well, it was refreshing and unexpected. I almost felt like I was back home." She smiled playfully at him.

"We aim to please. " He tipped his hat and smiled back, then could not help himself from asking, "Have you been spending much time with your cousins?" Hopefully, she could not detect his ulterior motives in asking, but finding out what hold Nathaniel held over her was nagging at him. He could not help but think Nathaniel was the key to solving the Elinor mystery.

She stared straight ahead and took her time answering. "No, that is not exactly a comfortable situation. Grandmother, Andrew and I are keeping each other company at the moment."

"Did something happen?" *Well, that came out wrong.* "Forgive the impertinence; please pardon my intrusion." He had not realized their family situation was strained. He was merely curious to know if she was spending time with Nathaniel. She had said she was not going to marry Nathaniel, but he knew there had been something between them and wondered if she wanted there to be. Elinor sighed heavily, clearly pondering what she should say to him. "Elinor, if you do not wish to tell me, please do not feel pressure to do so."

She shook her head, "No, it is only I did not realize you had not been told everything. The morning you spoke with my uncle, he called us all together for a family meeting." They mutually grimaced— nothing good ever came from family meetings with the Duke. "Apparently my uncle overheard Beatrice spreading the rumours about our having travelled on the ship together."

"It was your cousin, not Lady Dunweather?" He looked genuinely astonished.

"Yes, it seems she has not seen the benefits of my being in England and views me as either competition or too ignoble to be a relation." She grinned. "So, Uncle withdrew her pin money and banished her to the country for a year to learn manners." She managed to glance over at him, and he started laughing, which was contagious.

"That makes it all almost worth it! I still would not have believed Beatrice would sink to this," Easton said. They both laughed at the absurdity of it all. "No wonder you three are keeping company at the Dower House. I would stay clear of Beatrice as well." He shook his head, "So, would it be too forward of me to invite you for Christmas dinner, if you are avoiding the Abbey?"

"It is not too forward to ask, but I will have to consult with Grand-mama to see what her plans are. How is your father? Is he up to partaking of Christmas dinner?"

"He will be if he thinks you are coming," he said with a pleasant laugh.

"You issue the invitation to Gran yourself. I doubt she could say no to your charming self."

"You think I am charming?" Flashing his dimpled grin at her, he cocked an eyebrow mischievously as they handed their horses' reins to the grooms, then headed for the house.

"That is not what I said. I implied Grandmama finds you so." She tapped him with her riding crop and flashed him a brilliant smile. Before he could reason himself out of it, he leaned over and brushed his lips across hers.

~

She stood there, unable to move. Adam had just kissed her and was standing there waiting for her to do something. She should chastise him and walk away, but all she wanted to do was kiss him back. He had not felt *anything* like oysters. She looked up into his eyes and realized she had utterly, completely, fallen for him. How had that happened? He was supposed to have been a rake, a hardened soldier, a wastrel libertine lord. It was supposed to have been easy to walk away. Now, she could not have the one thing she never thought she could want. He deserved the truth, but she could not bear to see the disappointment on his face, so she turned and walked back to the house.

Easton followed slowly behind. *The devil!* He had pushed too far. He could see it on her face. It seemed like she was softening toward him, then her face changed, and she had talked herself out of it. This was irony at its finest. He had spent years fending off and hiding from women's advances. Now he had found one he did not think he could live without, and she was having none of it.

They made their way into the parlour in silence, both refusing to speak, for to do so would acknowledge something neither was ready to speak out loud. Expecting to see only her grandmother, Elinor pasted a smile on her face to hide her inner turmoil and entered the room only to find her uncle there taking tea. *No. No, No, No.* She had the worst sort of sinking feeling in the pit of her stomach. He would tell Easton. She loved her uncle dearly, but he would think it was for her own good. She flashed a look of panic at her grandmother as Easton and the Duke greeted each other.

The Dowager only gave her a look as if to say, *What do you think I can do?* Her uncle turned to face her. "Elly," he reached out his arms for a hug, and even though Elinor was still upset with him, she could not bring herself to deny his affection. "Will you please forgive me? I did not mean to hurt you."

"Uncle, please…" She tried to whisper and warn him off, but he was not listening to her. She looked up at Easton, but he was looking away, void of any visible emotion. Maybe he had not heard…ay, and she was the Queen of Sheba. "I still think you should consider Nathaniel's offer. It would be for the best."

"Robert." The Dowager managed a whole conversation in one word. Elinor glanced nervously toward Easton.

Easton sensed Elinor was uncomfortable with him present, so he stood and bowed before the Dowager. "Ma'am, I had only come in to request your presence at Christmas dinner. I will allow you to continue your, ah, family discussion without my intrusion." He bowed over her hand. "A pleasure, as always." Easton bowed to the Duke, then turned to exit.

"I will show you to the door." Elinor walked back through the hallway toward the entrance. The butler handed him his coat and hat and discreetly left. "I am sorry." Elinor could not bring herself to tell him the part about Nathaniel. She felt tears threaten to fall, and she could not look Easton in the eye.

"There is nothing to apologize for." He hesitated, wanting to comfort her. "If there is anything I can do, please know you can trust me." He wanted to tell her that whatever it was, it would not matter to him, but he was not sure she would want to hear that. If only she returned his feelings. She nodded but still did not look up. "I will see you at church." He turned to leave, and she fought the tears rolling down her cheeks as she went back to face her uncle.

They looked up as she came back into the parlour. "Elinor? What happened? Did Easton say something?"

She shook her head violently and tried to contain her emotion. "No, Uncle. I wish you would please give up this idea of my marrying Nathaniel. That is not what I wish for."

"But no one else will have you if they find out."

She kept her eyes on her hands for fear of what she might do if she looked up.

"You have not told Easton, have you? Do you think he will want you if he knows? I do not mean to be cruel, Elly. You know I love you like my own daughter. But I also know what a gentleman expects when he weds a lady."

Oh, she knew, all right. That is why she had every intention of going back to America to run the plantation and remain a spinster. Only she had not expected to fall in love with Easton. Could Fate be any crueller?

"Sir. I cannot marry Nathaniel. Please try to understand and not ask this of me. I hope our friendship may recover one day, but never more than that. Never."

"But..." he protested.

She tried to stop him, willing him to understand without further humiliation.

"He will need to provide an heir eventually..." her voice trailed off.

Her uncle gave her a long, steady look, assessing and finally realizing her meaning. Had he not thought about what it would be like for her to have to fulfil the marriage bed with a man who had violated her? Or did he not know the whole truth? Nathaniel, as the future duke, would have to provide an heir. And he would have to rape her again to achieve that, for she would never be able to go to him willingly.

Easton left the Dower House against his better judgement. If Elinor had not seemed uncomfortable...but she had, so he had left when every part of his being had wanted to stay and protect her from her well-intentioned, but dominant, uncle who was used to doing everything his way. Why was the Duke so insistent? Was he not considered a good enough match for Elinor?

Or was she uncomfortable because she wanted Nathaniel, and she did not want to hurt his feelings? Somehow he needed to find out what was causing Elinor's pain. Maybe Andrew could help, but he had left for London with business for the War Office. There had to be a way.

The next day was Christmas. They would all attend church, and Elinor had sent over a message that she and her grandmother would be delighted to attend dinner. It was unknown whether Andrew would return in time from London. Nathaniel would be at church and the ball later in the week. Maybe all would reveal itself soon, and he could determine whether she truly had feelings for Nathaniel, or hopefully, himself.

~

Church was going to be awkward, for there was no way to avoid her family there. With the two large estates adjoining and despite there being two separate villages, there was a shared parish living. Normally, that seemed a logical idea. Today, Elinor wished it otherwise. For all of her discomfort with her family, she did not wish their current situation to be public knowledge. Therefore, she would have to pretend all was well—including sitting on the family pew with Beatrice and Nathaniel. If there were any dramatics today, they would not be initiated by her.

She sighed. The Christmas service was one of her favourites. She still remembered attending St. Christopher's as a child, when her family would spend the holiday at her uncle's estate. All had been normal and natural then. What had brought their lives to this pass? Now she would spend today alone with her grandmother, since her father, brother, and sister were all unable to come. Thankfully, Easton had invited them for dinner, but it would not be the same, knowing what was coming. She needed to tell him so he understood, but she was not ready yet. One more day.

She made her way downstairs, trying to convince herself to smile, while having a discussion with herself. "One more day. You only have to pretend for one more day, and then you can face this. Nathaniel will not hurt you any more, and once you do not have to look at *him* every day, it will not be as painful. You will see. Papa will be here soon to take you home."

"I will see what?" Elinor looked up to see Easton and her grandmother awaiting her. Had she been speaking out loud, and what was he doing here? And looking breathtakingly handsome at that. How was a girl to concentrate on a sermon with him in the room?

"I was only talking to myself." She forced a smile.

"Merry Christmas, Miss Abbott. I thought I would escort you ladies to church if you do not mind? Father is not strong enough to attend this morning." He bowed gallantly over her hand and brushed his lips over her knuckles.

"Of course not. That is thoughtful of you. Merry Christmas to you as well." Their gazes caught, and she swallowed a painful gasp. *He is good at this pretending.* She was not sure how long they stared at each other, but her grandmother coughed, stifling an amused laugh.

"Let us go on." The Dowager patted at them with her reticule, ushering them toward the door.

"Yes, ma'am," Easton said humbly, though smiling. After helping them into the carriage for the short ride to the church, he asked, "Would it be too bold to request you to sit on my family's pew since we are betrothed?" He leaned over to Elinor and whispered, "We are still betrothed, are we not?" She looked up at him wide-eyed. Did he not think she would have the decency to inform him she was jilting him? He was grinning that devilish-dimpled grin. He was bamming her of course.

He shrugged. "I was not sure if your uncle talked you out of it."

Her grandmother twisted her lips in thought. "I suppose it would be all right if I sat with you. No one would question that. Besides, I am sure it is common knowledge in the villages now after the two of you have been out gallivanting all over the place."

Though her words were reprimanding, she had nothing but amusement in her voice. Elinor silently blessed him, for that would keep her from having to sit next to her cousins. Though it would mean she would be sitting near, *very* near to him for the whole service, heaven help her.

They arrived at the church, and Easton helped each of them down from the carriage. He lent an elbow to both ladies, and the Dowager scoffed, "Nonsense. I am not so old that I cannot walk. You escort your prize in." She winked at Easton.

The Dowager sauntered in, greeting everyone as she passed each pew down the aisle. Easton escorted Elinor in behind her to openly curious glances. She tried to smile and hoped no one noticed how terrified she was. They arrived before the Duke and Duchess and sat in the Wyndham pew across the aisle. So far, all was good. The music began. Were they not coming? It would be unheard of when everyone knew they were in residence.

As the vicar stood to take his place, the Duke and family made their way in. The Duke glanced over with a raised eyebrow to the Wyndham pew, nodded his head in acknowledgement, and they proceeded to sit at the vicar's behest. *Maybe this will not be horrid after all.* If they could sneak out with naught but a few pleasantries, she could manage.

Soon, Elinor was caught up in the service with the old traditions of the children singing and performing the nativity. A small, angelic girl of four or five sang, *O Come All Ye Faithful*, and Elinor felt warm tears threaten to fall. She had sung that same song in this same church the last Christmas she had known with her mother. Her mother had practised and practised the song with her and had sung her to sleep with it as a small child. Her grandmother knew what the tears were for and took her hand and held it lovingly as they remembered together. Easton discreetly pressed a handkerchief into her other hand and squeezed her hand as he did so. Fortunately, the song ended, and the humour of herding children and live animals through the nativity scene was enough to overcome her tears.

After the service, the two families handed out the traditional baskets of gifts and food to their respective tenants. Elinor assisted Easton, since he would otherwise have been left to tend to it all on his own. She had helped arrange them, after all. As they stood and greeted the tenants, it struck Elinor how natural it felt to be there with Easton. She even knew many of the tenants from visiting with Easton. She felt a pang of sadness knowing that next year would be different.

The lines drew to a close, and Elinor found herself standing across from her cousins. She made eye contact with Nathaniel and found herself able to return his gaze. He bowed at the waist in acknowledgement of her, but did not come over to speak with her. He did seem different, sincere. Beatrice did not speak, which was for the best. Neither did she glare, which was surprising. Unfortunately, her aunt did speak—with barely masked civility.

"Christmas joy to you, Aunt Wilhelmina, and to you, Uncle." She curtsied. Her uncle took her arm and began walking toward the carriage with her.

"Yes, and to you, Elinor." He stopped and looked her in the eye. "Elly, I must beg your forgiveness. I have thought much about what you said. I will not force the issue any longer. I wanted to give you and Easton my blessing. We are still holding our tenants' ball next week, and we will make an announcement then." He bent over her hand. "This will all get better, my love. I dearly want you to be a part of our lives again."

"Thank you, Uncle." He gave her a paternal hug, which still surprised her.

"Will you be coming for dinner?"

"No, sir. We are dining with the Wyndhams." The Duke nodded with disappointment, shook Easton's hand and then turned to walk toward his carriage. The Dowager was already waiting inside. Easton helped Elinor in, and she sat back against the seat with a huge sigh. It was barely past noon, and she was exhausted.

They made their way into the manor house, and the dowager excused herself to refresh her toilette. Elinor handed her pelisse and bonnet to the butler then looked around with astonishment. Garlands of holly and ribbon adorned the banisters, and the rooms were lit with hundreds of glowing candles. The effect was magical. Easton started laughing. Elinor looked back at him to see what was amusing.

"Be careful where you walk, my dear. Father is plotting against us. Or for us, depending on how you view the situation."

Elinor looked up to see masses of mistletoe hanging from every door and candelabra. She chuckled along with him until she noticed she was standing right under some. Before she could retreat, Easton was next to her with his devilish grin and said, "That, dearest, is as good as giving permission."

She knew she should stop him, but every part of her wanted him to kiss her. She wanted to savour every feeling, every touch of him, this person who had finally breached the wall of her fear and insecurity. *Before he no longer wanted her*—for when he found out, she knew it would all end. And her heart would be broken. So, she was greedy and accepted his kiss. He brushed his lips to hers, and when she did not resist, he cupped her face in his hands and kissed her harder and longer. When he pulled his lips away, he placed his forehead to hers, still holding her face. "Elinor. I want you to stay. For this to be real."

Her heart was going to jump from her chest. Embarrassed at her reaction to his kiss, she tried to pull away, but he refused to let her go. She shook her head. "I cannot."

Before he could argue, there was a knock at the door, and they turned around to see Andrew and Sir Charles.

~

"Papa!" Elinor nearly screeched as she ran to Sir Charles and threw her arms around him. "Are you actually here?"

"Yes, truly, my love, I am here. Season's Greetings! I cannot think of a more welcome gift than a hug from you!" He held her at arms' length and assessed her with approval. "I see England is agreeing with you, after all. And I hear there is much to tell." He hugged her again and kissed her cheek. He looked up with a smile to Easton, who promptly came over to greet his godfather.

"Sir, it is a pleasure to see you again, a most welcome addition to our Christmas festivities." He smiled a smile he did not feel, for his heart was in his stomach. If Sir Charles was here, then the war was over. If the war was over, he should rejoice, but all he could think about was Elinor leaving and the ache in his heart at the thought. What had he been thinking? He should have kept his distance—no, run in the opposite direction instead of stealing every moment with her he could get. Now, her leaving would only be more painful. He realized Sir Charles was speaking to him and forced his attention back to his godfather.

"You look much better than when last I saw you! I knew Elly would take care of you." They made their way into the parlour to await the others before dinner. "Andrew tells me the two of you are betrothed. I feared it was all my fault for forcing you on that boat together, but from the look of things when we walked in, it is not an unwelcome event."

Elinor's cheeks burned red. She saw the corner of Easton's lips turned up, and he looked away.

"I could not be more pleased," Sir Charles said.

"Thank you, sir. I am happy to know we have your blessing." Easton glanced at Elinor, but she would not meet his gaze. He turned back to Sir Charles. "You must be exhausted from your trip. Would you like to rest before dinner?"

"I would prefer to greet your father, first." Easton nodded and led the way.

Elinor decided to find a place to wash before dinner, and found Buffy and Josie embracing again under some mistletoe. She backed away quietly, trying hard not to giggle out loud.

They were a small, intimate group for dinner. Some footmen helped Lord Wyndham to the table. He looked frail but was in good spirits at seeing his best friend returned and his son with his betrothed. Elinor watched the two old friends conversing and felt a calm she had not felt since leaving America.

"So, Papa, is the war ended, then? I assume that you bring us good news?"

"We offered a peace treatise; however, it must still be presented for ratification. It will be some time for it to cross the Atlantic and be ratified by the United States, but I do hope this means the war has ended."

"Excellent, excellent. To peace." The elderly Earl raised his glass in salute, and the others followed.

"Are we free to return, then?" As soon as Elinor said the words, she winced. It had slipped her mind that she and Easton had not told anyone of their agreement to break their betrothal, especially the Earl. "I mean, is it safe for you to go back?" That was a poor attempt to cover her slip. Everyone was glancing at her, but the only one who seemed to notice anything was amiss was Easton. Was that a look of pain in his eyes?

"It will still be a while before we know that. It may be months before we get word here. The treaty was only signed last night, and we made haste directly here. It will take much longer for the treaty to reach Washington and be ratified there." He sighed, and Elinor sensed he was holding something back from her, but she dared not pry during dinner for fear her tongue might slip again.

Elinor nodded and turned to her stuffed pigeon so she would not have to look at Easton. It was time to end the farce and tell him the truth. She pushed the food around on her plate, suddenly finding herself without appetite. Her grandmother was not to let her off the hook so easily.

"Are you so eager to be rid of us, Elinor? What has Easton to say to going back to the colonies?"

"Her wish is my command?" He smiled and lifted his glass to Elinor. She could not help but smile back at that.

"I would be envious of you two, if it were not for the nausea about to overtake me!" Andrew parried, causing everyone to laugh.

"You will get your turn, dear. Do not worry. And it better be soon!" The Dowager tried to give him her stern look, but he only laughed at her and kissed her on the cheek.

"I will begin tomorrow, Gran."

"Do not be impertinent, child."

"Not I."

"All right, all right. We will let Andrew off the hook for now. We still have this wedding to plan," Sir Charles said gleefully, waving his hand toward the betrothed couple. Elinor must change the topic before the wedding plans got carried away. She would speak with her papa and with Easton on the morrow.

"Yes, I am glad you are here, Charles. I wanted to hold the ceremony soon so that I might attend," the Earl said. "I keep being told by the doctors that they do not know how many more spells I can survive." The Earl stopped to take a sip of wine. "Do not look so glum. I do not intend to stick my spoon in the wall tonight. I only want to make it long enough to see Adam and Elinor wed. I could not have hoped for a more happy union. My son and your daughter, Charles. It brings me such joy. Max showed no signs of settling down, and the women he did pay attention to….well, I am delighted to welcome you to the family, Elinor."

"Thank you, my lord. I am honoured." She ducked her head back to her food to hide her blush. Her papa and the Earl were discussing the wedding, and she could not come up with anything to divert them. She peeked a glance at Easton, and he was looking at her, smiling. She mouthed, "Do something", nodding her head to indicate their father's plotting to him, but he flashed those dimples at her and shrugged. She had a flashback to that first night in the parlour at River's Bend, when he'd flashed her that same grin and she had thought him the highest level of rake. Suddenly, August felt like a lifetime ago, with all that had happened between them. He was no rake, and she would miss his friendship dearly. She owed him honesty and would do her best to help him not let his father down.

She glanced back at him. That was a mistake. Her heart gave a leap at the look he was giving her, and she could not tear her eyes away.

"We will ride out immediately after New Year's Day." They both heard Sir Charles's proclamation, and their heads simultaneously swung toward him.

"What did you say, Papa? I apologize, I was daydreaming." Andrew snorted and gave her a one-eyebrow-raised smirk. She ignored his non-verbal barb, and looked to her father.

"I was merely telling Wyndham that I need Adam to accompany me back to London to wrap up some business with the war." Elinor looked up, glancing from her father to Easton. Easton looked distracted, contemplative.

"But you only just arrived!"

"It cannot be helped, Elly."

"I know, I have just missed you."

The sweet Earl chimed in, "Well, it looks like you will have to keep this old codger company." Who could not love him?

"It would be my pleasure, my lord."

"We can have the wedding all planned by the time they get back."

The small party made their way into the great hall, where the servants had gathered for the traditional lighting of the Yule log. Adam and Andrew took the pieces from the year before and lit either end of the large log. The servants all cheered and wassail was served as the Earl handed each loyal retainer their Christmas gift. This was one of Elinor's favourite parts of the festive ritual.

Once the servants had departed to celebrate with their own families, the Wyndham family traditionally exchanged gifts with each other. Elinor had thought they would wait until they had returned to the Dower House, but the Earl insisted she be given his present to her. He smiled at Adam and instructed him to retrieve the gifts for her.

Easton placed a small parcel in her lap. She looked up expectantly at the Earl, who looked as excited as a child with a present. She unwrapped the pretty ribbon and paper and beheld a beautiful, leather-bound journal that was worn with age. She opened the pages and found handwritten recipes for every type of ailment from ague to rheumatism. She scanned the pages in awe.

"That was the village healer's book before she passed on. I thought you might find some use for it. With the way you took care of my Adam and the village smith, I think you are going to have your hands full." He chuckled. "Of course, you might already know everything in the book..."

"No, it is perfect." She crossed the floor and kissed him on the cheek. "I actually know very little, and this is fascinating." The parcel also contained a newer book of medicine, but she found the ancient book of remedies held more interest for her. "I am honoured that you think I am capable."

"There is no think about it, my dear. The proof is in the pudding, as they say."

"And now for my gift." Easton went into the hallway and came back lugging a large, awkwardly-shaped bundle wrapped in a blanket and tied with a bow. She looked up at him with curiosity. "Well, open it. I am hardly going to spoil it now, though I have wanted to give it to you for weeks." *Weeks? He got me this weeks ago?* She unwrapped and uncovered as fast as she could and almost cried when she saw a beautiful leather saddle in front of her. For riding *astride*. She looked up at him in astonishment.

He shrugged his shoulders and smiled. "For use in the country. I know how much you miss riding. I thought it might make you a little less homesick."

Despite the impropriety, she threw her arms around him. "Thank you, thank you, thank you!"

~

Sir Charles, Andrew and Easton excused themselves to the library after the Earl retired, and the ladies went to the parlour. Easton dreaded this intimate gathering for multiple reasons, but the main one being the inevitable return to London for 'war business', code for hearing-for-questionable-behaviour-on-the-battlefield. Sir Charles had been supportive in Washington, but had events transpired in the meantime to change his mind or his allegiance?

Easton strolled over to a hidden cupboard and pulled out his favourite whisky, he received from a friend in Scotland. After pouring two fingers for each of them, he distributed the tumblers to Andrew and Sir Charles and took a seat near the fire. Content to sip their drinks and ponder the flames dancing in the fire, it was several minutes before they actually discussed anything.

"So, it appears that you and Elly are getting along rather well, despite the forced betrothal."

Easton looked up, a bit stunned that Sir Charles was speaking of Elinor and not the war. How much had Elinor told Sir Charles? Did he suspect it was all a farce to her?

"Yes, she seems to be adjusting to life here, despite her previous determination that it would be otherwise." All of the men chuckled. "Though she has been quite gracious about renouncing her prejudices." He sighed and looked into his whisky as if searching for the right words.

Sir Charles glanced at him sideways, then prodded, "And how do you feel about marrying her? It is one thing to be honourable, but I want to reassure you that I want both your happiness and I will not be the one to force you into something that will ensure your misery."

"Thank you, sir, but I find I am quite agreeable and that I care for her very much. I cannot speak for her feelings. I suspect she would jump at the chance to return to America tonight and never look back."

"Interesting. That is not entirely the impression I have, but time will tell. Besides, going back to River's Bend is no longer an option." That caused Andrew and Easton's full attention to be placed on Sir Charles. "I would prefer to tell Elinor myself, but I do not plan to return to America. The plantation house was burned after you left, Adam. And after being here, I find I want to spend my later years with family. I have run away too long."

"Elly will be devastated. When do you plan to tell her?"

"Soon. It is not fair to keep her hopes up if that is truly where her heart lies. Perhaps after we return from London."

Easton wanted to be excited that Elinor would be staying here, and that she might be more willing to have him, but he was distracted by what the War Council had planned for him.

"Ah, yes. London. Am I to be tried and condemned?"

"Thus far, all I know is that Knott is back, and there is to be a panel to review what happened in Washington and Baltimore. I have not heard your name associated with anything specific, only that your presence was requested. Recall, I witnessed everything—unbeknownst to Knott. Granted, the case would have been stronger had Ross survived, but the scar on your back is proof of Knott's own poor behaviour. We can call other soldiers in if need be, but I doubt it will progress to that point."

Easton was not so confident as Sir Charles, but what could he do? "There is one favour I must ask. Can we please keep this from Father as long as possible? I fear his days are numbered, and I would not have him burdened unless there is no alternative."

"Of course. The worst case is you were insubordinate. However, the orders were beyond questionable as was his method of punishment. Besides, you are the heir and selling out." He shook his head. "I should hope there is little chance you will be called to account for your actions." Easton suspected his godfather was only trying not to worry him.

Easton nodded slowly. Would that Sir Charles could be right. But Knott would not be thwarted at any cost and would not hesitate to use any opportunity to make an enemy look bad or punish him. No matter honesty, integrity or gentlemanly considerations.

CHAPTER 17

*E*linor spent the night tossing and turning, for she was trying to decide how to tell Easton about what happened with Nathaniel. She also knew she needed to tell her father, but that was the most agonizing of all. She rose and dressed herself quickly in a simple, rose muslin frock and sought out Andrew so she could find out how much he had already told her father.

Fortunately, she found Andrew in the breakfast room, drinking coffee and reading a newspaper. He rose and strolled over to give her an affectionate peck on the cheek. But when he looked into her eyes, he was filled with concern. "Elly, you look awful! Has something happened?"

"Thank you, dearest. No nothing new. It is only with Papa being here I realize I need to tell Easton the truth. I am trying to gather the courage to do so. I wanted to see how much you had told Papa. I would rather Easton hear it from me. Since they are going to London together, I did not want something to slip out. I gather Papa does not know, but I needed to know for sure."

Andrew shook his head. "I told Papa nothing of what occurred with Nathaniel. I only told him that you and Easton had become betrothed since it was put about that you were unaccompanied on the ship with him. Did not think it was my place to tell the rest. However, since the whole family knows, it will not be long. I think it best you tell him soon. You know Uncle will not keep it from him!"

Elinor laughed harshly. "Yes, as much as I love dear Uncle, he certainly thinks marrying Nathaniel to be in my best interest. I explained to him that he would not have an heir if he forced the marriage, and that was the only thing that made him stop pushing it."

"By Jove, Elly, did you truly say that to him? Oh, to have seen his face!"Andrew looked at her appreciatively.

"More subtle statements did not seem to give him the hint." She buttered her toast thoughtfully. "Any suggestions on how to go about breaking the news to Easton? I must confess to you I have come to care for him and would not like to see him hurt. That assumes, of course, that he cares enough for me to care about my lack of purity."

"Surely you jest? I have never seen Easton smitten before. If you cannot see how he feels about you, then I question your eyesight, *dearest.*"

"Do you think so?" She shook her head in disbelief. "Andrew, can you keep a secret?"

He looked offended that she had even asked.

"I only wanted to make sure! Do not look as if I stole your puppy!" She laughed. "It is only that Easton and I made a pact of sorts that we could pretend to the betrothal while I was here, and then when it was safe, I could jilt him and go back home with Papa."

She looked up, and Andrew was not smiling any more. In fact, he looked rather angry.

"Oh, Andrew! Please do not look at me so. You must see why we did such a thing! It has become so carried away. Now Papa seems so pleased, and the Earl seems so delighted, and I must confess I would not want to hurt him. Then there are the tenants and society. I do not wish to let everyone down, Easton included. I do not think he will want me once he finds out about Nathaniel!"

She was speaking so fast, her agitation rose to match it, and tears were threatened to fall.

"Elinor! Elinor! Slow down!" Andrew came over to her and

wrapped his arms around her and rocked her back and forth. "Hush now, it will work out. You must tell Easton, but I think you will be surprised by his reaction. If he is upset, it will not be with you, I promise."

Once she was able to calm down, she asked Andrew to ride over to the Wyndham estate with her before she lost her resolve. If she did not go alone she would not be able to back out.

On arrival, they were immediately shown into a parlour, warm and cosy from the blazing fire in the grate. Andrew went to inquire of Easton, and Elinor looked around the room with longing, but with small hope that it could be hers. She had finally found a man she was comfortable with, someone she could be friends with even, but it would most likely be unattainable. Fate was toying with her. All those offers she had refused. How many offers would there have been if any of them had known? Perhaps Nathaniel would have still been forced into offering for her. She shuddered at the thought. She must keep her courage. She still had a life she could go back to, and with a prosperous plantation as her inheritance, she could at least be a self-sufficient spinster. If only she had not met Easton, she would not have known what she was missing. She would have been content. Now she had no choice but to make the best of it.

She could always go through with the marriage and let him find out later. That is what many people would do. However, she was not most people and did not want to start a marriage with this between them. Besides, she did not know if she could go through with the marriage act without having a panic attack. The fact that she was even considering it with Easton was a miracle. But he could be in for a rude surprise if she reacted badly, and that would not be fair to a bridegroom. She had a small glimmer of hope that Easton would still want her, but would it change everything? She hoped she could tell by his reaction. If he was repulsed by her news, then she would leave and not hold him to the betrothal.

Andrew came back into the room alone. "Well, my dear, you are going to have to find courage another day because Easton is out on estate business, and they expect him to be away all afternoon."

Elinor covered her face with her hands and groaned. "I do not know if I can find any more, Andrew. I want to get this over with!"

"I know, dearest. You will see him at the ball, tonight. Maybe you will have a chance to tell him then." He led her to the stables.

"I completely forgot about the ball. I suppose we must go. But do not leave me alone with Aunt or Bea. Please!" She pleaded and pulled on his arm dramatically.

He chuckled. "They will not eat you. Well, at least not with Uncle around." She punched him in the shoulder, and he laughed, and they made their way back to the Dower House.

~

That evening would be the annual New Year's ball, held by both estates at Loring Abbey to honour the hard work and harvest of the year. There was no way for Elinor to avoid her family there, for they had to put on a united front for the people. Would this charade never end? Hopefully she could spend more time with the Wyndham tenants and avoid the Loring family as much as possible.

Lovely; now she had the rest of the day to contemplate how to break the news to Easton. She did not want to tell him at the ball. To be sure, it would provide an easier environment for escape than a solitary meeting. But that would demean the significance of what she had to say. Perhaps she would ask him to meet in the morning at his special place overlooking the sea. At least there would not be any other witnesses to her shame and mortification, but then she would not seem flippant about it either.

She walked into the parlour for tea, and conversation ceased abruptly. She stopped at the doorway to see her grandmother, her papa and Andrew all attempting to look normal. What was the matter? Should she ignore the awkwardness? She decided to make light of it.

"Am I interrupting a tête-à-tête? I can come back." She sensed hesitation. When the quiet continued and no one looked her in the eye, she began to feel uneasy.

Elinor looked at each of them, holding her gaze on Andrew. "Papa knows?"

"Yes," he said quietly.

She slumped into the nearest chair and threw her head in her hands and began to sob. Andrew rushed to her and enveloped her in his arms. She never would have expected him to be the one whom was always comforting her. "Who...who told him?" she managed through her sobs. She wanted to run and hide, but her legs would not budge.

"He went to the Abbey this morning to greet Uncle." He hesitated. "Right now he is sorting through it all. Anger, hurt, disappointment... we were telling him all you had been forced to endure at the hands of our *family*."

"How dare Uncle interfere? He had no right to tell!" She rose to leave and felt her father's hand on her. She could not bear to look him in the eye. Andrew released her to be replaced by Sir Charles.

Her grandmother and Andrew silently left the room with a quiet click of the parlour door behind them. Why were they abandoning her? Elinor had never felt so ashamed. She had dreaded this moment above all others, even more than facing Nathaniel.

Sir Charles wrapped his arms around her, and she reluctantly fell into his embrace. Sir Charles began to cry, saying, "I am sorry, Elly. I am so sorry. Can you ever forgive me?"

"There is nothing to forgive." She lost all control of the tears, and once they started, the floodgates opened until they had run dry. She did not know how long they had cried, but when they stopped, she no longer felt anything but numb. She pulled back, ready to speak of the inevitable once and for all.

"I suppose you have a lot of questions." She willed herself to look into her father's face. She was sorry she did. He looked vulnerable. He looked exhausted, weary, tired. She had hoped to spare him from this. She had borne it all so he would not have to know. She did not regret not telling him six years ago, because if he felt this way now, it would have been that much worse when he was grieving for her mother.

"No questions." He took her hands into his. "I know you did not tell me because I was so distraught over losing your mother. I do not know if I will ever forgive myself for being so selfish." She started to protest, but he held up his hand so she would let him continue. "I should have supported you. I knew there had been an alteration in you, but had assumed it was your way of grieving and going through your womanly changes." Tears began to fill his eyes, and he looked away.

"We cannot undo the past, Papa. I only hope you understand why I cannot stay here. There have been some nice parts about being here. I am still not a lover of society." He chuckled at that. "But the country is much like home. However, I know that I cannot marry, and it would be easier to simply go back."

"What of Adam?" He looked at her and what he saw broke his heart. "You cannot tell me you are indifferent."

"He does not know." She walked over to the window and stared out as if the garden might hold the answer. She twirled the tassels mindlessly through her fingers, not ready to answer the question.

"Does he know you plan to leave?" She nodded, and a lone tear rolled down her cheek.

"I see." Silence. The cliffs were looking more enticing by the minute. "Do you not think you should at least give him a choice?"

How to answer that? What choice was there?

"Elly, he is a man of honour and integrity. I know it may not always be obvious; a soldier learns to mask his emotions. However, you must realize he also has much to contend with, from his brother dying and thrusting him unexpectedly into running an earldom, to dealing with an ailing father, not to mention the effects of war. I tell you this because I think he cares deeply for you and you may not realize how much. Please give him the opportunity."

Please do not make this harder, Papa. "I tried to go tell him this morning, but he was out." He gave her an affectionate squeeze.

"Good girl. It will work out, my love. It will work out."

If only.

~

Unfortunately, the ball had to go on. Fortunately, her papa had taken the news better than she had ever imagined. True, she felt relief having one of her burdens out of the way, but she was not happy. Perhaps if she had told him years ago, she would not be in this situation now. Tonight she would have to face the rest of her family again. She knew she needed to forgive Nathaniel in order to move on with her life, but she wanted to ignore it all and hope it would go away.

Elinor forced herself to go to her room to dress. Josie had selected a simple, demure gown of lavender satin, empire-waisted, with a modest neckline and capped sleeves. The unadorned gown reflected Elinor's sombre air. The last thing she wanted was for any more attention. Blending in with the tapestries was more in line with her mood. She pulled her hair back in a simple chignon and placed a single string of pearls around her neck; she did not even wish for Josie's help tonight.

~

Easton raised his eyes to survey the ballroom after the endless greeting line to welcome all the tenants. Normally, this was one of his favourite activities of the Christmas season. This year, however, there was so much at stake in his life that he was trying to come to terms with. Being thrust into English society after eight years away was bad enough, but to come back to a dying father *and* having an entire estate to run—that he was not trained to run—was daunting. He looked out at all the tenant families he had known his entire life, and desperately hoped he would not fail them. He also prayed Sir Charles was correct about being called before the War Council in London next week. If he were called up on charges—he shuddered to think. What would happen to the Earldom then?

Then there was Elinor. Spirited, passionate, genuine, beautiful Elinor. His eyes were drawn like a magnet toward her across the ballroom. How different she was from society misses. She was simple and stunning. He eyed her, his heart full of love. She could be his, if he could only convince her! But she deserved so much more than him.

How would she take the news about her home being burned and her father staying in England? Would she resolve to take him since she had no better choice? Was his love for her enough to make a happy marriage? Many marriages were based on much less. But what if he were found guilty of something at the War Council? He had to get his thoughts away from that. He could torture himself to death with speculation.

He saw Buffy twirl by with Josie and chuckled out loud. If Elinor did not stay, he had a feeling he would be losing his batman soon. His gaze drifted yet again to Elinor. She was like a beacon, shining her light for him. Lord Vernon was dancing attendance on her. What was Vernon about? They had all been friends practically from the cradle, along with Andrew and Nathaniel. None of them would knowingly encroach on another's betrothed. Perhaps he was simply being friendly to his distant cousin. He watched as Elinor threw back her head with laughter, as Vernon was apparently the wittiest cad alive. If that was friendly, Easton was in major trouble because he did not care for it one bit.

Nathaniel approached Elinor, and Easton watched with trepidation and curiosity, hoping the interaction would reveal Elinor's true feelings about him. She was smiling politely at him. What did that mean? That she had feelings and was being shy? Or that she was merely being polite to her cousin? He would welcome any outlet for his frustration at the moment, because it was taking every ounce of restraint he could muster not to plant facers upon two of his oldest friends!

Elinor tried not to notice Easton's every move, but she knew where he was nonetheless. Trying to convince herself she was indifferent, she watched with growing jealousy as females hung on his arm and practised their flirting skills. Lord Vernon approached and did his best to make her laugh. He was diverting, though most of his humour was derived from sarcasm at the expense of others. Nathaniel joined them, and she found each interaction with him a little less painful. Then she saw Beatrice approach Easton and managed to be led toward the dance floor. So when Nathaniel asked her to dance with him, she was not thinking completely coherently when she consented.

~

Beatrice had watched Easton's reaction to Elinor as he noticed her cousin across the ballroom. He did not seem to mind that she was used goods. Or perhaps he did not know? In fact, her fast behaviour had not been much of a deterrent to any of the men if the continuous parade of fawning gentleman was an indication. *Had the hussy thought to have her stowed away in the country so she would not have any competition? She leaves for six years and does not want to play by the rules when she comes back?*

Beatrice approached Easton from the side as he continued to watch Elinor with Nathaniel. "They will always have a special bond, you know. I wonder if they still have feelings for each other after all these years? Perhaps Papa is right that they should wed."

Easton glanced at Beatrice and followed her glance to Elinor and Nathaniel. That was what he was afraid of, and Beatrice had given voice to those feelings. If only he knew what that special bond was. He glanced back to the pair in question. A friendly conversation, by the looks of it. If only he knew what there was between them, he would feel more secure.

"Come, let's dance and take your mind off her. It is not gentlemanly to brood," Beatrice cooed as she pulled Easton toward the floor.

He shrugged slightly, then held out his hand to lead Beatrice to the floor. The orchestra began to thrum a waltz, not the typical type of dance for the tenants' ball. *Brilliant.* Now he would have to listen to her spew her malicious venom for an entire dance. That was all it was, was it not? Beatrice was trying to poison him against Elinor in retaliation for her success? If only he could will himself to ignore the well-placed barbs at his insecurities.

To top it off, he would be subjected to Elinor waltzing with

Nathaniel. Beatrice saw him watching Nathaniel and Elinor as they came closer to the couple on the dance floor. Nathaniel was looking down at Elinor as if she was a precious china doll.

Bea continued, "You must admit, they make a charming couple."

"I suppose I would still pine for the person I gave my innocence to as well," Beatrice said rather loudly just as Elinor and Nathaniel brushed up against them. Easton stopped abruptly and dropped Beatrice's arms as if they were on fire before turning on his heel and exiting the ballroom, not realizing that Elinor had overheard. Elinor turned toward Beatrice with a look of mortification. Then she turned the opposite direction and fled.

Nathaniel led Elinor to the dance floor, and she found she was not as nervous as she had been the last time he touched her. She tried to relax and will herself to stay calm, but she could not make the trembling stop. She noticed Easton dancing with Beatrice across the floor, and suddenly she was not thinking about dancing with Nathaniel, but what mischief Beatrice might be creating instead. She had hoped Beatrice would not be allowed at the ball, but Uncle had said no more London or society, so perhaps he considered she could not do much damage here. *Clearly he underestimated her*, Elinor thought to herself as she saw the cat-who-got-the-cream look on Beatrice's face as she danced with Easton.

Elinor averted her face as she realized Nathaniel had asked her a question. When she had seen the look on his face, she felt confused and apprehensive at the same time. He had gazed at her as if she were fragile porcelain. She was not sure why he looked at her like that, but she hoped it was only because he was grateful for her dancing with him. She could not begin to imagine what else he might be hoping for.

She noticed Easton and Beatrice coming closer to them. Elinor wished it were she in Easton's arms, not Beatrice. She needed to plan a time to speak with him if nothing else. They drew so close to the other couple, it was a near miss when she thought she heard Beatrice say, "I would still pine for the person I gave my innocence to as well." Elinor stopped abruptly and found herself staring into Easton's retreating back, then to Beatrice's face that had a malicious smile on it. Elinor realized what knowledge Beatrice had just imparted then turned and fled to the stares of the now-hushed crowd in the ballroom.

Elinor ran out of the terrace doors and continued across the lawns and woods, finding some comfort in the pains beginning in her side and the difficulty breathing. She did not know how long she ran, but it must have been a while because she could no longer feel the blisters on her feet and she could make out the outline of the Dower House ahead in the moonlight. She forced herself to a walk, trying to recover her breath, then leaned against a tree as she kicked off her ruined slippers and revelled in the relief of the frozen ground.

While running was not as comforting as riding, it had served to get her blood pumping and help her find a small measure of comfort in clearing her head. Plus, it was rather hard to cry while running. She knew that the farce was over. She wished she had been able to tell Easton herself. But maybe it was better this way having seen his reaction tonight. It was worse than she feared. She had thought he would be disappointed and back out of the betrothal quietly. She had not expected this reaction, however.

She should not be surprised, but she was. She did not think she was capable of these feelings any more, but she had let herself get in over her head, and it hurt more than she could have imagined. Nathaniel's betrayal had hurt because she had loved him like a brother and she had been too young to know what was happening. But this was a different sensation entirely. She did not know if she could ever get over this.

Right now, she had to focus on surviving until Papa returned from London. At least Easton would be with him so she would not have to see his disgust with her on his face. Papa had taken it better than she had expected. She knew she could not have borne it if her papa had been disgusted with her too.

Grateful for the fire already burning in the grate in her room,

Elinor gravitated toward the flames without thought. She slumped onto the floor from exhaustion and sat staring at the sparks leaping from the hearth until she thawed out. She began to consider her options, and the only thing she could bear was to pack and be ready to leave when her father got back from London. He would surely understand. When they had spoken earlier that day, he did not seem to want to talk about going home, thinking that Easton would still have her. Obviously, that would not be the case.

Chastising herself at her foolishness for hanging on to the hope that he would be different, she got up and marched over to her wardrobe and began to throw things onto the bed. She threw open her trunks and started filling them without regard to method. She had no idea when her papa would return from London, but, by God, she would be ready! She could not be away from here fast enough!

She heard a tap on her door and she assumed it was Josie. "Come in," she said without turning to look.

"Can we talk?" Her head popped up to see Andrew standing there.

"About what?" she murmured in the most unaffected manner she could muster.

"Well, for a start, why you ran from the ball like the hounds of hell were chasing you, and why you apparently kept going all the way here. I spent the last two hours frantically searching for you, only to find you here packing furiously."

"I would have thought it rather obvious."

"I suspect I know, but I would still like to hear what happened from you."

"Must I?" She threw up her hands then turned to face him. Noting the look on his face, she acquiesced. "Very well. Beatrice told Easton, and he stormed off. There's nothing more to it than that. I am leaving as soon as Papa gets back from London." She turned back to her task as if the discussion were over.

"You are going to run away?"

"Papa did." She winced as she said it, knowing that was unfair. But she was hurt and she had to lash out somehow.

"I see." He only stood there, arms crossed without expression. It was disturbing.

"Do you? You will not fight me?" He sighed and stood in silence for an eternity.

"No, I will not fight you. Father needs to know, though. Did you not have a chance to talk to Easton about it?"

Elinor kept her head down and shook it. She felt tears threaten and refused to let them fall. She had known how it would end, so why did it hurt so much? "He knows what he needs to know, and his reaction was quite clear. I do not think there's anything more to say. However, I will write him a note and apologize."

"Very well." He came over and gave her a hug and kissed her on top of the head, then saw himself out. Elinor sat on the bed and sobbed until there was nothing left.

～

Easton heard what Beatrice said and was furious. Was she telling the truth, or was she merely spewing more venom? He looked at the smirk on her face, and his only thought was to remove her filthy hands from him and get away. He marched off the floor not caring what people thought of his behaviour. He could take her no more! He needed to think this through.

Easton found an empty path leading away from the house. He began to pace, trying to sort his thoughts, but nothing made sense! He had to admit there was something between Elinor and Nathaniel. He could tell from her reaction around her cousin. But to have given her innocence to him? She had been but a child when they left for America. He did not think they could have done such since she had been back. He supposed they could have hidden the relationship, but to what purpose? Her uncle, the Duke, clearly wanted Nathaniel and Elinor together. He shook his head. Perhaps he should speak with Andrew. He could not march up to Elinor and ask her such a thing! Did it change how he felt? He did not want to answer that yet, but did not think he could handle a marriage to her knowing she preferred someone else. He stood for a moment, drawing in several deep breaths in an effort to calm himself before returning to the house to search for Andrew.

Hushed whispers and eerie quiet greeted Easton when he walked back into the ballroom. He dismissed them as he usually did and went on the hunt for his quarry. He questioned a few of his acquaintances, but no one had seen Andrew in some time. How long had he been outside, anyway? He checked his timepiece and was surprised to find he had been wandering for over an hour. He grabbed a glass of champagne from a passing waiter, and a swig of false courage.

"She is gone, dear." Easton looked up to find the knowing eyes of the Dowager Duchess upon him. "She made her own dramatic exit immediately after yours. In fact, it seems I have been abandoned by both of my escorts. Would you mind seeing me home, since it is on your way?"

Knowing the question to be rhetorical, and not wanting to be there any longer, he agreed. "I will go and call for the carriage."

Easton asked Barnes to call his carriage for her Grace, then spotted Nathaniel sitting alone in the entrance hall.

"Outside, Fairmont."

Hearing his name, Nathaniel looked up in surprise, having been deep in thought and not noticing Easton's presence. He rose to follow.

"I suppose you would like to have a go at me as well," Nathaniel said quietly.

"That among other things," Easton said clenching his jaw, barely controlling his temper. "I do not know what happened in the past, but for the future, you cannot have her." He knocked Nathaniel down with his best right hook, and, with considerable satisfaction, sent Nathaniel sprawling across the marbled floor, drawing his cork in the process. He then turned on his heel and went to assist the Dowager into the carriage.

Silence reigned for the first few moments once they were ensconced within the carriage as they made their way to the Dower House.

"Things are not always as they seem, my dear. I do not pretend to know what you might or might not have heard this evening, but seeing you and Elly both run from the ball in opposite directions gives me pause. I will remain vague, for it is not my wish to interfere. However, I will say with many years of wisdom behind me, it is best not to make assumptions, especially in matters of the heart."

Easton opened his mouth to speak, but found there were no words. Elinor had run from the ball? Had she overheard Beatrice? Shock and realization assailed him. He wondered why the Duchess was saying this to him. He rubbed his aching knuckles, in deep thought.

"Your expression gives you away, my dear. Take your time and remember what I said." The carriage rolled to a stop, and Easton disembarked and assisted the Dowager from the carriage. As they reached the front door, it was opened by Andrew.

"Thank you, Easton, it seems you have saved me a trip. I was coming back to retrieve you after making sure Elly was safe." He reached over and kissed his grandmother.

"Well, that answers my question about her whereabouts. I assumed someone would eventually notice I was still there. Good night, dears. I am off to check on my granddaughter." The Dowager turned and made her way up the stairs.

"Andrew, might I have a word?"

Andrew noticed the solemn look on his friend's face and obliged.

"Of course." He gestured toward the study and stoked the fire before pouring generous fingers of whisky for them both. He handed one to Easton and sat down in the chair opposite, waiting for him to speak when he was ready. Easton finally looked up from the fire and downed his drink in one swallow.

"I am sorry, Andrew. I seem to be at a loss for words. I suppose you know some of what happened tonight." Andrew nodded subtly but remained silent. Easton raked his hand through his hair and attempted to compose his thoughts. "Would you mind clarifying the relationship between Fairmont and Elinor for me?"

Andrew almost winced at the question, his loyalties torn between his best friend and his sister. He knew that he could fix this mess with one sentence, but he had given Elly his word that he would not inter-fere. "I would love to, but I have given my word that I would not. It is not my story to tell, and I would that you would listen with an open mind and not make assumptions."

"That is all I am to know?" He jumped up and began pacing back and forth across the carpet.

Watching his friend's anguish, Andrew suddenly realized that Easton cared for Elinor beyond friendship. He had thought perhaps Easton was trying to ascertain how to quash the scandal that would ensue, but seeing his reaction, it dawned on Andrew that might not be the case.

"You have fallen in love with her."

Easton looked up with agony written on his face. He did not deny the accusation.

Andrew had assumed Easton knew the whole truth, since Elinor had merely said that Easton had overheard.

Easton thought Elinor loved Nathaniel and had given her inno-cence to him willingly. Andrew had not denied it.

"How can I compete?" Easton felt a squeeze at his heart at the thought of losing her, but if she loved Nathaniel he would have to let her go. What choice did he have? If he had a choice.

"You will have to fight for her." Andrew said bluntly.

"I feel like fighting." He felt murderous as he rubbed his still-throb-bing knuckles. *Would this be a losing battle?*

Easton left, pondering Andrew's words and wondering how in the world to accomplish winning over Elinor's heart. He was leaving early in the morning with Sir Charles, so he would not have the chance to speak with Elinor before his trip to London. Perhaps time to sort his feelings out was for the best. He wished his mind were not so consumed with Elinor, and feared he would be far from his best before the War Council.

CHAPTER 18

*A*fter Elinor finished packing, her grandmother came to her room. She took one look about her and did not say anything about the packed trunks. Instead, she glided regally to the settee and sat down, indicating with a pat next to her, for Elinor to do the same. The last thing Elinor wanted to do was talk, but she owed her grandmother some explanation. She assumed her father was too absorbed in the card room to have noticed her absence yet, or he would have already been here with the inquisition as well.

"Do you care to talk about it?" The all-knowing, inquisitive eyebrow thrust high on her forehead.

Elinor shrugged as if nothing of substantial import had happened. "No, but I know I will not be let off the hook so easily. What do you know?"

"I do not actually know *anything*. I overheard much, I saw some, and I believe there is a misunderstanding."

"There is little to misunderstand, Grandmama. I overheard Beatrice tell Easton that I lost my innocence to Nathaniel. Right in the middle of the dance floor!" Elinor felt the anger bubbling up inside her again.

"And that is all you heard?" Elinor nodded, again fighting tears.

"You do not know if he was told the whole story?" Elinor shook her head.

"Does it matter? He knows I am ruined. That is all that matters." She looked down at her aching feet.

"Nonsense. It matters very much. And he cares very much. But give him a few days. He needs time to sort this out. When he comes to you, you must tell him everything. Right now, without knowing the whole of it, he is likely worrying that you prefer Nathaniel to him."

Elinor shook her head vehemently then looked away, ashamed."No, Grandmama. I have to confess something to you." She willed herself to look her grandmother in the eye, though she knew she would hurt her feelings.

"Hmm?" Her grandmother made a questioning noise. She pulled her close and she began stroking her hair soothingly.

"We do not have a real betrothal. We had an agreement that I would jilt him and go back to America. His heart is not engaged. His pride might be pricked, but not his heart."

"And you wish it otherwise," the Dowager said, quite matter-of-factly.

"My wishes matter not. All I can hope for is a return to life as it was before."

The Dowager smiled as she pulled her closer for a hug. She kissed the top of Elinor's head.

"Sometimes we have to surrender the past before we can make our path to the future."

The Dowager rose and made her way out, but instead of retiring, as she longed to do, she made her way back down to find Sir Charles and enlist his help in her plan.

Elinor awoke to her curtains being drawn and maids carrying in buckets of water to fill the bath. She heard the sounds carrying on around her, but she could not seem to clear the fog from her brain to open her eyes or form coherent words. She felt a hand shake her.

"Miss Elly! Miss Elly! Your bath is ready. Your father has requested your presence before he leaves, so you best get out of bed." Josie got more aggressive with her shakes.

"All right, all right." Elinor managed to sit up but could not open her eyes. She ached all over from running so far the night before. Josie led her to the bath and helped her discard her nightgown and climb in. She wondered, was there anything better than a bath? She was sorely tempted to doze off again and prolong the inevitable conversation that awaited her, when she felt a pitcher of water being poured on her head. Josie then proceeded to scrub her hair with soap, none too gently, either.

"That ought to wake you up." *Indeed.*

Josie rushed Elinor through her toilette before she made her way to the library to join her father. She stopped at the door and was immediately taken back to the last day of blissful ignorance when she had been perturbed that Mr. Wilson had offered for her and assaulted her lips. Her body scrunched up in distasteful remembrance of the occasion. It seemed like an age since that day. Had it only been a few months? She knocked lightly on the door, and her father looked up and smiled.

"There you are, my dear. Feeling rested?" He looked too cheerful.

"I could do with some tea." She smiled sleepily.

"I already requested it." He stood and came around the desk. He gestured her toward the chairs in front of the hearth. "Have a seat, dear. We need to have a talk before I set off for London." The butler came in and placed a tea service down on the table between the two wing-back chairs. Sir Charles dismissed him, and Elinor sat and began to pour. She remained quiet at her task, waiting for her father to begin as she handed him his cup.

"Do you care to tell me what happened with Adam?"

How many times would she have to go through this? She had only just built up enough courage to tell Easton before everything had come crashing down on her at the ball last night. She was beginning to grow numb and shut herself off from it all. Before she could speak, he must have sensed her hesitance.

"I thought you might want to talk about it, Elly. I have already heard what happened, if you do not wish to tell me."

"From him?" Her eyes were wide with shock.

He shook his head as he swallowed a sip of tea. "No, from your grandmother. She wanted me to know before I went to London with him. Probably so I would not make the situation worse."

"I see." Maybe she would not have to have any discussions with Easton. She had written an apology down—several times—since it had taken her forever to fall asleep last night, but perhaps this was the easy way. She still felt she needed to explain. "He knows everything?"

"I assume so, but I still feel you should talk and make sure. Something was on his mind. You know Wyndham wants to see you married, and soon, but I want you both to be sure."

"If not, then we can leave for home?" She stared into his eyes and saw hesitance, then sadness. "What is it, Papa?"

He sighed, then spoke quietly. "I am not going back, Elly."

"What?" The word came out as a screech. Her mouth was gaping open; she could not help it. "But you promised me."

"The plantation was burned." He spoke softly, but she heard.

A cry escaped her. She finally managed words as she thought of all of the beloved plantation workers and loyal servants. "Is everyone safe?"

He nodded. "It was only the manor house. Abe is overseeing everything."

"Thank God for that." She jumped up and began to pace. "When were you going to tell me?" She threw her hands out for emphasis. "Going home has been the one thing keeping me sane throughout this whole ordeal!"

"Elly, please." He looked guilty.

"That has been my life for six years. You promised we could go back! Everything is falling apart here, and now I have nowhere to go." She fell back into the chair and threw her face into her hands. She hated being emotional and knew she sounded dramatic, but there was only so much a person could handle. She had not asked for any of this.

He reached over and took one of her hands. She refused to look up, willing the hot tears streaking down her face to dry. "I intended to tell you as soon as I saw you, but when I arrived there were many mitigating factors. Then, I was hoping you would want to stay of your own volition." He paused and stared into the fire. "Elly, seeing the house burned, watching the battle and what happened to Adam, then being back here with family, I realized I want to grow old here—with all my family. I ran once, and I do not want to run any more. Learn from my mistakes, Elly. Face them now, and fight for what you want."

It was all she could do not to run from the house and ride away on her horse. He made it sound so simple. How does one fight for someone else's love? Their good opinion? After all *a good opinion once lost is lost forever*. She laughed in a self-deprecating manner as she thought back to the hours she'd spent reading from the beloved book to everyone on the ship. They had certainly come full circle. She had spurned him, and now he would surely spurn her. How had she let it go this far? How could she have failed to guard her heart and lost it?

"I will speak to him, Papa, but I have little hope it will have the desired outcome," she said with resignation in her voice. After all, she had nothing left to lose.

He rose and guided her to her feet. "Let us go, then."

The day of reckoning was here.

～

Elinor and Sir Charles crossed the threshold into Wyndham Court and were shown into the parlour. Easton strolled through the door and hesitated when he saw Elinor, but he kept moving and greeted them as if nothing had happened the night before. Sir Charles excused himself to say goodbye to the Earl and left them alone. There was a disturbing silence, and neither wished to face the conversation ahead.

"Easton, would you mind walking with me in the garden? Unless you have time for a ride? There are some things I need to tell you," she said nervously, but was determined to explain the whole and have it over and done.

He nodded and glanced out of the window, seemingly as resigned to the talk as she was. "I think a walk. The skies look uncertain, and we can find shelter more quickly if we stay near the house."

She agreed, so he assisted her from her chair and they gathered their hats, gloves and coats. He offered her his arm, which she accepted, trying to ignore how nice it felt to be so near him. They walked in silence for a while, adjusting to the abrupt change in temperature from the cosy parlour. Eventually Easton broke the silence. "I will not force you to go through with this if you love Nathaniel. Father will simply have to understand," Easton said quietly as they headed down the path through the garden.

"Pardon? You think I love Nathaniel?" She stopped and looked up into his eyes, then turned and continued walking. "I suppose I deserve that. I have been afraid to tell you the truth."

"Afraid? Do you not trust me?" He raised his eyebrow, and he appeared truly hurt.

"I—I suppose I do, but this is not something you say casually. I have wanted to tell you since I knew of my feelings for you, but I could not bear to see your disappointment in me. I was selfishly holding on to your good opinion of me." She kicked some pebbles in their path, unable to face him.

"You have feelings for me?" He stopped and held on to both of her forearms, but she could not look him in the eye. "Elinor, I have been torturing myself by thinking you had feelings for him! I realize you most likely did not understand what was happening with him at that age and calf-love can make you do things you regret." She looked up, then.

"Is that what you think?" She shook her head violently. "Oh, Adam. That is not how it was, at all. But promise me you will do nothing foolish if I tell you."

"Why do I have a feeling I am going to regret this agreement?"

"You will not, because it would do more harm than good." He pondered for a moment, then begrudgingly, he nodded and held her hands.

"I promise to carefully consider before acting." Her pulse raced at his touch, but in a wholly unexpected way.

"Nathaniel was intoxicated—no, possessed was more like it—and he took me against my will." She released her breath with relief of having said it out loud.

Easton drew her in his arms. He also released a gush of air, but instead of a string of curses, he surprised her. "Shhh. You do not have to say more. I am so sorry. I had no idea."

She felt relief as the warmth of his arms surrounded her. She had imagined much worse. "I—I needed to say it. To have it all in the open. I am sorry I did not tell you sooner." He led her to a bench and sat with his arm still around her holding her close. "If you want to end the betrothal, I will understand why."

He gently tilted her chin so she would look at him. "I could never think less of you for something not in your control. I knew something was not right, but I never could have imagined this. Can you forgive me?"

She laughed with relief. Who would have thought she would be able to smile after that revelation? "Forgive *me* for doubting you. I knew you were different; now I know you are truly special."

"That is not what you thought at first," he retorted playfully.

She snorted. "Ha. Very well, not at first. It took me a while to realize all of your attributes. You appeared and acted the handsome, arrogant rake. And, you must admit society is cruel about a ladies virtue, or lack thereof. How was I to think differently? No one save Josie knew until a few weeks ago. It was hard to know what to think at that age. Had I been older, I might have been more rational, but I was also grieving for my mother. Then it became harder and harder to try to tell anyone. It was easier to push everyone away."

He gazed at her tenderly and spoke softly. "Believe it or not, I understand that. I feel much the same about the war. It is not the intimate violation that you experienced, but I feel emotionally violated." He looked off and made a noise in his throat. "Men are not supposed to feel these things."

"I understand. I think it just as difficult, only in a different way." She reached over and held his hand.

"Thank you for telling me." He looked back to her. He saw the tears of relief in her eyes and took her in his arms again. He placed his chin on her head and relished the feel of her in his arms. He longed to tell her how he felt, declare his love, but he did not dare until he knew he would make it through the Council unscathed. There was a chance he might not make it back at all, and though he thought she had feelings for him beyond friendship, he dare not tell her she owned his heart and make her burden worse.

"Elinor, I must warn you that things might not go well in London." He looked her in the eye to see if she understood. "There is a chance I might not make it back." He had just voiced his greatest fear out loud.

She swallowed visibly and spoke quietly. "I know."

"Promise me you will look after Father while I am gone—and if anything happens."

Elinor tried to interrupt. "Adam, please..." He held up his hand.

"I have sent for my sister, Olivia, to be brought home from school. My aunt will assist with her of course, but if you could help her through things as well. Olivia has not had a mother for years, and I am afraid if Max and Father and then..."

Hot tears poured down Elly's face again. "Please do not speak this way!"

"I need to know they will be looked after. Please." He cradled her face in his hands and leaned down to touch his forehead with hers.

Elinor nodded her acquiescence. "You know I would do anything for you."

"I do." He placed a chaste kiss on her lips, not willing to torment himself with anything more. They walked back into the house in silence. There was nothing more to say.

Elinor buried herself in riding and seeing to the needs of the Wyndham tenants, since she could hardly bear her own thoughts these days. She paid scant attention to her own needs. Eating held little appeal for her, and idle time was the devil for her morose thoughts to take hold. She had finally found a man she loved, who seemed willing to overlook her impurity, and now he might be tried for war crimes. To think he might be held accountable to hideous Colonel Knott, insufferable man! It should have been he, not General Ross whom the sniper's bullet found!

The hardest part of all would be spending time with the Earl, pretending to be happily besotted and betrothed as they planned the wedding that might never be, having to keep all of her worries to herself. The third day after Easton and her father left, Elinor made her way to visit the Earl as promised. Instead of being greeted with cheery anticipation of wedding bells, the Earl did not look well. His face was ashen and tired, and the drooping she had seen after one of his spells was more pronounced. He barely had the energy to greet her and had not actually spoken any words. After she greeted him, she excused herself to use the necessary, but instead found the butler and requested he send for the physician immediately.

She went back into the drawing room, and it appeared that the Earl had fallen asleep. Elinor took the liberty of drawing his feet up onto the couch, settling him with pillows and tucking a blanket around him. He opened his eyes and tried to smile at her. He reached out to grab her hand, and she met it with hers. His hands were clammy, which worried her further, and she reached up to feel his forehead to check for heat, as her mother had done when she had nursed Elinor as a child.

He felt feverish and began a coughing fit that seemed to start from deep within his chest. She pulled the bell rope and sent a footman off immediately to fetch Josie and her herbal remedy book, not knowing when the doctor would arrive. She then started penning a note to Easton, hoping that he would be able to return in time, for she feared the feeble Earl would not have the strength to fight off an inflammation of the lungs.

While she waited, she thought she might as well try to see what was happening with Lord Wyndham, even though she doubted her ability to help. Her knowledge was fairly limited to war wounds and mild ailments of the children from her village. "Lord Wyndham, can you tell me when this spell started?"

He opened his mouth to speak, but he struggled for his voice. Elinor held a glass of water to his lips, but swallowing, too, was a struggle. He did finally manage to say, "This morning," though even that was difficult to understand.

"Is this the same as your usual spells? You seem feverish, and you have quite a cough."

He shook his head, finding that easier than speech. Josie arrived with Elinor's bag of herbs, and Elinor sorted through them with a frown. At a loss for what to do, she decided on the willow bark, knowing it might at least help his fever. Perhaps the doctor would arrive shortly and take the decisions from her hands. By the time the doctor arrived, the Earl's fever seemed improved, and he was resting more comfortably.

"Good evening, sir." Elinor rose to greet Dr. McGinnis.

"I am pleased to finally meet the infamous Miss Abbott." He smiled pleasantly at her. She smiled in return, but was unsure about what he meant by infamous. Sensing her discomfort, he continued, "I beg your pardon, Miss Abbott. I was referring to your work with the smith— and Lord Easton, of course."

She blushed. "Oh, yes. Thank you, sir." Unused to praise, she quickly turned toward Lord Wyndham and recounted how she had found the Earl and had given him willow bark tea for his fever. The doctor examined and listened to the Earl, then sighed as his gaze came back to Elinor.

"It would appear you are correct that he seems to have an inflammation of the lungs. I will leave you some elderberry syrup, and, of course, continue with the willow bark. I expect we will have to wait and see, but with his recent spell, I am afraid this will be most difficult for him to fight in his already compromised condition. Is Lord Easton available? I feel I should speak with him."

Elinor shook her head. "He is away in London with war business. I found Lord Wyndham in this condition when I came for tea."

"I fear you should have him sent for. Shall you stay with him? He would benefit from someone with your expertize at his side, especially since his family is away." The doctor then directed some footmen to carry the feeble Earl to his chambers.

"Of course. I would not think of leaving." Not yet, anyway.

~

Easton felt wretched as he sat through yet another day of dreadfully mundane testimonies at the War Council. He could not focus on anything that was being said, and he had no desire to relive any of it— the strategy, the battle, or the aftermath. The last thing he had wanted to do was to come to London. The last person he had wanted to see was Colonel Knott. For some reason, he had a sick feeling about leaving home, and the feeling had only grown as they went further from Sussex. His father had not looked well, and, of course, he had left without declaring himself to Elinor, never mind the fact he was finding it difficult not to obsess about murdering Nathaniel.

He refocused his gaze back toward the proceedings and felt the hair stand on his neck as he watched Knott take his place to begin his testimony. Catching his scrutiny, the Colonel cast a pointed stare at Easton. His pulse raced; a bilious taste pervaded his mouth. He saw his future flash before his eyes as he heard Knott began to recount his version of Easton defying his orders and trying to draw the troops to his side contradicting his commands. *This could not be happening,* he thought. *This could not be happening.* Of course Knott was giving his side and making Easton look as black as possible. Sir Charles reached over and touched his arm in a reassuring way, but it did not ease the panic growing inside of him. Several members of the committee glanced over at Easton from time to time throughout the testimony with questioning eyebrows, but none interrupted Knott.

Easton did his best to keep his face impassive, unaffected. He sneaked glances at the faces of those who would be his judge and jury. Many of them were familiar to him, whether having served with them, or having association through society. Easton could only hope that Sir Charles' testimony would save him, because Knott's testimony as he gave it would utterly damn him.

After Knott was satisfied with his recollections of the battle against Washington, the Council decided to adjourn for lunch. When they returned, the presiding general took his seat. He looked directly at Easton and indicated for him to stand. Easton promptly stood at attention.

"Major Easton, due to the testimony by one of your superior officers, Colonel Knott, we feel there is enough to warrant a trial. You are hereby ordered for court-martial. We will resume three days hence in order to allow you time to prepare your case. You will be released into the care of Colonel Sir Charles Abbott due to your impeccable record of service. You may not leave London. Do you understand?"

"Yes, sir."

"Very well. We are adjourned until then."

Easton should not have felt shocked; he had known this was coming. But he did. He felt shock and despair. He had never before had anyone that he wanted to live this much for.

CHAPTER 19

*A*s Elinor started awake to another of the Earl's coughing fits, she wondered if this attack would be the last. The convulsions wracking his body and the sounds emanating from his chest would overtake the strongest of men, let alone this frail man debilitated by years of spells and sorrow. She spooned some elderberry syrup into his mouth, and he finally managed to swallow it and settle back down. She refilled the pot of water placed over the hearth to moisten the air and hopefully ease the cough, then soaked another rag to place over his forehead to lessen the fever. Elinor stood watching over this sweet man who was the father of the man she loved. She felt helpless to save him just as she had when standing near her mother's deathbed, years ago. Tears welled up in her eyes, and she tried not to let herself give up on him.

Elinor could not help but think about the promise she and Easton had made to him, and how delighted he had been at the thought of their marriage and his future grandchildren. She choked back a sob and went over to stare out of the window at the gardens ensconced in moonlight. Elinor willed herself to be strong, and not to grow melancholy over the what-ifs, the what-would-never-bes, or the what-might-have-beens. She had received the message from her father that the War Council was proceeding with a court-martial. She wanted to scream! This could not be happening when she finally had a glimpse of happiness in her life again. She had to hold on to the hope that her father's testimony would be enough.

At least things had gone well with facing Nathaniel. She was grateful for the peace she had gained from having faced Nathaniel and told her secret. Now she had found a man she was comfortable with, a man she loved, and it might have to be enough. She never would have thought so much possible. She began pacing across the carpet, growing more and more concerned Easton would not make it back in time to see his father—or at all.

Whatever could be taking them so long? Had the messenger not been able to find them? Surely they could not be so cruel as to forbid him leave when his father was deathly ill? Realizing her fretting was not helping matters, she sat herself on the settee next to the Earl's bed, with a prayer that he could last until Easton made it home.

The three days of house arrest in London was torture. He would rather be in a battlefield without food or shelter, fighting off twenty of the fiercest warriors, than play this never-ending waiting game. He had not even been allowed to present his side of the story before the court-martial was announced. Then he had received the letter from Elly, stating his father was not expected to live. Not only would he not be with his father when he died, he would not even be able to take over for him. He could not even allow himself to think about Elinor, for the pain was beyond bearable.

The third day finally arrived, and Sir Charles and Easton made their way into the courtroom. The general started the proceeding by reading Major Easton his rights and how they were to proceed. Easton would be allowed to present his case first. Easton trembled with nervousness and anger that this was happening, but took a deep breath and prepared to begin. He gathered his papers in front of him and cleared his throat.

Before Easton spoke, Sir Charles requested permission to address the court. The general looked up in surprise. "This is highly unusual."

"I am able to provide firsthand witness to the attack." Easton looked to Knott, who immediately paled. Then it was true he was unaware of Sir Charles' presence that night. The General who was overseeing the proceedings looked astonished by Sir Charles' pronouncement.

"I was unaware of your presence on the battlefield that night, Sir Charles. However, the charges that Colonel Knott brings against Major Easton are serious indeed, and quite contrary to Easton's prior record of dedication and bravery to the Crown, not to mention the earldom he is soon to inherit. I welcome any account that will verify these claims."

"But he is Easton's godfather! Easton is betrothed to his daughter!" Knott could not contain his outburst. "Sir Charles is hardly unbiased!"

"Enough, Colonel! You insult this court! We shall hear the testimony and decide for ourselves. You undermine yourself with your outburst. You yourself will be held in contempt if it occurs again."

Knott's face was reddish-purple, and his veins were visibly pulsing, but he sat down and held his tongue. Sir Charles rose and handed some parchment to the General, then returned to his seat.

"I was concerned this might occur after witnessing the events that night. I took the liberty of having each soldier who observed the events write his account if able; some are dictated. You will notice that General Ross's account is included, God rest his soul."

Several of the members gasped and looked to the Colonel, who was in a visible rage. He continued to hold his tongue, however. The general spoke quietly to the other members of the court.

"We will adjourn these proceedings so the court may read these accounts. Normally we would require testimony in person, and some of the soldiers may be required to do so. However, that is not possible with Ross, therefore, we will read these accounts, then hear from Sir Charles and Major Easton as required."

The court adjourned, and it was over three hours before they were called back in to the session—three hours of complete hell for

Easton. The General cleared his throat and looked pointedly at Easton, Sir Charles, then Knott. Easton tried not to squirm. He felt as a child standing before the headmaster at Eton, awaiting his lashes.

"Colonel Knott, it seems that your account is remarkably different from that of Sir Charles and General Ross, in addition to a dozen other well-respected soldiers. Major Easton's record of eight years also reflects the accounts of these officers. I assume, were we to ask Major Easton to remove his shirt so we may witness the gunshot wound to his back, that these accounts would be verified." He looked to Easton, who nodded.

"The actions as you describe would have been a complete reversal of character for him and his service record. Major Lord Easton has already decided to resign his commission to take over his duties for the Earl of Wyndham, and there is no evidence to support your claims, only refute them. Therefore, we dismiss your charges against Major Lord Easton." He turned to Easton. "Lord Easton, we accept your resignation and we thank you for your years of service. You may go."

Easton let out the breath he had not realized he was holding. He would not even be required to take the stand! He nodded and saluted to the court. "Thank you, sir." Taking his elbow, Sir Charles led him from the room, then shook his hand as soon as they were through the doors. He felt an enormous surge of relief knowing the ordeal was over with. They made their way to await their carriage.

"Well, what a pleasant turn of events. I am shocked he pursued you, but all is as it should be now. Shall we try to make our way back this evening?" Sir Charles was utterly serene, as if Easton's neck had not been on the line a quarter hour past. Easton shook his head in disbelief.

"I was fairly certain that Knott would seek revenge. It is a character trait in the prideful. I am unbelievably grateful for Ross, and your foresight to have written it all down." He felt a wave of sadness for his mentor, Ross.

"I cannot take full credit. After sending you back to the plantation,

I consulted Ross, and I thought it best to have it written, not knowing what can happen from one battle to the next."

"Thank God for that." Neither one spoke aloud of where Easton would be now if he had not. They settled in the carriage and journeyed south toward the country.

"Well. Now that disagreeable business is over with, what are you going to do about Elly?"

Easton tried not to choke on Sir Charles's bluntness.

"I only want what is best for her. I want her to be happy, and I will not force her to marry me," he said with determination, trying to convince himself as well. He desperately hoped she had not changed her mind.

"Your father might." Easton chuckled despite his fear his father would not live to see them wed. He prayed he was not too late to say goodbye. Easton nodded, and they fell into silence as the countryside passed by.

Easton watched out of the window anxiously, as they pulled onto the drive of the estate, for any indications they might be too late. Thankfully, he detected no signs of mourning, but the dawn was only beginning to hint over the horizon. The staff might not yet be aware if something had happened. After being delayed several hours by sudden, torrential rains and muddy roads, Easton was beyond relieved when the carriage finally pulled to a stop outside the manor house. He alighted as fast as he could and ran into the house, barely managing a greeting to Hendricks. He made it to his father's chambers and stopped himself in time to catch his breath and prepare for what he might see.

He eased the door to the sitting room open, then peeked into his father's chamber, where the door was slightly ajar. The Earl was still on the bed, and Easton pushed the door open, his pulse beating frantically, and rushed to his father's side and grasped his hand. He breathed a huge sigh of relief when the hand was still warm. He felt the hand gently squeeze against his then looked to his father's face to see him awake with a lopsided smile. The Earl tried to hold up a finger to say *shh*, and indicated toward Elinor sleeping next to his bed. Easton glanced over in surprise to see an exhausted and dishevelled Elinor looking more beautiful than ever. He nodded in acknowledgement and leaned over to whisper.

"Are you feeling better then, Father? I came as soon as I could." The Earl nodded weakly but did not speak. "Is there anything I can do for you?" The Earl shook his head. Easton looked sceptical, unsure of what to do, but overwhelmed to find his father alive.

Elinor began to stir and sat up with sleep in her eyes and dark circles under them. Seeing the Earl awake, she shot straight up and rushed to his side. "My lord! You are awake!" She quickly put her hand to his head, then sank back down next to him with visible relief. "Oh, thank God. Easton should be home soon."

The Earl's eyes moved over to his son, and Elinor's followed his gaze. She jumped when she saw Easton had been there some time. Her gaze locked with his, and she lit up the room with her smile.

"Welcome home, my lord. I am most happy to say it looks as if my note was premature."

"Miss Elinor." He nodded his head in acknowledgement. "As am I." She looked incredibly beautiful in her dishevelled state, it was all he could do not to scoop her up and run away with her. With a small knock, Sir Charles poked his head around the door. He came over and greeted his friend.

"I cannot say how pleased I am to see you awake, old friend." The Earl managed a smile, but still did not speak.

"Miss Abbott, can you tell us what happened?" Easton asked, concerned that his father was not talking. Elinor explained how she had found the Earl weak with fever. The doctor had visited several times and said the Earl had an inflammation of the lungs, and she had been giving the Earl the infusions the doctor had prescribed.

"Have you not left his side, Miss Abbott?"

She looked offended he would ask such a thing, not answering. She turned away and began preparing medicines for the Earl. She heard a small chuckle from him, which brought on another round of coughing. She reached over and pulled him back up from where he had slipped during the night and directed them to prop him up with pillows while she gave him some more cough syrup and barley water.

"Well, it seems you were made for doctoring." Easton smiled at her. "I am most grateful, as I am sure Father is." The Earl reached out his hand to hers, and then Easton's. He held them together, and Elinor attempted to still the trembling. The Earl cleared his throat to speak. Elinor tried to discourage him from speaking, but he shook his head insistently. All they could do was wait. Eventually, he was able to get out the word, "Wedding."

Elinor could not help but glance at Easton. She froze for a moment, then smiled a little. He squeezed his father's hand, and then he chuckled. Elinor released the breath she had been holding.

"Patience, Father. Elinor is exhausted, and you have only awakened. We will speak of this once everyone is rested." The Earl looked as if he were about to protest, but then looked to Elinor and nodded.

Sir Charles and Elly left, promising to visit later to see about the Earl. For the first time, Easton was able to breathe easily. His father was better, and he was free. Now would Elly want to marry him? He hoped so, because he did not think he could live without her.

Sir Charles wrapped his arm around Elinor and kissed her head, as they walked silently back to the Dower House. She felt as though she was sleepwalking by the time they crossed the threshold. Josie hurried in to assist her, but she did not remember much past the blissful feeling of her head meeting the pillow.

Sir Charles was to escort her back to Wyndham Court later that morning, and Easton joined them shortly after their arrival.

After the usual greetings, Elinor voiced her concern for the Earl, "How is your father now?" It had only been a few hours since they had left, but she knew fevers could return with a vengeance.

"Dare I say better? He is almost chatty, fussing about the wedding."

They exchanged glances and she could not read what was in his eyes. Nervousness?

"I forgot to enquire how the trial went in London. I assume your presence is a good sign?" She could not believe she had been too tired to ask. She had been relieved to see him and for the Earl to have broken his fever.

"Better than I had hoped." Easton paused to gather his thoughts, but Sir Charles interjected first.

"I was not expecting Knott to attempt revenge, the arrogant traitor. Clearly, he thought himself above reproach and had no idea there had been witnesses to his atrocities. Gentleman indeed," Sir Charles scoffed.

"I was not surprised to receive the note that you had been court-martialled," Elinor said shaking her head. "I was afraid he would do something of the sort. Men like that think they can do no wrong. Obviously something convinced the council of your innocence, or you would not be here."

"Aye. Your father." She nodded as if it were just as she suspected. "I did not even have to testify after he produced written accounts from multiple witnesses."

"Thank goodness." They all nodded, then fell silent. They finished their tea, and Sir Charles stood and announced he was off to visit Wyndham, which left Elinor and Easton awkwardly alone.

"Would you care to take another walk? I believe we have a conversation to continue."

She nodded and wrapped her arm through his. It felt good to have him back. "I am relieved everything was resolved with Colonel Knott. I hope he receives his just desserts. Also, with your father's health. I cannot tell you how worried I was."

He stopped and turned to face her. "I am sure it has been horrible for you. I know how it felt being there, unable to do anything for myself or knowing if Father was still alive." He sighed. "Elinor, I will not prolong my point. I love you no matter what happened and want you to stay—here, with me, as my wife. I want no more pretending." She laughed, then sobered. He noticed the change. He watched the emotions play out on her face. "We can even go back to America to visit?" he pleaded, trying to convince her. Now she looked away.

"Easton, I am not sure if…" She let the thought trail away. She did not know if she could talk about it. They were quiet a few moments. He seemed to realize what her hesitation was. They walked out to the gardens and sat down on a bench.

"Elinor, are you afraid of me?"

She shook her head. "No."

"Are you afraid of touching me?" It suddenly occurred to him, though the fact she thought he would force her hurt a bit. Did she not realize what they would experience would be completely different from what happened to her before?

She took a deep breath. She did not want to say it, but she knew she had to. "I—I am concerned." She hesitated. "But, I do not feel nauseous around you."

"That's encouraging," he said dryly.

She chuckled nervously, hoping she could explain. "I mean, if a gentleman tries to touch me, I feel ill. I do not feel that way with you."

He took both of her hands in his. She looked up and held his gaze. "Elinor, I promise you, I will never push you further than you are comfortable with. Even if it means my father never has any grandchildren, then so be it. I only want you to be happy. And I will take whatever part of you that you are willing to give me." *And hope that I can be worthy of you.*

"Is such a thing even possible? I thought a man had to, to…" She gulped, unable to say the words.

He laughed. "We are not all controlled by our baser urges. That is not to say I would not be very happy if you were to oblige them from time to time."

She laughed nervously then stared boldly at his mouth. She leaned over and kissed him tentatively.

He pulled back gently, pleasantly surprised. "Are you feeling ill?" She shook her head. "Good." He took her face in his hands and drew her lips to his again, kissing longer and deeper, leaving them both breathless.

"How are you now?" he asked catching his breath.

"I feel dizzy," she said trying to reorient herself while feeling new sensations inside.

"It means we did it properly." She thought about it, then a smile spread across her face.

"Adam, can we do it again?" He laughed.

"As much as you like. However, I think for now we had best oblige my father and hold the wedding. Now."

CHAPTER 20

*B*y the time the two made it back to the house from their walk hand in hand, the Earl and Sir Charles were ensconced in deep conversation near the blazing fire. The Earl looked up at their approach with a lopsided grin spread from ear to ear. Sir Charles also appeared pleased, with a twinkle in his eyes.

"Are the two of you ready at last?" Adam and Elinor looked up at each other. What did he know? Adam shrugged one shoulder up.

The Earl raised an eyebrow, and then did his best attempt at a stern look while crossing his arms over his chest. It made him look innocuous at best. "Did you think I did not know something was afoot?"

Elinor chuckled at his feigned reprimand.

He carried on, "Your feelings for each other are obvious to everyone else; I am glad the two of you finally came to realize them."

So he had known all along, the conniver.

"My favourite part was the look on her face when I made you propose and kiss."

Elinor gasped and sat back on the settee. Adam sat *right* next to her.

"Oh, I knew, Father. The hard part was convincing Elinor." His betrothed looked up at him, incredulity written on her face. "I did not properly thank you for arranging the lovely scene that day." She gave him a good shove with her elbow. He merely laughed and rubbed the soon-to-be-bruised area. The Earl returned to business, ignoring their banter.

"I have already sent for the bishop. He should be here in two days with the licence." *Two days?* The Earl responded to her jaw hanging ajar. "Yes, dear, the rest of us have been waiting for months. I think I have been quite patient, considering." The frail Earl gestured at his frail body as if that were explanation enough.

"Perhaps I should be allowed to ask my godfather for permission first, Father?" Easton interjected.

Sir Charles chimed in, shaking his head. "Nonsense, Adam. You have my permission and my blessing." They crossed the space and embraced each other.

Elinor held back tears. She suddenly had a longing for her mother to be there. The Earl reached over and squeezed her hand as if he sensed her thoughts.

"I think a nice wedding, here at Wyndham Court, would be just the thing. Hopefully, your grandmother has finished all of the arrangements by now."

"Of that I have no doubt. I expected her to be scheming, not you." This produced another wide grin.

"The two of you had best go inform your grandmother and brother." He shooed them away and turned back to Sir Charles as if nothing of significance had occurred. *Rascal.*

"We have been mere puppets in this show all along, my dear," Easton whispered loudly and kissed her on the temple. The two older gentlemen *giggled.*

"Apparently," Elinor agreed. He proffered her a gallant arm, and they left for the Dower House.

On a cold but sunny January day, as the sun glistened off the crystals in the snow, she peeked out of her bedroom window. She could not believe this day was real. Easton actually wanted to marry her, in spite of her past. She had found someone who did not hold her past against her. She thought about how she and Adam had been brought together through connections, trials and tribulations—and she knew there must have been divine intervention. Some called it fate, some coincidence, but Elinor knew it all to be the same thing.

She smiled at a few lone snowflakes falling through the sun, and she felt her mother's presence with her, a pervasive sense of peace and rightness. She opened her window to catch the chill on her face and held out a hand to provide a perch for some of the snow crystals. She shivered despite the exhilaration she felt, and she pulled her dressing gown tighter. A gentle knock broke her out of her reflection, and her grandmother peered around the door.

"Good morning, dear."

"Good morning, Grandmama." She pulled the windows closed and crossed the room to greet her grandmother with a kiss on the cheek.

"I do not know how you can stand the cold. It seems as if it goes straight through to my bones at my age." Her grandmother shivered and walked toward the fire. "I came to see if you needed anything." Josie sauntered in behind her with a tray of hot chocolate and scones and deposited them on the table next to the settee. She bobbed a curtsy, winked at Elinor and promised to be back soon with her bath.

"I cannot think of anything, Gran. I am remarkably calm for such a day. It feels so right." And it did. She had not felt this happy since her mother was alive.

"I cannot tell you how relieved I am to hear you say that. I know Adam to be a wonderful man, but I was afraid we had pushed you into what we wanted, with selfish motives." Elinor shook her head in protest. "I find I have grown a conscience over this matter overnight."

"Please do not feel that way, Gran. I know you all want what is best for me. I promise I could not have been *pushed* into this if I was not willing." Sitting on the settee, the Dowager sat next to her and reached for a cup of chocolate.

"I know you must feel the absence of Elizabeth greatly today." She paused to gather her emotion. "And I know Sarah would be here if she could, but you must be satisfied with me for now." She held up her hand to stop Elinor's protest. "I also know the last thing you want to hear from an old woman is advice on the marriage bed." Elinor giggled and turned pink. Her grandmother winked back at her. "However, I do want to impart a few bits of advice."

All Elinor could say was, "Oh." *Please, no mental pictures.* She had hoped to be spared the little talk most ladies received before their marriage.

"Firstly, the experience with someone you love or even *lust* for will be completely different from your unfortunate incident with Nathaniel." *Leave it to Gran to not skirt around the issue.*

"Secondly, relax and try to enjoy yourself." *Of course. Relax.* She nodded her head.

"Thirdly, use your imagination." The Dowager cocked her eyebrow and smiled a knowing smile. *That was all she was going to say?*

"That is all?" Thank God it was over.

"Yes, Adam will teach you what you need to know." Elinor choked on her chocolate. Her grandmother laughed and then gave her a hug before departing. Josie entered with bath water, more excited than Elinor.

After bathing and dressing her hair, Josie pulled a cream coloured gown from the dressing room, and Elinor let out a gasp when she saw the dress.

"Is that...my mother's wedding gown?" She rushed over to touch the familiar gown she had seen her mother in daily in one of the few portraits she had of her, "I had not even thought of what Grandmama had picked out for me to wear. Oh, it is even more beautiful in reality!" She lovingly fingered the silver- knotted buttons that adorned the layers of silk.

Josie helped her into the gown, and Elinor felt dreamy as she was enveloped in the same gown her mother had worn to marry her father. She could not have felt more perfect. Josie placed her mother's pearls about her neck, then after one last glance, she hurried down the stairs to where her father was waiting to take her to the church.

She was wrapped in an ermine cape and a furry muff for the brief ride. A sleigh awaited them to pull Elinor and her father to the church. "A sleigh! How wonderful, Papa!"

"Your mother was brought to St. Christopher's in this sleigh as well. The Duke had it built for our wedding. It only seemed fitting. It does not get much use in Sussex." She climbed in and held her father's hand as she looked up to the heavens, feeling her mother's presence blessing her this day.

"I feel her with us, Papa." Until now, she had managed to hold tears at bay, but sitting in her mother's wedding gown, in her sleigh, on her way to be wed at the same church, with her father at her side, the tears flowed.

"She would be proud of her beautiful daughter." Her papa was struggling to hold his own tears back. "Your papa is more than proud of you." He handed her a handkerchief with a smile and a hug.

"Oh, Papa. I know. I love you."

He barely managed, "You too," while struggling to maintain his composure.

As they pulled into the churchyard, Elinor could not help but smile as she saw all the children from the orphanage lined up in matching dresses and suits. They could not control their excitement when they noticed the horse-drawn sleigh pull up. Elinor was beyond pleased that they could attend and have a nice holiday from London. She would make sure they enjoyed themselves later.

As she was handed down from the sleigh, the children each handed her a white rose and curtsied before her, then went into the church. The two littlest girls, one being Adam's little Susie, preceded Josie into the church, tossing rose petals everywhere. Elinor could hear the chuckles from those gathered inside. Then Josie sauntered down the aisle. Elinor could only imagine the huge smile on her face. It was finally her turn. As the door opened, she took a deep breath and was surprised at the crowd gathered in the church. She should have known her grandmother would make it a grand affair. She tried not to think about everyone staring at her. As her papa led her down the aisle, she barely heard the music or saw the familiar faces of the villagers. She did notice her grandmother wiping her eyes with a handkerchief, the Duke smiling proudly at her, and Nathaniel standing next to him as if to remind her that this was right. She realized she had forgiven him, and it felt right. Forgiveness was a beautiful thing indeed.

The Earl sat in his pew on the other side, smiling bright enough to light the church. She was delighted to please him, but not half as delighted as she was to be marrying the man standing behind them at the front of the church, next to the vicar, her brother and Buffy. She finally dared look up at Adam, having consciously not looked for fear she would not be able to walk up the aisle.

He was more stunning than usual, if possible, in black tail coat, with a silver waistcoat and snowy white neckcloth. He held out his hand to her, then handed her a single red rose. Love. Her father placed her hand in his and told Adam there was not anyone else he would rather give her to. Elinor remembered little else of the ceremony, except that it was over blessedly fast.

After the wedding, she was finally able to relax and truly laugh again. She felt a peace that she had never known before. It was wonderful to feel herself again. She knew she still had a major obstacle to overcome, but she was not worried about facing it with Adam. Somehow she knew it would be different with him. She was even a bit curious and excited.

The wedding breakfast at Wyndham Court was a virtual feast. She finally was able to see everyone she had not noticed at the church and was surprised how many had travelled for the ceremony. She fleetingly wondered to herself how long ago her grandmother and the Earl had set the date, as she spied Andrew dancing with one of the triplets, and Buffy and Josie enjoying themselves in a set. She sensed a pattern there.

There did not seem to be any particular type of dances occurring with the children about. It seemed like a reel-waltz-cotillion with giggles and joviality. The girls held hands and turned in circles while the adults tried a modified waltz. She turned and laughed as she watched the children dancing, particularly Susie as she held on for dear life to Adam with her feet atop his. If he had not already captured her heart, she would have lost it then.

"Can you spare a dance for your old papa?" Elinor turned and saw her father standing there watching her.

"I think I can arrange that." She took his proffered hand, and he led her to a safe spot on the floor.

"What is next for you, Papa? Are you able to stay here a while?"

"Perhaps, though I want you and Adam to have some time to yourselves without all of us interfering old folk." She made a playful face.

"Where will you settle down? We would love to have you here, of course."

"I have not decided anything other than it is time to move on. I could go to London, or maybe back to the country when the tenants move out, though I am not sure I want to live there again." He paused. "And, I am not so old yet."

"Of course you are not old, Papa!" she interjected. He chuckled.

"But I am not a spring chicken either. Your mother's love and companionship were everything to me. I truly felt like part of me died with her. Nevertheless, I know she would be disappointed in me for dwelling in the past for so long. So, henceforth I am determined to live each day for that day and see what happens."

Elinor smiled up at him. "I think there is a lesson in it for all of us, Papa." She embraced him and he led her over to Adam, who was surrounded by doting children.

"Pardon me, everyone, but if you will allow me one dance with my beautiful wife, then we will go outdoors for snowball fights and sleigh rides before we return for chocolate."

The news was met with loud cheers from the children, and Adam grabbed hold of Elinor and whisked her off to the dance floor.

"Finally, I have you to myself for a moment. Even if I had to bribe the children."

She looked up at him adoringly and laughed. "You love every minute of it, and you know it."

He smiled lovingly back at her and twirled her around. "How does it feel to be Lady Easton?"

"Surprisingly good, though I believe I prefer Mrs. Trowbridge."

"Surprisingly? Should I be offended?" He raised his eyebrows in mock indignation.

She slapped him playfully on the arm. "No, you should take it the good way."

He chuckled. "Marriage lesson number one noted." He twirled her again. Buffy and Josie were still dancing. "It looks like there will be another marriage soon."

"Yes, she found her handsome beau." Elinor smiled wistfully.

"I am glad to have been of service." He made a small half bow while dancing.

"Yes, it worked out nicely. You did not have to go to so much trouble to introduce them though."

"Noted for the future." He pulled her closer and continued to swirl her around. Nathaniel and one of the triplets passed them and smiled greetings. When they were back across the room, Adam inquired about the situation. "How are you feeling about things with Nathaniel? I am still unsure of how I ought to react, myself."

"I feel relieved it is over with. Although I suppose there will still be Beatrice to deal with somehow."

"Where is the termagant?" He made a half-hearted effort to scan the room.

"She conveniently has a head cold." Meaning her father would not let her ruin another day for Elinor.

"Ah." He pulled her closer and revelled in having her in his arms for the remainder of the dance, letting everything else around them fade away. When the music stopped he did not let go, and there were chuckles all around them.

They heard a spoon clinking against a glass and looked up to see her father, the Duke and the Earl on the dais ready to make a toast. A footman handed them flutes of champagne and watched as the Earl was lowered into his chair and rolled over to them.

"I will not bore you all with long speeches. I shall only say I am ever grateful that I was able to witness this wonderful event, and I could not be happier. Now here are the keys to the cottage, my son. I do not want to see you for at least two weeks. You have grandchildren to make!" He made shooing motions indicating that he meant straight away.

She felt her cheeks burning with embarrassment. There was no good response, except, perhaps, to empty her glass. She handed her glass to a footman, then felt Adam pulling her towards the door. They made hasty farewells, ensured certain Andrew would see to entertaining the children, and then she was packed into a carriage.

As they made it into the woods toward the cottage, Elinor nestled in close to Adam. He raised an arm to allow her to snuggle in close. "Am I to assume this means you do not find touching my person offensive, Mrs. Trowbridge?" He smiled and wiggled an eyebrow at her.

She looked up with her big green eyes and with an equally mischievous grin. "You assume correctly, Mr. Trowbridge." And, he was correct. And so was everyone who had told her that when she found the right man, she would not be afraid.

Adam took that as a good sign and tapped on the roof of the carriage for the driver to make haste.

PREVIEW SEASONS OF CHANGE

As Beatrice watched Elinor and her betrothed flee in opposite directions, she felt rather pleased that her plan had come to fruition effortlessly. Until she felt a large hand grab her and spin her around. Her brother stood over her, eyes blazing with fury. She then noticed the music had stopped, and the crowd stood still watching her every move. Bother!

Nathaniel hissed through clenched teeth, "Smile and walk off the floor with me before Father throws you over his shoulder."

Beatrice glared, but walked with him, her head held high. She was not going to cower away with her tail between her legs. Nathaniel led her into the library and shut the door behind them. He crossed his arms over his chest and glared at her without a word. She refused to back down. "Well?"

"Do you care to explain yourself, Bea?" he asked calmly. "You'd better come up with an explanation before Father finds out and wrings your neck."

"I did nothing wrong." She crossed her arms over her chest and held her head high.

"Nothing wrong? You think this is all about you? I am beyond disgusted. I do not know what happened to you while I was away, but I am ashamed to call you my sister at this moment"

"Well, that is the pot calling the kettle black. You have no right to judge me!" She threw up her hands haughtily. A duke's heir could get away with murder, and she was being reprimanded for this?

"I understand how you feel, but I know of what I speak. You are heading down the same path I did. In fact, I might recommend Father implement the same treatment for you." Nathaniel began to pace the floor in front of the fire.

"As if I could join the army." Beatrice walked over and laughed in his face. "Do you think you are protecting your beloved? She has eyes only for Easton, you idiot!"

He stopped and towered over her. "You have no idea, do you?" He placed his hands on her shoulders and looked her in the eye. He hesitated then said quietly, "Bea, I violated Elly."

"Do not be ridiculous!" Beatrice retorted.

"I am in earnest, Bea," Nathaniel said sombrely.

Beatrice stood there as if she had been slapped, too stunned for words. "V-violated?" She slumped down into the chair behind her, and her face fell into her hands. "Oh, God, what have I done?" She had wanted to put Elinor back in her place when she thought her loose and pretending to be something she was not.

"You cannot toy with people like they are game pieces, Bea. What changed you into this malicious scheming shrew while I was gone? I want to keep anyone from hurting her more. That is the least I can do."

She shook her head. That angered her. She did not try to suppress the indignation building within. "Pray, do not imagine to understand how it was for me when you left!" She stood and marched toward the windows then spun around back to face him. "Father has never recovered from having to send you away. I was never a substitute for you. Then, he wanted me to be like her! He paid no attention to me, and I was left with Mother."

He scoffed. "Like mother, like daughter." He shook his head. "Bea, you cannot use Mother as an excuse. You and I have both wronged

Elinor, and I plan to spend the rest of my life trying to make it up to her."

She still did not speak. He sighed. "You'd best consider what to say to Father. At this point, you will be fortunate if he does not send you to a convent."

A booming voice resounded from the doorway, "I think a convent is an excellent idea."

The Duke entered the room calmly and sat in his chair behind the desk. He was eerily silent. He was never silent. He stared at Beatrice for what felt like eternity, and then finally spoke.

"Beatrice, best you go to your room. We will discuss this in the morning."

She stood there, shocked into silence for a moment, unable to believe what she had heard. Never before had he dismissed her without a lecture. Too afraid to protest, she meekly obeyed without further eye contact.

〜

Nathaniel closed the door behind Beatrice and waited to see if his father wished for his presence or not. The Duke looked up and waved him into a chair.

"Do you think a convent will make any difference?" The Duke looked as miserable as he felt. He did not even have to ask Nathaniel what Beatrice had done. "I still cannot fathom how you managed to become so disguised that you forced yourself upon Elly in the first place. And now your sister is so demented she thinks to ruin Elly further," the Duke said as he continued staring into the fire.

"The army managed to reform me. I think Bea must feel true pain in order to have a chance at seeing what she has done and surmise there is a world beyond herself." Nathaniel knew this from personal experience.

"Pray tell, where did I go wrong? You have had the best of every-thing, and this is the thanks I receive in return." He shook his head in dismay. "If you were not the only heir, I would send you back. I still cannot believe I urged her to marry you." That was as near as the Duke ever came to admitting he was wrong.

"I will work the rest of my days to be worthy of her forgiveness. No one regrets what happened more than I. I can never take away what I did, and I have to live with that," Nathaniel said quietly.

The Duke looked back at him with pain in his eyes. There was a soft knock at the door, and the Duke waved Nathaniel over to answer, too choked to speak. Lord Vernon followed him back into the room.

"My lord." Vernon made a quick bow.

"I suppose you do not want Beatrice any more, either. Cannot say that I blame you." The Duke sighed loudly. "Nathaniel thinks we should send her to a convent," he said resignedly, looking to Vernon to give his opinion.

Nothing could have astonished Vernon more than the thought of Beatrice in a convent. They sat in silence a few moments, then Lord Vernon looked up. "Perhaps there is another way. It is just shy of a convent, but Easton has convinced me to start another orphanage up at my Scottish property. I use it as a hunting box mostly, but it is well enough. Perhaps she could help out there. See the less fortunate and all that."

Nathaniel laughed mockingly. "How would we keep her there? She would be on the first equipage that rode by."

"No chance of that. The place is so remote you cannot find it unless you know it is there. Even Bea would not dare run away from there, especially in the winter. And my spinster aunt Mary lives there. She can look after her."

"Do you honestly think it would work?" The Duke looked sceptical.

"We have to hope there is still a shred of decency left." Vernon walked over and stared into the fire.

"She has no choice but to understand the delicacy of her situation. She has already defied me once. I will not condone this behaviour any longer," the Duke said, clearly out of patience.

"I must say she seemed shocked when I told her the truth of what happened," Nathaniel interjected in Beatrice's defence.

"May I speak to her before she goes?" Vernon asked the Duke.

"Are you sure you wish to do so, Vernon?" the Duke asked, surprised.

"Considering I have been planning to marry her since the nursery, I think I should at least say goodbye," Vernon pointed out.

"Very well. I am going to inform her of her fate in the morning. You may see her then," the Duke consented.

Beatrice walked to her room in shock. If she could reverse the last few hours—no months—she would. Why had not anyone ever told her what happened? Elly had been violated? By Nathaniel? Beatrice could not believe her brother capable of such an atrocity, even though he had certainly sown his wild oats before going into the army. So many things began to fall into place when she thought back. Beatrice felt ill to the core of her being, suffered pangs of conscience she had thought long gone. A tear of remorse fell down her cheek. She knew her father would send her to a convent. She had never seen him so angry, so quiet. She had no idea what would become of her there, or what she would be expected to do.

Even though Beatrice knew she had done Elly an injustice, it was still hard to swallow her pride. When she thought about what Nathaniel had done, the offences were incomparable and it brought back all of the old hurts from her childhood. She determined she would take whatever punishment he doled out and not flinch. If she was on her best behaviour, she would be able to come back soon. She would prove them wrong. She would.

The next morning, the dreaded talk with her father arrived. Beatrice had just received the summons. She had barely managed to sleep at all, knowing she had been awful, but not knowing what to do to make things right. There were some things that could not be forgotten. She glanced in the looking glass and saw dark circles and red, swollen eyes. Jenny helped her into a dress and pulled her hair back without so much as a word or look in the eye. She walked slowly through the house with an impending sense of doom.

Beatrice knocked on the door to the library, and then entered quietly at her father's command. She stood alone before him, her mother noticeably absent.

"Sit." He was still eerily quiet. She did as she was ordered.

The Duke looked as if he had been up all night, but he had taken the time to change clothes and shave. "I only have one question. What inspired this change of heart in you?" He looked long and hard at her, searching for the answer. She remained silent. What good would it do to answer anyway?

After several minutes of silence, the Duke stood and walked over to the window. When he finally spoke, he did so quietly without looking at her. "First, you will write and apologize to Elinor. I will not force her to suffer your presence." Beatrice looked up in surprise, though she should not have been. "Secondly, you will release Lord Vernon from your betrothal. He deserves better." Beatrice looked away trying to hide the tears. This was worse than she had ever imagined it would be, and she could tell he was not finished yet. "Thirdly, you will leave all of your possessions, save two dresses. I recommend something warm since it gets quite cold where you are going." She felt a deep sense of foreboding when he uttered those words. "Lastly, Lord Vernon has asked to speak with you, though I cannot pretend to know why. The carriage will be ready to leave in one hour." He walked out the door without a look backwards, never asking for her side of the story, assuming the worst.

She sat in stunned silence. Though she should have expected nothing less. He never had affection for her like he did for her cousin and brother. At least she had held her tongue. She would not humiliate herself further. She looked up and Rhys, Lord Vernon, stood there before her. He looked hurt, disappointed. She dropped her eyes to her hands, unable to meet his gaze.

"Why, Bea?" he asked so quietly she could barely hear him.

She shook her head but did not look up. She did not want him to see the tears. She could not bring herself to admit to him that she was jealous.

"I have lost my best friend, my love. Does she still exist? Or is it only in my imagination?" he asked with anguish.

She could not speak for the lump in her throat and trying to hold back sobs. He took her silence as her answer.

"Very well," he said curtly. "This is goodbye then." He turned on his heel and walked away from her.

AFTERWORD

Unfortunately assault on women and children has been a problem since the beginning of time. While some people may be frustrated a bit with the ending, forgiveness was the key to healing in my situation. The circumstances of the story and characters are fictional, but I hope that through this story others might also find the gift of healing.

ABOUT THE AUTHOR

Like many writers, Elizabeth Johns was first an avid reader, though she was a reluctant convert. It was Jane Austen's clever wit and unique turn of phrase that hooked Johns when she was "forced" to read Pride and Prejudice for a school assignment. She began writing when she ran out of her favourite author's books and decided to try her hand at crafting a Regency romance novel. Her journey into publishing began with the release of Surrender the Past, book one of the Loring-Abbott Series. Johns makes no pretensions to Austen's wit but hopes readers will perhaps laugh and find some enjoyment in her writing.

Johns attributes much of her inspiration to her mother, a retired English teacher. During their last summer together, Johns would sit on the porch swing and read her stories to her mother, who encouraged her to continue writing. Busy with multiple careers, including a professional job in the medical field, author and mother of small children, Johns squeezes in time for reading whenever possible.

ACKNOWLEDGMENTS

Many thanks to:

Wilette Youkey for being the role model, friend (the word doesn't do her justice) and mentor anybody would be lucky to have, not to mention talented author and design artist.

Wilette, Staci, Tammy, Judy, Melynda, Jill, and Dad for suffering through reading all of my rough drafts and providing invaluable advice.

My high school teachers, who "made" me read *Pride and Prejudice* and *Jurassic Park* as make-up work during convalescence one year.

Jill well, for just making me laugh and for "getting" me.

Holly for caring enough to notice something was wrong and for forcing me to talk about it.

Mom and Dad for raising me to believe I could do anything I put my mind to, and for being a constant source of love and support.

CJ for encouraging my dreams.

Nicholas and Ella for the smiles and hugs that make everything worth it.

AUTHOR'S NOTE

Author's note: British spellings and grammar have been used in an effort to reflect what would have been done in the time period in which the novels are set. While I realize all words may not be exact, I hope you can appreciate the differences and effort made to be historically accurate while attempting to retain readability modern audience.

Thank you for reading *Surrender The Past*! I hope you enjoyed it. If you did, please help other readers find this book:

1. This book is lendable, so send it to a friend whom you think might like it so they can discover me, too.

2. Help other people find this book by writing a review.

3. Sign up for my new releases at www.Elizabethjohnsauthor.com, so you can find out about the next book as soon as it's available.

4. I would love to hear from you! Come like my Facebook page

www.facebook.com/Elizabethjohnsauthor follow on Twitter @Ejohnsauthor or write to me at elizabethjohnsauthor@gmail.com

Read on for a preview of the next book in the series, *Seasons of Change*.

Made in the USA
Monee, IL
24 July 2022